REKINDLED

REKINDLED

TITANIUM SECURITY SERIES

By Kaylea Cross

★ ★ ★ ★ ★

Cover Art by Syd Gill Designs

★ ★ ★ ★ ★

This book is a work of fiction. The names, characters, places, and incidents are products of the writer's imagination or have been used fictitiously and are not to be construed as real. Any resemblance to persons, living or dead, actual events, locales or organizations is entirely coincidental.

ISBN: 978-1494878344
Print Edition

Dedication

I dedicate this book to the men and women out there trying to rid the world of chemical weapons, and the ones who stand ready to protect us all.

Author's Note

This is the fifth and final book of my **Titanium Security** series, and I'm so excited to finally bring you Alex's story. They might not be Luke and Emily (from ***Absolution***, which most of you probably know is my favorite book I've ever written), but their story is also about healing and second chances. I hope it pulls on your heartstrings as much as it did mine.

Happy reading!

Kaylea Cross

PROLOGUE

Four years earlier
Mombasa, Kenya

Blood and death surrounded her.

Grace shut her eyes. People were screaming. Blasts of gunfire echoed through the cavernous ballroom at one of Mombasa's most luxurious resorts. Rounds continued to punch into the polished marble pillars and floors. Fear paralyzed her, choked her with icy fingers.

She lay on the cold tile floor of the ballroom, curled into the fetal position. Pain engulfed her in its white hot burn. She kept her hands pressed to her middle where two bullets had plowed deep into her belly. Warm, sticky blood stained her turquoise satin gown. It pooled around her in a glistening scarlet puddle.

She squeezed her eyes shut and prayed. It hurt to breathe. The wounds burned like acid inside her. She lay still, afraid to move lest it make her a target again.

The masked gunmen had stormed the room a few minutes ago.

What is the name of the Blessed Prophet's mother?

When no one had answered in the stunned silence that followed, they'd opened fire on the crowd without warning.

She'd been one of the first hit when they'd begun spraying the room with bullets.

Another burst of gunfire shattered the air. More screams. Grace cringed. The panic in the room pressed in on her, heavy and suffocating. There was nowhere to go, no place she could hide. Rounds impacted around her, so close they showered her with sharp shards of marble and plaster. She winced as they peppered her skin like shrapnel. She curled tighter, trying and failing to stay calm. Her heart thundered in her chest, accelerating the blood loss. Already she could feel her body weakening.

Then suddenly the lights went out, plunging the ballroom into instant darkness. The shooting stopped instantly. Frantic shouts from the gunmen filled the room.

Grace eased one arm away from her belly and set it on the cold floor, slippery with her blood. She had to crawl somewhere safe before those lights came back on.

Before she could move, someone grabbed her by the shoulders and started pulling. An agonized scream tore out of her dry throat. She tried to pry the hands away but they wouldn't let go, determinedly dragging her across the floor. Her eyes flew open as more shots rang out in the darkness. Illuminated by the quick bursts of light from the muzzle flashes she could see the dark, glistening blood trail spread out along her path and the bodies that lay everywhere. The gunmen were still shooting…

But not at the guests now. Toward the open double doorway at the back of the room instead.

"Stay down," a male voice hissed close to her ear.

She was too weak to move anyway, in too much pain to speak.

As she curled up once more the volume of gunfire suddenly doubled. Another wave of terrified screams rivaled the volume of the deadly blasts. Grace clenched her eyes shut again and prayed. *Please get me out of here. Please let me live. I have to see Jack. Tell him I love him.*

She didn't care if it was wrong or that people would judge her for it. She only knew that it was true and she had to tell him.

But no one was coming for her now. She was going to bleed out on this floor in her gown and Jack would never know how she truly felt about him. The thought brought a rush of hot tears.

Blood spilled between her numb fingers as everything slowly faded out. She slipped in and out of consciousness for an unknown amount of time, then urgent voices reached her through the fog of pain and fear.

She struggled to force her eyes open, squinting in the sudden glare of the overhead lights, and realized the shooting had stopped. People all around her were crying, moaning. More hands grabbed her, strong and sure. Lifted her.

She tried to cry out, to stop them because the pain was too much. Only a whimper escaped her tight throat. She had the sensation of floating. Dizzying flashes of light and a rush of confusing sounds bombarded her. She closed her eyes and retreated back into that dark space she could hide in.

The hands lowered her onto something softer than the floor. She could feel the cushioned surface beneath her as she lay twisted on her side, her shaking hands still pressed to her belly.

"*Grace.*"

Her heart clenched at the sound of that deep, urgent voice. She fought to pry her heavy eyelids apart. In the flashing red and blue strobe lights around her she looked up into the face peering anxiously down at her.

Beautiful silver eyes stared back at her, liquid with unshed tears.

Jack. She tried to say his name. Her lips moved but no sound came out.

He cupped a warm hand against her cheek, cradled the side of her face. "That's right, baby. You stay with me. I'm right here. You just look at me and hold on." His voice was hoarse, on the edge of breaking. The agonized look on his face tore at her, because it confirmed what she'd already feared. She wasn't going to make it.

She forced one hand away from her belly, intending to reach for him, then realized he was pressing something to her wounds. His jacket. Tears flooded her eyes. Ragged sobs building in her throat. She didn't want to die like this. Not when she'd just found him.

He bent to press his stubbled cheek to hers, his voice a raw whisper against her ear. "Stay with me, baby. Please hold on. *Please.*"

I don't want to go! She found his wrist, gripped it with her remaining strength. Jack wasn't the sort of man who begged. For anything. But he'd begged her to hold on. She had to, for him. For their future together. *Help me!* she silently beseeched him. *How do I hold on?*

Two men appeared beside him, dressed in paramedic uniforms. She refused to release Jack's wrist. He didn't let go. He merely shifted to the side to give them room and wrapped her hands between his larger ones, infusing them with warmth as the men worked on her, applying pressure to her abdomen. The pain intensified so suddenly that she cried out. Jack's worried face turned blurry. She felt herself falling back into the blackness.

"Grace!"

Jack. I have to fight for Jack. She forced her heavy eyelids open once more. She was so tired and weak. But Jack's face was close, so close. She wished she had the strength to touch it. She wanted to stroke away the worry lines in his forehead. Her tongue was dry, thick as she forced the words out. "Don't…d-don't leave…me," she managed, terrified of dying alone. She was so cold already, death pulling at her with merciless force.

His strong hands squeezed harder, kept her anchored to him. He stared straight into her eyes. "I won't. I swear I won't." A vow. And Jack would never break his word to her.

Knowing Jack was there and wouldn't leave her no matter what, Grace relaxed and let herself go. She floated beyond the pain, beyond the fear.

When she came to again, she was in a hospital bed.

I'm still alive.

Pain still burned in her belly, but it was duller now and she wasn't as cold. She cast a frantic look around the room. Where was Jack?

"He's not here."

She glanced toward the window. Robert pushed away from the wall and walked toward her bed. He still wore his suit and tie, though it was badly rumpled and his hair was mussed as though he'd been repeatedly running his hands through it. Her estranged husband's handsome face was blank, distant. "He left when you were in recovery."

Jack had left her.

She shook her head in denial. A hot ache lodged in her chest. *No, he'd promised. He wouldn't have left me.*

"You're going to be okay, but it was close," Robert continued, only his eyes holding any emotion. Pity. Sadness. Regret. "There was a lot of damage though…" He let his voice trail off, as if he was trying to decide how to break the bad news to her.

Grace put a tentative hand on top of her abdomen. She could feel the padding of the bandages beneath the thin covers. Her entire middle felt bruised, hot, swollen. She licked her dry lips. "What did they do?" she rasped.

Robert blew out a breath and ran a hand through his still dark hair, something he only did when he was severely stressed. Throughout the political rollercoaster that had been their lives since he became a member of the foreign diplomatic service, she'd never seen him this rattled. This year-long posting in Mombasa had taken its toll on both of them, and now had culminated with this disaster. "I'm sorry, Grace, but they had to do a hysterectomy. And they took out your spleen as well. They had to."

Shock rippled through her. They'd saved her life but had taken away her dream of having children of her own. At forty-two she'd known she was getting too old to think of getting pregnant, but then she'd met Jack and a part of her had dared to hope that maybe—

"And…"

She looked up at Robert again. He glanced away. Folded his arms across his chest. She knew there was more. Something even worse to come. Her pulse thudded in her ears as she waited.

He met her gaze again and she saw the pain and anger there. "I'll wait to tell you after you get some more rest—"

"Say it." The words came out hoarse, a bare whisper. Whatever it was, she had to know.

Robert sighed, shook his head. He looked weary. Resigned. "He isn't who you think he is."

Her heart lurched, then started beating faster. *Jack?*

Robert's expression was shaded by deeply buried anger. Apology. And she knew that whatever he was about to say next brought him no pleasure, despite the pain they'd caused each other over the last few years of their marriage. Before they'd finally done what they should have found the guts to do years ago and separated, two months before.

"He's an NSA agent. His name isn't even Jack Davison."

She stared at him, aware that her breathing had turned shallow, almost frantic as the panic shot through her. *No.*

"He was using you to get into your social circle to get information on the terrorist group that carried out the attack last night."

She pressed her lips together and shook her head, not wanting to believe it. She wanted to scream at him. *You're wrong! You're lying!*

"They cracked the case last night, but…too late to stop the attack."

Grace barely heard the last part. Whatever faults Robert had, whatever anger he still harbored toward her for seeking their legal separation, she knew he wouldn't lie to her about this. Not now.

Horror reverberated through her, then pain, almost worse than the bullet wounds. Could it be true? Then, slowly, the numbing fog of denial took hold. She turned her face away from him and closed her eyes, trying and no doubt failing to hide her agony.

She'd risked everything for the man she loved, and had lost it all.

Because everything Jack had ever told her was a lie.

CHAPTER ONE

Islamabad, Pakistan
Present Day

Arms folded across his chest, Alex Rycroft leaned back in the hard plastic chair and stared across the stainless steel table into the prisoner's dark, defiant eyes. For more than five minutes now they'd been playing eye contact chicken. Neither one of them wanted to be the first to blink. *I got all day, asshole.* "I give final clearance on them taking you outta here for your next surgery. You don't tell me what I need to know, and I can cancel that surgery slot with a single phone call."

Malik Hassani glared back at him in defiance, that deep set stare fixed on his. "I know how this game is played. Far better than you ever will," he replied in nearly unaccented English.

Alex hid a smirk at the pointed reminder. Hassani had been a high ranking official of the Pakistani Inter Services Intelligence for many years before he'd left to pursue his terrorist agenda. He'd earned his ruthless reputation for a reason, but whether the bastard believed it or not, that didn't intimidate Alex. This piece of shit sitting opposite him had ordered several attacks on his team over the past few weeks and had just attempted to pull off a full-scale military coup that had almost succeeded. "How's that hand doing right now?" he asked the prisoner instead.

Hassani's mouth, framed by a short, dark goatee, twitched ever so slightly in annoyance. His face held a grayish cast that had nothing to do with the sickly overhead lighting. A fine sheen of sweat dotted his forehead. He didn't answer, even though Alex knew he was hurting pretty bad. Surgeons had gone in there once already to patch up the mess made by a SEAL Team Six member's point blank 9 mm round prior to capture. They had to go in again to reposition the pins and screws if Hassani was ever going to be able to use his hand again someday. Not that Alex gave a shit about that.

Maintaining his relaxed posture, Alex switched tactics. This man would never bend for something as meaningless as pain relief or even the chance to use his hand properly again. Alex decided to cut through the usual bullshit and dangle the only bait he knew Hassani would be tempted to jump at. "You haven't asked me about Bashir yet."

A tense silence followed. Alex didn't move. Every word they said was being recorded, and others watched from the opposite side of the two-way mirror in the hallway.

Something flickered briefly in those nearly black eyes. That hard slash of a mouth tightened ever so slightly.

Little tells a less experienced interrogator might have missed, but Alex knew he definitely had the bastard's interest now. "I guess no one's told you?" he continued casually, even as urgency hummed inside him. They had to nail this asshole *now* to get charges pinned on him and start the lengthy legal process that would follow. And they had to make sure they exposed the rest of his network to stop any future terror operations they might have planned and maintain the fragile balance of power in Pakistan. A destabilized nuclear Pakistan was the personal nightmare of every intelligence officer in the region.

"Told me what?" Hassani growled. "That he's dead?"

"No, not dead. Worse. He's alive…and willing to talk."

"You're lying." That hard mouth twisted into a cold sneer. "If Bashir's alive, he won't talk." He said it with total confidence that, coming from any other man, Alex might have seen as naiveté.

But not this one.

"No? Huh. Guess that must have been some other five-foot-ten former ISI officer we pulled out of that cave with you then." Alex shrugged, tilted his head to the side. "We know he's your most loyal man. Care to tell me about the others yet? Because I can guarantee you they're not as loyal as you seem to think. And that thumb drive the SEALs found on you in the cave?" He gave a low whistle. "Lot of interesting stuff on there. You play dirty." Hassani had documents and incriminating photos on dozens of big name players in the region. Government officials, intelligence officers, politicians and military higher ups. All held by the balls because of Hassani's blackmail. Teams of people in the NSA and CIA were combing through the drive now to uncover and begin unraveling Hassani's corrupt network of power.

The hard stare turned disdainful. "You're fishing, Rycroft. And I'm not in the mood to play."

Alex clenched his jaw. *I'm sick of* playing *with you too, asshole.* For two days now they'd been circling each other like wary combatants, with little result. Even with Hassani in chains, in pain and sleep deprived, Alex couldn't force anything out of him. Not without taking much more drastic and forceful measures, and those methods had unfortunately been prohibited by the U.S. government. Especially with such a high profile prisoner as this.

"What about the traitors, then?" Alex said.

"What about them?" Hassani shot back.

"All the politicians and law enforcement people you control. Even the military. When it looked like you were going to be captured, they all caved and turned on you. Want to know who sold you out to us?"

The man's jaw flexed, then one side of his mouth curled in bitter amusement. "Fine. Who sold me out?"

"General Sharif." Alex watched his reaction closely, noted the flare of rage in Hassani's eyes just before he masked it. "For a whopping two hundred K in cash. U.S. dollars, of course."

Hassani's nostrils flared. Alex could feel him seething underneath that calm exterior. The beast was right there, clawing for freedom. Alex was going to enjoy pushing him until the chains holding the animal snapped.

"He and his men were already deploying to the border when the firefight started in that valley. Between us, the American forces out hunting you and your own military and police changing allegiances at the last moment, there was no way you were getting across that border, Malik. Zero."

Hassani raised a taunting brow. "If you know all of that, then you don't need to question me."

"Oh, but I do. Until I unearth every last one of your sources. And you and I both know there's one key player who hasn't been mentioned yet." The informant within the ISI itself. Whoever it was, he was the key. Once Alex discovered his identity, he could shut down Hassani's entire network and expose every last one of his followers to the international intelligence community.

"You'll have to be more specific," Hassani answered, sounding bored this time.

Alex gave him a cold smile. He and Hassani were both in their early fifties. They'd both served their countries in Special Forces before going on to intelligence work. But that was where the similarities ended. "We're close, you know. There's new intel coming in every day from your former supporters. Plenty of them jumped at the chance to change sides once they got a better deal from us. Whether you cooperate or not, we're going to find out who you've got in the ISI and make it all disappear like a bad memory."

"Well, I'd hate to spoil your fun, Rycroft."

Would he. Alex noted the shadows beneath the other man's eyes. So dark they looked like bruises. Doctors had already told him that Hassani was feverish due to him fighting an infection. Even if his condition deteriorated, Hassani would continue to be a formidable opponent. Alex knew he wasn't getting anything more out of the bastard for now, maybe not ever. Might as well do the right thing and get Hassani's medical situation resolved before their next session.

Alex uncrossed his arms and stood up. "We're done." He strode for the door, motioned for the guards to open it for him. The heavy steel lock clanged into place behind him. He spoke to the dark-haired Fed waiting outside the room by the two-way mirror. Jake Evers, another member of the NSA taskforce Alex had set up. A former Army officer in his early thirties who now worked for the FBI. "Take him in for the surgery."

Evers gave a wry chuckle. "That went well."

"I thought so," Alex replied pleasantly. "You saw his reaction when I mentioned Bashir?"

"Oh yeah. Looking forward to seeing you keep needling that sore spot."

Alex smirked. The way things looked now, Bashir was about the only weapon he had at his disposal to crack Hassani with. "Perk of the job."

"Yeah, rub it in, you bastard." Evers got on his phone. "Alert the medical staff. We're bringing Hassani in."

Alex stood by the large two-way mirror that looked like a window cut into the wall as two burly Pakistani guards entered the interrogation room. They approached Hassani from behind, yanked a black hood over his head and hauled him to his chained feet. Evers waited for them on the other side of the door with two heavily-armed Feds. "Let's go," he told them. He gave Alex a nod on his way past.

When they were gone Alex texted Hunter and received a reply that the SUV was parked out front. He slid his tactical vest on before heading outside into the bright October sunshine. He walked up to the vehicle just as the convoy taking Hassani to the secret medical facility left the parking lot.

As he got into the back and slammed the door, Hunter turned in the front passenger seat to face him. In his early thirties, the dark-haired former SEAL and now co-owner of Titanium Security was part of Alex's current personal security detail. His light brown eyes twinkled with amusement as he met Alex's gaze. "So. How'd it go?"

Alex shot him a wry grin. "Same old same old. You guys find anything of interest on the surveillance front?" For the past day and a half they'd been watching two different men with ties to the Taliban suspected of being involved with Hassani.

"Nada," Gage responded from the driver's seat in his North Carolina drawl, his tatted forearms flexing as he gripped the wheel. Alex had met the forty-two year old redhead back in his SF days, when he'd been a lieutenant and

Gage had been a master sergeant. Hiring him and the rest of Hunter's Titanium team had been one of the best decisions Alex had made in recent months.

"Both dead ends as far as we can tell," Hunter added. "If they were involved with Hassani at some point we'll find out, but so far it looks like they've cut all their ties with him. Still got a long list to work through though."

Alex grunted a response as he scrolled through his new e-mails. A few urgent, though most he could deal with later.

"So, where to, bossman?" Gage asked as he fired up the engine. "Back to HQ?"

They'd set up temporary headquarters in a nondescript building near the outskirts of Islamabad, choosing a different location than the one they'd used during Hassani's capture for security reasons. "Yeah, I've got some files to review. Any word from Claire yet on that latest encryption?" Before being brought onto the NSA taskforce Alex had assembled that included the Titanium team, Gage's fiancée was one of Alex's best employees. She was currently back at NSA headquarters in Fort Meade, Maryland, working her cryptology magic.

"She's still working on it," Gage replied as he turned out of the parking lot. "Zahra's helping out from the hospital when she can."

At the name, he felt a tiny twinge of guilt. In some ways she was like a daughter to him. There'd been so much going on since Hassani's capture that Alex hadn't had a chance to go back to the hospital yet. He felt bad about that, like he'd let Zahra down. "Any change in Dunhpy's status yet?" The team's spotter—Zahra's boyfriend—had been badly wounded in an IED attack on the Khyber Pass the day before Hassani's arrest and had no sensation or motor control from the waist down. It made the entire team even more motivated to bring down the rest of Hassani's network.

Hunter shook his head. "Nothing. We're gonna go visit him later if you wanna come. Got a present for him."

"Yeah, but this present's way nicer than the last surprise we gave him," Gage added with a grin.

Alex could only imagine what they'd gotten for the team prankster this time. Hopefully something to yank him out of the depression Zahra had told Alex he was sinking into. "Maybe." Though when he did pay a visit, he'd prefer to do it on his own. The guys fell silent and let him be as he scrolled through the last of his e-mails. His muscles tensed when he saw the subject of the reply his NSA contact had sent while Alex was interrogating Hassani.

Grace Fallon

He opened it, aware that his heart was kicking hard against his ribs. This was it. The message gave the name and address of the hotel where Grace was supposedly staying.

"Change of plans," he said to Gage, unable to stem the surge of excitement that raced through him. "Got one more location to check out first." He gave him the address, praying she would still be there.

Gage didn't say anything but Hunter swiveled his head around to look at him and raised his eyebrows. "What's up?"

Alex kept his expression blank. "Just something I want to check on." *Someone.* He had to see her. Had to find a way to talk to her, get her to listen. Ever since he'd thought he'd spotted her in that Peshawar marketplace a few days ago, he hadn't been able to stop thinking about her. About what he'd do if he saw her again. Now he might finally get the chance.

He put his phone back into his pocket and stared out the window, wondering what the hell he was going to say to her if he saw her. He still couldn't believe she was in Islamabad right now. Normally nothing could distract him while he was on the job, but knowing she was here had kept him from sleeping. For the past two nights he'd had nightmares and flashbacks about the last time he'd seen her—things he hadn't experienced in well over two years. He thought of the first time he'd seen her, in that crowded restaurant in Mombasa one night when he'd met up with his CIA contact.

"There's someone I think you need to meet," was all the man said before dragging Alex over to a table in the corner.

Approaching her from behind, he noticed the sleek curve of her auburn hair glinting in the candlelight, heard the American accent as she spoke. She turned when her male dinner companion noticed them and broke off in mid-sentence. Those gorgeous aqua eyes flashed up to his and he found himself staring, dumbstruck for a moment. Something about her glowed, drawing him in from that first sight.

"This is Dr. Grace Fallon," Alex's contact told him. "Grace, meet Jack, a friend of mine."

Grace pushed her chair back and stood to offer her hand, everything about her poised and confident as she smiled at him and shook his hand in a firm grip that surprised him. And her body. He couldn't help but rake his gaze over all those seductive curves outlined by her snug skirt and the blouse that hugged the round swells of her breasts. "Pleasure. And please, call me Grace. I'm not much for answering to 'doctor' outside of work."

"What kind of work?" Alex asked, acutely aware that he was still holding her hand and was in no hurry to let it go.

"Grace would never toot her own horn, so I'll do it for her. She's got a PhD in chemistry with an undergrad in chemical engineering, and she does freelance work for OPCW," his contact answered. "But your real dream is to work for the UN one day, right?"

The Organisation for the Prohibition of Chemical Weapons, based in The Hague. Alex's eyebrows shot up at that. "Chemical weapons?"

Not something he heard too often, let alone about such a beautiful, intriguing woman.

Grace smiled faintly and withdrew her hand, her cheeks taking on a pretty flush of color, as though the praise had embarrassed her. "Yes. And what do you do, Jack?"

"Nothing even remotely that interesting," his contact said with a laugh.

Intrigued by her, Alex glanced at the table and noticed it was covered in papers and folders. "Sorry to have interrupted your meeting," he said, already wondering how he could arrange to meet with her again.

She waved his concern away with an elegant hand that he couldn't help notice bore no wedding ring. "Not at all. Would you like to join us?"

He knew she was just being polite, but without even glancing at his contact for confirmation, Alex nodded. "We'd love to."

He didn't even remember eating, he'd been so caught up in his conversation with her. Afterward the two other men murmured excuses and left, obviously having picked up on the not-so-subtle attraction brewing between them. He and Grace had closed the restaurant down. They'd spent the entire night talking, hadn't realized how much time had passed or that they were the only customers left until a waiter came over and politely asked them if they'd be leaving now. Alex had already been hooked.

It had taken nearly six weeks for her to let him past her defenses and open herself to him completely. Six weeks of long late night phone conversations, leisurely dinners and walks on the beach when he could get the time, then scorching make-out sessions that had left them both trembling and desperate for more. He'd known she was leery of getting involved with him so soon after her separation, so he hadn't pushed her. He'd never earned anything as important as her trust, before or since.

But he'd shattered it. He'd hated hiding his true identity or the reason he was in Mombasa, especially after getting to know her better and learning about her recent separation, but he couldn't tell her the truth.

A horn blared close by, pulling Alex back to the present. The traffic was heavy but Gage knew the city better than most local cab drivers did. Without even bothering with the vehicle's GPS he took several short cuts that got them around the downtown core and to the luxury hotel.

"We looking for someone, or something?" Hunter asked as they turned onto the street where the hotel access was.

"Someone," Alex said evasively, already staring at the front of the hotel. He already knew why she was here: as part of a secret chemical weapons inspection team attached to the UN. Her dream job. While he hated the thought of her being in potentially dangerous situations that came with that line of work, he was damn proud of her for achieving her dream.

Hunter turned around again and shot him an annoyed look, making it clear he didn't appreciate being left in the dark. "Fill us in, man."

Alex didn't take his eyes off that entrance. "I just wanna see if—" He broke off as a flash of auburn hair caught his attention. Beneath the porte-cochere at the hotel's entrance, a group of people stood next to two minivan cabs parked at the curb. Including a red-headed woman who was in the process of covering her head with a shawl. Alex leaned forward to peer harder out his window. His heart was pounding. His mouth was dry. The woman was the right height and the right shape, all sexy curves…

She and a man climbed into the back of the second cab.

"What?" Hunter demanded, his voice tense as he stared at Alex.

The minivan pulled away from the curb and headed toward the exit.

Alex ignored him and leaned to the side to maintain his sight on it, aware only of the urgency and elation surging through him. "Follow that cab, *now*," he commanded Gage.

Gage and Hunter exchanged a *what-the-fuck* look for a second, then Gage hit the accelerator. The SUV's engine revved as it tore after the minivan. Alex gripped the door handle and willed his heart to slow down. After four long years she was finally right there in front of him.

And this time, he wasn't going to let her go.

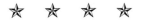

"So, Dr. Fallon, do you need to go over anything before the presentation?"

Grace looked up from the calendar on her phone at her assigned twenty-something assistant, David, and smiled. He was new to the job and had only been working with her since she'd arrived in Pakistan a few days ago. "No, I'm good. But thanks." He nodded, but she couldn't help but notice the way he tapped his fingers anxiously against the armrest. "You're not nervous, are you? I'm the one they're going to grill, not you."

He laughed softly and some of the tension seemed to melt out of him. "Just want to make sure I don't screw anything up."

His self-deprecation and earnestness was a refreshing change from a lot of the arrogant know-it-alls she'd worked with in the industry over the years. Grace reached over and patted his knee. "You'll do great. I have faith in you."

She adjusted the slim briefcase on her lap and glanced out the window at the heavy traffic surrounding them. The cab driver turned left at a light. A second later he sped up and jerked the wheel hard to the right to zip into the next lane. Grace threw out a hand to brace herself and exchanged a wry look with David. She'd managed to make it all the way here from New York without dying. Would be highly ironic if they didn't make it to this meeting in once piece.

David still seemed anxious, however. "Would you feel better if we went over something?" she finally asked.

One side of his mouth tipped up in a sheepish grin. "If you don't mind."

"I don't mind at all." She settled back against the seat and tried to ignore the driver's heavy hand on the wheel and the way he kept hammering the brake and gas. Not an easy task.

David began sorting through the papers in his briefcase. "What about the last report we received from—"

"Is someone supposed to be following you?" the driver interrupted in a heavy accent.

Grace blinked at him in surprise, sure she'd heard him wrong. "Pardon?"

"A black truck is following us. Very fast and aggressive." He was frowning, eyes on the rearview mirror as he stared at whatever was behind them.

Instinctively she turned around to peer through the back window. Sure enough, a big SUV was cutting its way through the lines of cars toward them. "Are you sure they're following us?"

"Yes, I'm positive."

"For how long?"

"Since just after we left the hotel." He glanced around as though searching for an escape route and at his anxious expression, Grace felt her pulse accelerate.

She looked at David, who'd gone a little pale. He turned in his seat to look out the back window, pushing his glasses up on the bridge of his nose. "The other two cabs are in front of us. Is it a security team or something?"

"I can't tell, but I don't think so," she said. They were here for a secret meeting barely anyone knew about. Were they really being followed? They couldn't be. The team was travelling in unmarked cabs rather than UN vehicles they used while on official inspection missions, but… Grace's palms grew clammy. She turned back to the driver. "Can you get us off this road and take another route instead?" Then they'd know for sure whether they were being followed or not.

He nodded, checked over his shoulder then yanked the van to the right and forced his way into the far lane. When Grace looked behind them, the SUV was mirroring their movements, cutting off other traffic and narrowly avoiding a collision as it did. No, she didn't like the feel of this at all.

"Okay, get us out of here." She yanked out her phone to call the head of the team in the lead cab. Their security guards were in another vehicle somewhere nearby. The driver finally got them clear of the tangle of traffic and hit the gas just as Dr. Travis answered her call. "We're being followed," she said quickly. "We don't know who it is, but they're not stopping so we're taking a different route to the—" She yelped as something slammed into the right rear corner of the van, hard enough to jerk her head backward and send her phone flying into the foot well with a thud.

Shaken, she swiveled around to look at the car that had hit them. Its driver was already out of the vehicle, yelling and shaking his fist at the cab driver, who shot out his own door to shout back. She instinctively reached for David, who was rubbing the back of his head where he'd smacked it against the door frame. Before she could ask if he was all right, his eyes suddenly went wide as he stared over her left shoulder.

Grace whipped around in time to see the black SUV roar past, only to veer in front of them and screech to a halt perpendicular to the hood of the cab. Before it had settled the passenger side doors flew open.

Oh, shit. Memories of the attack in Mombasa flashed through her mind. On instinct she undid her belt and started to scramble across the seat toward David, intending to escape out his side, when her door was suddenly wrenched open. A scream lodged in her throat as hard arms reached in and grabbed her, hauled her up and out of the cab.

She barely had time to drag in a breath before those strong hands turned her around. Gasping, she caught a glimpse of a light blue dress shirt stretched across broad shoulders an instant before those powerful arms closed around her back and crushed her to a hard male chest.

"*Grace.*"

At that hauntingly familiar voice she snapped her head up—and found herself staring into a pair of silver eyes she'd never expected to see again. Shock immobilized her.

Jack.

No, not Jack, she corrected herself angrily. *Alex.*

A tremor snaked through her as his achingly familiar scent wrapped around her, a hint of spice and warm, clean male. His dark hair had more gray in it now, especially around the temples. His face was still the same, all hard angles. Was she hallucinating?

"Are you okay?" He released her to take her face between his big hands, his eyes scanning her face anxiously. "Are you hurt?"

She wasn't sure, because she had to be imagining this. "N-no." She was vaguely aware of the sound of sirens close by, of police officers exiting a patrol vehicle behind the cab.

Alex relaxed visibly, then wrapped his arms around her again and hugged her tight as he buried his face in the curve of her neck. The embrace was urgent, on the verge of desperate. *No.* She shuddered in confusion, still trying to comprehend what was going on. Her hands automatically came up to press against his chest. Dammit, he couldn't just show up like this, grab her and knock her world off kilter again.

She pushed but got nowhere and he didn't ease up on his hold. He was hot and hard against her, his big body practically vibrating with suppressed emotion. He dragged in several deep breaths against her neck, as if he was inhaling her scent. She froze as goosebumps broke out across her suddenly violently sensitive skin.

Feeling like she was surfacing from a strange dream, Grace shook herself and found her wits. She flattened her hands against the solid muscles in his chest and shoved until he raised his head and she could lean her upper body away to get some badly needed space. "What are you *doing* here?" He'd been in that SUV? Why had he been following her?

His eyes bored into hers. "Had to see you."

What? Why? "*See* me? What are you talking—"

"Where are you going right now?" His voice was clipped, taut.

Anger punched through her, sharp and powerful. "To a meeting. A very high level meeting I'm now going to be late for." *Thanks to you*, she added silently, fuming. Her team was meeting with certain high-ranking Pakistani officials in preparation for the upcoming undisclosed summit with an envoy from Syria. And she was a key part of the presentation.

Grace glared up at Alex, who stood there blocking her path. He'd cost her everything. Her marriage—hopeless though it had been near the end, he'd sealed its fate in her mind nonetheless—her heart, her reputation, even her ability to have children by hiding the truth from her.

"Let me *go*." She pushed harder, didn't stop until he released her, even though she could tell he didn't want to. As she pulled away she felt colder all of a sudden, unsettled. God dammit, how could he still shake her to her core like this? She'd sworn to herself years ago that she was over him, that he could never affect her again. She'd also never expected to see him after leaving Kenya and had no defense against this bombardment. Alex had always been shockingly protective and demonstrative with her, even in public. They'd burned so hot together, like thermite. She'd never felt anything like it. It scared her that he could still elicit such a strong, primal reaction from her even after all the damage he'd done and all the time they'd spent apart.

She took a hasty step back but had nowhere to go. Her spine hit the side of the van, and she put a hand over her pounding heart. It wasn't fair that the man still looked incredible. He still emitted that vital, commanding presence and seemed to have barely aged since she'd last seen him. Even the scruff on his face was still mostly dark. And his body was as powerful as ever, all hard lines and taut muscle. That razor sharp edge that clung to him was clear in his eyes and posture, giving him a predatory vibe that drew her even now.

She swallowed and found her voice again, refusing to give into that dark lure. Realizing they were being watched, she glanced past Alex. A powerfully built dark-haired man stood at the open front passenger SUV door. Beyond him in the vehicle, another muscular man with red-gold hair sat behind the wheel, both his arms covered in full sleeves of tattoos. The men shot each other a wary look before focusing back on her. Clearly they didn't know what the hell was going on here anymore than she did.

Grace tore her gaze from them and met Alex's intent stare once more. "How did you find me? How long have you been following me?" Had he been spying on her?

He shook his head. "I only found out the other day that you were in the city. I went to your hotel just now and saw you get into the cab."

She had no way of knowing if he was telling the truth or not—though she doubted he was being honest—but she'd be stupid to just take him at his word. "And so you decided to chase me across the city like that? You scared the hell out of us all, I thought it might be—" She broke off, not wanting to say it aloud. *Terrorists.* She suppressed a shudder, glared at him instead. In her peripheral vision she noticed that her team's security had finally arrived on scene. The four men in suits climbed out of their own vehicle and approached the police officers, who were talking to both drivers and David. She kept her gaze locked on Alex. "You could've landed us in the hospital with that stupid stunt." God, what the hell was wrong with him?

His jaw flexed. "I needed to talk to you."

She felt her eyes pop wide. "Well too damn bad! I've got nothing to say to you, I thought I made that clear last time you contacted me. Now let me go and stay the hell away from me."

Rather than apologize or appear embarrassed by his over-the-top behavior, he took a step closer and lifted a hand to cup the back of her neck, just below where her chin-length bob ended. His touch froze her. Firm, commanding, but tender. A lethal combination that had the power to bring her to her knees if she let it. His hand was warm, hard, and she remembered exactly how perfect it felt when he stroked it over her naked skin. She drew in a sharp breath, stiffened her spine.

Those sexy-as-hell eyes locked on hers, and in that moment she was suddenly terrified that he could see through the anger and resentment to the fear and hurt hidden inside her. To the shocking need only he'd been able to elicit from her. "Grace. I *need* to talk to you," he said in a low voice. It was deeper than she remembered. And it still slid through her like warm honey, heating her blood, melting away the icy shock and replacing it with something that scared her far worse than this whole scenario had. "I've waited so long to tell you what I…" He shook his head tightly, the frustration pulsing off him in tangible waves. "Just give me a chance to explain. Please," he added softly after a slight hesitation.

She huffed out an exasperated breath. The man had serious balls, to chase her down and corner her here like this in public while she was on a supposedly secret mission. Especially when she'd made it more than clear two years ago that she wanted nothing more to do with him. "Why the hell should I?"

"Because there's so much I need to say that you weren't willing to listen to before."

She wanted to laugh at that, but none of this was funny. Not at all. "And you think I am now?" He'd shattered her trust, her entire *world.*

He shook his head once, regret etched into every line of his handsome face. "God, I hope so."

For some reason the stupid, soft-hearted part of her wanted to believe him. Wanted to believe she'd meant more to him than just a means to an end on his last job in Kenya. It pissed her off.

Grace narrowed her eyes at him. "You don't deserve the chance to explain. You don't deserve *jack* from me." She used the word deliberately, telling him exactly what she thought of him and his lies. She was shaking with a combination of anger and shock. And even then her body was at war with itself. Part of her wanted to ball her hand into a fist and punch him right in his handsome face, while the other wanted him to hold her in those strong arms and make everything okay. For him to say something that might make her understand his actions in Kenya, that might make her listen to his pleas for forgiveness.

He made a frustrated sound. "I know. Christ, you don't think I know that? I've lived with my mistakes and regrets for four years, Grace, without being able to explain myself to you. All I'm asking is for you to listen."

She searched his eyes, fighting the anger with effort. He seemed so earnest, so desperate for the chance to explain, and she couldn't deny that a part of her longed for the closure. Maybe once she heard him out and had her final say, she'd be able to move on for good. But not here, not now. More people had gathered around to stare at them. She wanted to get out of here and the quickest way to do that was to agree to the talk. If she didn't like what he had to say, she'd walk, pure and simple.

But first she intended to let him know he no longer held her under his spell the way he once had.

Raising her chin, Grace reached up and shoved his hand away from the back of her neck. "I'm busy until after dinner. You'll have to meet me in the lounge of my hotel tonight at nine." Her schedule, her terms.

A muscle flexed in his jaw at her physical rejection of him, but he nodded. "Nine it is. Now let us get you checked out with the paramedics."

When he reached for her arm, she yanked it away. His touch had always weakened her and she couldn't handle that right now. Aside from being shaken and a little stiff in the neck from the impact, she was okay and had a tight schedule to keep. "I'm fine, except I'm about to be late. If you want to help, just move out of my way."

"We'll take you to that meeting," he said instead, gesturing to the SUV where the muscular dark-haired man even taller than Alex stood next to the open passenger door, watching them intently. The man wore shades so she couldn't see his eyes, but his eyebrows were drawn together in a deep frown as he watched them. The redhead with the tats was still at the wheel. Both hard men, both lethal. From their bearings and appearances alone, she knew they were former military, and bet they had served in Special Ops. Alex's personal security detail?

She faced Alex once more and narrowed her eyes in warning. "I don't think so. I've got my own security here now. We'll take another cab. You can stay and deal with the police for me." It was the least he could do, since her driver had gotten into the fender bender by trying to escape Alex in the first place. God, the man confused and infuriated her.

She pushed past Alex to find her assistant staring at them with a wary expression. The cops were still talking to the drivers and security team. "Come on, David." Head held high, Grace walked around the back of the damaged cab, trying to mask how much her legs shook and her insides quivered. Of all the things she'd anticipated handling in Pakistan during this trip, Alex Rycroft hadn't been one of them.

"Grace."

Nope. Been there, done that, got the scars to prove it. She shook her head at Alex and didn't look back as she strode toward David. "Nine tonight," she called out. Behind her she heard Alex curse. Ignoring him, she walked with David over to the curb where another cab sat, and waited for one of the team's security guards to give them the okay before climbing inside. "Did you pay the other driver?" she asked David.

"Yeah, but the police still want our statements."

"We'll deal with it later." She told the new driver the address of the meeting location and settled back in her seat, feeling disoriented and shaky as hell. Alex was here and he'd somehow found her. Not by chance. Likely using his connections within the NSA. He wanted a chance to explain. About what? His lies? Did he seriously think there was any way he could justify what he'd done?

"Who the hell was that?" David finally asked once they were moving.

"A ghost from my past," she murmured, rubbing the back of her neck where she could still feel the tingle of Alex's hand there. The muscles were already stiffening, promising a bitch of a headache later on.

Not a ghost, she corrected herself bitterly. *More like a figment of my imagination.*

Because as it turned out, she'd never really known him in the first place.

CHAPTER TWO

Malik Hassani eased toward consciousness slowly, gradually becoming aware of a soft beeping close by and hushed footfalls moving around him. He peeled his heavy eyelids apart to find a nurse at his side, checking the machine that connected to his IV line. He shifted a bit, feeling groggy and strangely heavy, as though his limbs were weighed down.

"Ah, you're awake. How do you feel?" the nurse asked, a white woman with pale blue eyes and a crisp British accent.

In all honesty, part of him was still surprised that he was alive. When they'd put him under this last time he'd been sure it was for good, so they could call his death while in custody an accident. But here he was. They must not have figured out yet who the big players involved in his network were. "Fine."

She nodded, checked his line and his pulse, then made notes on a clipboard she carried. "The doctor will be here to talk to you in a few minutes. Go ahead and rest a while longer."

Rather than respond, Malik gazed around the room to get his bearings as he fought the haze that clouded his mind. He was alone in here. The small space had no windows, only a single door that appeared to be made of steel. Other than the quiet beeping, the place was nearly silent. Quite possibly he was the only patient in the entire facility, wherever it was. With the hood on he hadn't been able to see where they'd driven him, much less the layout of the building itself. But he knew without a doubt that armed guards waited on the other side of that door.

Once he was sure he was safe for the time being, he examined his hand. They'd cuffed his right wrist to the bedrail and wrapped his left hand up past his wrist where the surgeons had gone in to access some of the damaged tendons. The tips of his fingers extended from the edge of the bandages. He flexed them slightly, sucked in a sharp breath at the searing pain the slight movement caused. After setting his hand carefully on his stomach, he took stock of his situation. He was sleepy and his mind felt fuzzy, but he knew what would happen from here.

As soon as he got clearance from the doctors, the FBI team would hood him again and take him back to the detention center where he'd undergo countless more rounds of "interrogations" from members of various agencies. Malik curled his right hand into a fist. Arrogant, power hungry Americans, always interfering with and controlling other countries' affairs. Did they really think they could break him just by depriving him of sleep and asking him the same questions over and over? Anger churned deep inside him. He'd spent years on the other side of this equation, using methods much more severe than they had the guts to employ. He would never give them what they wanted.

He hated feeling like a caged animal. The thought of spending months locked up like that and going through the lengthy process of a trial before they sentenced him to a prison term was depressing as hell. It outraged him. He was stronger than the international intelligence community realized. He'd do his time, pull whatever strings he had available to him from within the prison walls, and plan his next strategy for when he was free.

A wave of fatigue hit him. He allowed the residual anesthetic in his system to pull him back into a doze. The nurse came back to check on him awhile later, then the doctor, who told him the surgery had been a success. With therapy, in time he should regain nearly full use of his hand. Malik knew he should have been more grateful about that but he was too caught up in his failure to care. He'd been *this* close to achieving his dream of seizing control in Pakistan, the dream he'd been pursuing for so long. Then it had all been taken away.

After the surgeon left he dozed some more, this time slipping into a deep sleep.

"Malik."

He jerked awake at the low male voice next to him. Blinked against the glare of the overhead lights when he peered up at the man who stood at his bedside. The newcomer wore hospital scrubs, the surgical mask pulled down to reveal his mouth and dark mustache. There was something vaguely familiar about him—

"Wake up," the man said urgently as he unlocked the cuff on Malik's right wrist. "We have to—"

A sudden, unmistakable blast of gunfire outside the room cut off whatever he was about to say. Malik shot upright, wincing as his injured hand hit the mattress. His heart slammed against his ribs. Were they coming to kill him now? He was trapped, chained to the bed. He had no weapon.

"Hurry," the man snapped as he reached for the IV pole. He seemed totally unaffected by the shots.

A rush of adrenaline helped clear the lingering grogginess away. Malik twisted around to get a better look at the man, sizing him up as a threat. "Who are you?" he demanded. Beyond the door the staccato shots continued, along with the sounds of screams and pounding footsteps.

"A friend," the man answered without looking at him. "Now get up and *hurry*. We don't have much time."

Not about to trust him, certain this was a trap to kill him and make it look like a botched rescue attempt, Malik swung his legs over the side of the bed and thought about what he could use as a weapon. The IV pole was the only thing in sight. Without taking his eyes off the man occupied with shutting off the IV drip, Malik yanked off the tape holding the catheter in his vein, tearing away hair with it, and slid it out. He pressed hard on the wound with his bandaged hand to get it to close just as the man grabbed him by the upper arm and hauled him to his feet.

Malik snarled a warning and wrenched his arm away, but the drugs in his system were too strong. He swayed, barely caught the bed railing to steady himself before his knees slammed into the linoleum floor with a jarring thud.

The man grabbed him again, his attention on the closed door as he drew a pistol from his waistband. Malik's gaze locked on the weapon. He prepared to grab it, wrestle it from the man's grip, but instead he was dragged to his feet again. Malik stumbled after him, hating how weak and disoriented he was. Two steps from the door he heard another barrage of gunfire outside, closer this time. A female screamed in the distance, then came the pounding of running footsteps. He focused on that door, every muscle in his body tensed as he prepared to either flee or attack.

The man holding his arm stood back as the door flew open to reveal four uniformed police officers standing there. The first one took in Malik with a single cursory glance, then barked, "Quickly," and stepped aside to let them pass. Malik felt as though he was floating as they ushered him out into the hallway. Spatters of blood covered the walls and floor. The bodies of several FBI officers littered the hallway.

"Come on," the first cop snapped, and hurried down the hall to the exit door at the end.

Malik shuffled along while the others surrounded him like a living shield, weapons drawn. More shots cracked down another hallway to the left. They didn't slow, didn't hesitate. Men were shouting over the gunfire, more women screamed. Malik saw the body of the British nurse lying on the floor on her back, eyes staring sightlessly at the ceiling. He quickly turned his gaze to the exit at the end of the corridor they were in. His heart was pounding now, most of the grogginess gone. Were they really getting him out of here?

"This way," the man who'd come into his room said, and pulled Malik through a door on the right that one of the cops held open. This hallway was dim, lit only by the emergency lighting. An alarm started up, the shrieking grating on his tautly stretched nerves. The men hurried him toward another heavy door at the end, carrying him helplessly on an unstoppable tide.

"Where are we going?" Malik finally demanded, still having no idea what was happening. He didn't know any of these men. Were they taking him to a different location? Maybe Pakistani officials were waiting for him, planning to kill him later. There were too many men around him to overpower, even if he'd been fully alert and had use of both his hands. But why kill all the guards and staff if their aim was to murder him?

"Somewhere safe," the first man answered, his attention locked on the far door.

Malik had taken four more steps when a tremendous boom shook the building. He instinctively ducked and raised his hands to protect himself, but the men surrounding him didn't stop. They dragged him onward to that door, ignoring the threat beyond it even as bits of plaster rained down from the ceiling and his ears throbbed from the concussion of the blast. A large bomb. Targeting the building? Something outside it?

At the exit the men formed a protective circle around him and waited. At some unseen signal one cop shoved down on the release bar and threw the steel door open. Brilliant sunshine blinded Malik. He put up one hand to shield his eyes, crouched as the men grabbed him and bodily dragged him outside into the parking lot at the back of the building. Chaos met his stunned gaze. Several vehicles were on fire, some lying on their roofs from the force of the explosion. Dead bodies lay scattered around two SUVs and an unmarked van, the corpses charred and blackened.

"Go, go!" the first cop urged the others.

The detail broke into a jog, keeping him in the middle of the living barricade. More shots rang out behind them, farther away this time. At the other side of the lot, two large SUVs suddenly roared up to the curb. More uniformed cops burst out, weapons drawn.

Malik automatically dug his heels in but the men surrounding him merely lifted him off his feet and kept running toward the vehicles. They shoved him through the open door of a rear passenger seat and jumped in beside him. He'd barely scrambled upright when someone put a hand on the back of his head and shoved his face toward the floor. Doors slammed, the engine revved, and then the big vehicle peeled away from the curb with a squeal of its tires.

"Stay down," that firm voice commanded beside him. "It's not safe yet."

Malik didn't argue. He kept his head down and struggled to figure out what the hell was happening. These weren't his men. "Who *are* you?" he snarled.

"I told you, we're friends. Just stay down and you'll see everything soon enough."

Helpless, resenting that, Malik had no choice but to obey. The driver took several sharp turns and drove at a fast clip. They drove for what seemed like a long time—maybe forty minutes or more—before they finally stopped and the doors popped open.

"Okay, come on." The man released his hold on the back of Malik's head. He sat up and looked around warily. They were at some sort of a garage. More vehicles were waiting next to a low concrete building. "Hurry. They'll be following us." He yanked Malik across the seat and out of the vehicle. His bare feet hit the pavement and he was once again surrounded by a wall of men as they hustled him to a silver cube van parked a few dozen meters away.

They helped him into the back of it, climbed in with their weapons at the ready, and slammed the wide doors shut behind them. There were no windows back here, the only light the tiny line of it that seeped in between the seam in the rear doors.

The man who'd pulled Malik out of the SUV knocked sharply on the van's ceiling and the driver took off. Once they cleared the lot and got onto the street, the man sighed and leaned back with a satisfied chuckle. He flicked on a slim pen light, illuminating his face. Malik narrowed his eyes, studying him. Savior? Or executioner?

The man's teeth gleamed in the light as he smiled. "Bashir sends his regards."

Malik stared at him as the blood roared in his ears, hardly daring to believe it. "What do you mean?"

"He initiated emergency procedures, orchestrated this whole thing from behind bars, right under the Americans' noses." The smile widened. "And here you are, safe and sound once more. Once you reach the safe location, you'll finally be able to take command."

Alex's whole body was strung tight as Gage drove him and Hunter from the accident site back to the hotel. Having just seen Grace face-to-face and wrapping his arms around her the way he'd dreamed of for so long, being forced to watch her walk away from him again was the cruelest torture. He felt like he was being torn in half. There was the rational, civilized part of him that told him to give her space, time to cool down before they talked tonight.

Then there was the primal, innate part of him that howled in agony at being separated from her again, even for only a few hours. He'd always been careful to keep that part of him locked deep inside where no one else could see it. Until now. Both men riding up front were a pointed reminder of that.

The atmosphere in the SUV was tense, the silence brittle. He saw Hunter and Gage exchange another questioning glance, then Hunter finally turned in his seat to stare at Alex. "So, care to fill us in on what the fuck that was all about?"

Alex let out a deep breath. When he'd come back to the vehicle after Grace left, both the guys had gaped at him like they'd never seen him before. He wasn't surprised, since they'd seen him reflexively haul her out of that cab and grab hold of her like he was afraid someone might try to tear her from his arms. "Dr. Grace Fallon," he answered tightly, knowing he owed them that much.

"Uh-huh." Hunter pulled off his shades, those light brown eyes pinning Alex. "Who is she?"

"A chemical engineer, now working for the U.N. as a chemical weapons inspector." Alex also knew exactly *why* she was here. He'd made it his business to find out from the moment a source at the NSA had confirmed she was in Islamabad.

Hunter kept staring at him with an impatient "get real" look that said he wasn't buying that bland description. "She's more than that."

Gage snorted. "Way more. Fuck, man, tell us. We want details."

Obviously she was *more* to him, and anyone who'd seen his reaction to her a few minutes ago would realize it. But he wasn't going to spill the details to anyone, not even these men whom he trusted with his life. Some things were just too personal, too raw.

Alex bit back a sigh and looked away to stare out the window. "Yeah." He wasn't going to tell them that she was the woman he'd never gotten over. The one he'd fallen so fast and hard for that every memory he had of her was permanently seared into his brain. Even four years ago he'd recognized that she was *the one*, the woman he could see himself settling down with to make a life together. Having already been through a bad marriage and a divorce, that stunning revelation had certainly knocked him on his ass.

But just when it seemed like life couldn't get any better, everything had suddenly gone to hell, and there hadn't been a single thing he could do to stop it. All this time later, losing Grace was still the biggest regret of his life. One he knew he'd never get over. Now that she was here in Islamabad, he had to make things right, had to fight for her.

When it was clear Alex wasn't going to say anything else, Hunter finally let it go and faced forward again. The rest of the ride passed in silence.

In his hotel room shower, Alex tipped his head back to let the hot spray of water pour over his hair and face, and groaned in relief. It'd been a bitch of a day so far and he was running on less than a total of six hours' sleep for the past three nights. The pounding water beat down on him, easing the sore, tight muscles in his neck and shoulders. His mind, however, was another story. It wouldn't slow down, constantly spinning at a hundred miles an hour. And of everything that had happened over the past few days, seeing Grace was what he kept coming back to.

God, it was so hard to believe he'd been able to look into those beautiful pale aqua eyes again, hold her in his arms after all this time…

Now she was here and he had one final shot. Damn, the mere memory of all those soft curves pressed against him today made his cock so hard it hurt. He braced a hand on the tile wall and reached between his legs with the other. He fisted himself and stroked the rigid flesh, letting his mind take him back to that incredible night they'd spent in each other's arms in Mombasa, before the attack had shattered both their lives forever.

That single, too-brief night had been the culmination of weeks of intense build-up for them, and it had resulted in the hottest sex he'd ever had. But it had been way more than physical for both of them. He'd never felt so connected to a woman as he had to Grace that night. Her naked body had been soft and giving beneath him as she arched on the plush hotel room carpet of his room and begged for more. The longing and absolute trust on her face as she finally relinquished control to him on that final night together had filled empty places inside him he'd never known existed until her.

Even as he took her he'd understood the magnitude of what it meant. She'd just gotten a legal separation from a husband who hadn't touched her in nearly a year, and Alex had been working undercover for seven months. They'd been starved for each other. He'd reveled in the way her eyes had gone all hazy as he'd pinned her hands above her head and finally slid into her tight, slick body, making her his at last. Everything about it had been intense. Something primal and untamed inside him had demanded he imprint himself on her, claim her in a way she'd feel forever.

Pleasure swelled as the images rushed onward. Alex squeezed his aching flesh harder, his strokes rough and urgent. Her breathless gasps sounded in his head, the soft cry of surrender coming from her throat as she gave herself to him. His breathing sped up, his muscles tightening as release built deep inside him. But just as he neared the edge, his mind fast forwarded to the night when he'd finally been allowed into her hospital room after the terror attack. The look of betrayal and utter devastation on her face when she'd looked at him was like a knife to the gut. His hand froze around his erection, his breath halted. And just that fast the pleasure disappeared.

Muttering a curse, Alex shoved the image from his mind. He released his rapidly deflating cock and grabbed the little bottle of shampoo from the shelf in the corner. Even though he scrubbed his hair and body clean, there was nothing he could do to wash away what that stricken look on Grace's face had done to him for the past four years.

He toweled off and dressed, mentally rehearsing what he would say when he met her at her hotel shortly. He'd gone over it at least a dozen times throughout the afternoon, and had changed it that many as well. When he'd seen that car hit her cab today, he'd almost lost it. It'd been his fault; the cab driver had seen the SUV coming after them and instinctively tried to escape, resulting in the collision.

The thought of anything or anyone ever hurting her again made him insane. He'd never reacted to a woman the way he had with Grace. It shook him that he still didn't know how to control that part of himself. Without even trying she'd brought out every base aspect of his personality, roused everything he kept hidden behind his cool, detached veneer. With her, there was no control, and that's what scared him. He never lost control. Couldn't afford to. And yet just by being in the same room with him, Grace managed to reduce him to the primal, territorial animal that lurked in his core. No matter what happened, he had to keep that part of him chained down when he saw her tonight.

Stepping out of the humid bathroom, he heard his phone buzzing over on the dresser. He strode across the room to get it, finalizing exactly what he was going to say to start the conversation tonight. He had to make her listen. Had to make her understand that he'd been more authentic with her than anyone else on earth, even his ex-wife. With Grace, he had no defenses. In some ways it made her more of a threat to him than Hassani had ever been.

The phone quit ringing just as he reached the dresser. When he picked it up he frowned as he saw all the missed texts and voice messages. He checked the call display, saw the same number had called him six times over the past ten minutes. The last text message read *CALL ME NOW, E.*

Evers.

Alex called him back, holding the phone to his ear with his shoulder as he did up the last of the buttons on his shirt.

His pulse beat faster as he waited for the call to connect. Something big was up.

Evers answered on the first ring. "Where the fuck were you?"

Alex blinked, his fingers freezing around the final button. "In the shower. Why, what's going on?"

Evers let out a tight sigh. "Hassani's escaped."

Alex's head snapped up. The mirror in front of him reflected the shock on his face. *No.* "What the fuck are you talking about?"

"I mean he's *gone.* A group of gunmen dressed as Pak cops attacked the facility right after he came out of recovery. Well-organized, well-armed. They blew up the team's vehicles and smuggled Hassani out in an unmarked van. They took out the medical team, guys from my team, the CIA guys. I'm talking mass fucking casualties."

Not possible. The Feds and CIA boys had that place locked down tight.

Alex whirled and grabbed the remote from the dresser. "When?" he demanded as he turned on the TV. A newscast showed a scene of chaos at the site. Upturned vehicles were still burning, strobe lights from emergency vehicles filled the screen.

"Forty-five minutes ago. We've got teams scrambling to find him. Apparently they took him in an SUV, possibly in a convoy. We're interviewing two survivors and tracking security camera footage now."

Holy shit, Hassani was really out there again.

Fuck. Me. Alex ran a hand through his damp hair, struggled to keep from exploding. He couldn't believe this was happening, not after everything it had taken to nail the bastard the first time. "Where are you now?"

"Detention facility."

"I'll be there in fifteen minutes. Have a team ready to brief me when I get there." He hung up before Evers could answer, and shot a text to Gage to meet him in Hunter's room. Yanking on his boots, Alex grabbed his sidearm and tactical vest before running down the hall to pound on Hunter's door.

Four seconds later the door swung open. Hunter raised his eyebrows and stepped out of the way as Alex stormed past him into the room. "What the hell's wrong?"

"Turn on the news," Alex told him. Hunter frowned but did as he said, just as another knock signaled that Gage had arrived. Alex let him in. "Hassani's escaped."

Both men's gazes snapped to his. "Are you serious?" Hunter asked, his body tensing.

Alex nodded at the screen, jaw tight. "Evers said the team posed as Pak cops. Killed everyone inside and blew up the teams waiting in vehicles outside. Whoever they were, they weren't amateurs."

"No fucking way," Gage muttered as he watched the footage. "No way he planned this from inside that cell. Somebody's helping him from the outside."

"No doubt," Alex agreed. "We need to find out who that ISI source of his is, A-fucking-SAP."

"So what now?" Hunter asked as he picked up his shoulder holster from the table and shrugged it on.

Alex was already shooting off more texts to his CIA and NSA contacts. "Get hold of Ellis and Jordyn, get 'em back here on the next flight out of BWI. We're going to meet up with Evers at the detention facility right now. Once we're briefed, we're gonna find that sonofabitch before he makes it out of the city. The attack was a little over forty-five minutes ago, so he couldn't have gotten far." *Yet.*

His mind raced as he tried to think what he would do in Hassani's place, where he would go to regroup and start planning. Not Peshawar again, not this time. Lahore? Karachi? Or would he make another attempt to get back over the border into Afghanistan to meet up with his surviving Taliban pals? Though Alex doubted he'd get a warm reception after the way he'd shot one of the fighters during his desperate attempt at escape in that tunnel beneath the village in the Spin Ghar Mountains.

Alex marched over and shut off the TV. "Let's go." He stepped out into the hallway with the others close behind him. They were in for another long night—and maybe several long days. He didn't care how long it took, he just knew they had to find Hassani, *fast*, before he reactivated more of his sleeper network and vanished.

As he strode down the hall, Alex's jaw clenched. Not only had they just lost their number one high value target, the meeting with Grace and the chance for forgiveness he'd waited four years for was now postponed indefinitely.

It only made him hate Hassani more.

CHAPTER THREE

Grace fiddled with her glass of sparkling water as she waited in the hotel lounge for Alex to show up. She'd love something stronger to fortify her for the coming confrontation—say, four or five glasses of strong red wine—but she didn't want anything to dull her mind. Or her tongue, for that matter.

She felt like she might explode if she didn't get the chance to finally unload everything she'd kept carefully locked up inside her these past four years. Talking to her sister on the phone earlier had only helped relieve the pressure a little, and she knew her sister had probably alerted their parents the moment she'd gotten off the phone with her. Grace felt bad about that. Everyone was already concerned enough about her without this new complication. Since the terror attack her entire family worried far too much about the dangers of her job. But Grace loved her work and had long ago accepted the inherent risks that came with it.

Those risks had never included Alex Rycroft before, however.

She rubbed at the back of her neck where the muscles were stiff and sore from the fender bender, and looked around the lounge. About a dozen other hotel guests were scattered amongst the other tables, mostly businessmen in suits, a few couples.

Turning her gaze toward the room's entrance where Alex would show up soon, the butterflies in her stomach stirred to life once again. All afternoon since the lengthy meeting to finalize the agreement they would present to the Syrian delegation, she'd gone over what she wanted to say to him, and the questions she wanted answers to. She didn't plan to give him the chance to take over the conversation. The man was lethally charming, and a skilled liar. No, she was going to get the information she wanted, say what she had to say, then leave.

Realizing she was still fiddling with her glass, she put her hands in her lap and laced her fingers together to keep from fidgeting. She would *not* let Alex know how nervous she was, or how much the sight of him affected her. Pulling in a calming breath, she turned her attention to one of the TVs mounted on the opposite wall. One of the staff members had turned the channel to an international news station broadcasting in English.

Grace read the *Breaking News* subtitle. From where she was sitting there was no audio, but she could see the picture clearly enough. Another bombing right here in Islamabad. Eleven people confirmed dead, more still unaccounted for.

Grace continued to watch the footage unfold, keeping an eye on the clock at the bottom of the screen. Alex was already a few minutes late. It wasn't like him. The man might be a consummate liar, but back when she'd known him—or thought she had anyway—he'd always been on time for everything, and usually a few minutes early. For the first time, doubt began to replace some of her anxiety. He wouldn't stand her up, would he?

Just then a hotel staff member walked up to her from the bar. "Ms. Fallon?"

"Yes."

"I have a message for you from a Mr. Rycroft."

Grace tightened her hands in her lap, steeled herself as she raised her chin. "What did he say?"

"He regrets that he won't be able to join you this evening. He's left a number for you to reach him at, and asked that you leave him a message when it's convenient."

Oh, did *he?* Grace took the slip of paper and thanked the man, stifling an ironic laugh. Had she seriously expected anything different? God, would she never learn? She shoved the piece of paper into her purse without looking at it and took a gulp of her water to ease the tightness in her throat. Her gaze strayed back to the TV as a new picture flashed onto the screen. A familiar-looking middle aged Pakistani man with deep set eyes and a neatly trimmed goatee. She stilled in shock as the subtitle changed.

Malik Hassani reported to have escaped U.S. custody

Grace couldn't believe it. They'd only captured him a few days ago—it'd been all over the news and in the papers and—

Understanding hit. Alex worked for the NSA. He'd undoubtedly been here because of involvement with Hassani's case. And now the most wanted terrorist on the planet was once again on the loose.

She snatched up her purse to fish the piece of paper out, her stomach sinking as she stared at the number scrawled there. *Alex, what have you gotten yourself into this time?*

Alex strode into the luxury hotel lobby at just before two in the morning after Evers and another Fed dropped him off at the front doors. When Alex had told him to drive him here rather than their hotel, Evers just grinned and shook his head. Alex wasn't sure how the Fed had found out about Grace, but was pretty sure either Gage or Hunter had spilled the juicy details about him going all territorial caveman with her after the fender bender. He might be dead on his feet and in desperate need of sleep, but this couldn't wait. The lobby was empty except for the single employee behind the front desk. Alex headed straight for him.

All night they'd been tracking Hassani, organizing various taskforces and getting people in place to hunt him down. At that moment, six different teams were out doing recon on various target locations, acting on tips from reliable sources about the terrorist's whereabouts. Alex and his intelligence community counterparts had been in contact with their informants to find out if anyone knew anything about the breakout from the medical facility today. So far nothing useful had been uncovered, and they still didn't have a firm location for Hassani. It was like the bastard had vanished into thin air.

Alex walked up to the front desk, shifting his mind to the present. Despite the crisis with Hassani, all night he'd been distracted about the situation with Grace. She hadn't called him, hadn't even left a text. A small, hopeful part of him had been waiting for her to contact him all night, so he'd kept checking his phone obsessively. It had frustrated the hell out of him that he couldn't concentrate fully on his job. At midnight he'd finally realized she wasn't going to call, and since there was nothing more he could do on the Hassani front until he got a fresh lead, he was here to take care of business.

Hunting Hassani down was going to take everything Alex had, and he couldn't give that without talking to Grace first. Whether she'd listen to anything he said was still anyone's guess.

"I need to speak with Grace Fallon," he told the guy at the desk. "It's an emergency." Well, it was to him anyway, and it was also the only reason the staff would ever disturb her at this hour.

The clerk's pleasant expression transformed into one of concern. "Of course, sir. Who shall I tell her is calling?"

"Alex." *And she might tell me to go to hell.*

"One moment." He looked up Grace's room number on the computer and used the desk phone to call up to her room. She must have answered because the guy relayed the message. Alex was aware of his pulse thudding in his ears as he awaited the response. The clerk hung up the phone. "She said you can go right up." He gave Alex the room number.

Relieved that she was at least willing to meet with him, Alex rode up to the eighth floor and strode down the silent hallway with his stomach full of knots. Even though he'd geared up for this and what might happen, he knew deep down he wasn't prepared to walk away from her again. Losing her had carved a chunk out of his heart and it had never stopped bleeding. He'd agonized over his decisions that had led to this result every day since. At her door he paused to take a deep breath and knocked quietly. His heart thudded hard against his chest.

The door opened a moment later. Grace stood there dressed in form-fitting yoga pants and a snug black top that hugged her full breasts, her chin length auburn hair all tousled from sleep and her face scrubbed clean. She looked soft and kissable and sexy as hell. Rather than say anything, she leveled those guarded aqua eyes on him for a few heartbeats of silent scrutiny, then stepped aside and gestured for him to come in.

Releasing the breath he'd been holding, he stepped into the suite and glanced around. The sitting room opened up into a kitchenette with granite counters and a stainless steel range. To the right a door led through to what he guessed was the bedroom and connecting bath. He walked toward the large window that overlooked the outdoor pool. At the couch set next to it, he turned to face her. Grace still stood near the door as though she didn't want to get too close, her arms folded beneath her breasts in a defensive posture.

The air was charged with sudden tension, so thick he could feel it crackling over his nerve endings. She stared at him for another long moment before breaking the taut silence. "Apparently you couldn't wait until morning to talk to me?"

"No," he answered simply, and caught the flare of surprise in her eyes at the forcefulness of his answer. "Something important came up, or I would've been here at nine like I said I would. Did you get my message?"

"Yeah, I got it."

At least she didn't deny it. "You didn't call, so I came to you." He'd waited too damn long to see her already.

"I was waiting to call you in the morning. You know, at a more human hour." She raised an eyebrow in a pointed reminder of how late it was.

Bullshit. He was willing to bet she'd just have texted him at best and then not returned his messages afterward. He set his hands on his hips. "Well, I'll be tied up all day, so I'm here now." He should be sleeping to catch whatever rest he could before he started his work day at five, but there was no way he could do that until they talked.

She tilted her head slightly, those intelligent eyes measuring him. "You guys lost Hassani, didn't you?"

She must've seen the news and figured it out on her own. Alex nodded, seeing no point in denying it. "Yeah."

"Did you find him?"

"Not yet." But they would. It was his top priority once he and Grace cleared the air. There was plenty he had to say.

"Well, what happened—"

"As much as I want to tell you everything, I can't talk to you about an ongoing investigation." Though he wished he could. Having Grace as a sounding board would take a ton of weight off his shoulders. She was fucking brilliant, her mind every bit as sexy as her lush body. He'd always thought she'd make one hell of a confidant and advisor for him.

She nodded once in acceptance, her arms still folded tightly beneath the enticing curve of her full breasts he couldn't help looking at. "Fair enough. So what *do* you want to talk to me about?"

"Us."

At that, her eyes widened and she snorted in disbelief. "First off, there *is* no us. Apparently there never *was* an us, only I was too stupid to see it."

And there it was. The knife in his gut twisted. He shook his head. "You know better than that."

"Yeah, I do now," she replied bitterly. Sighing, she squared her shoulders and lifted her chin like she was getting ready to do battle. "All right, let's just get this over with. Say what you came to say."

Even though he'd gone over it a thousand times, being confronted with the very real possibility that he might lose her forever after this filled his chest with lead. Four years ago she'd frozen him out, completely ignoring all his frantic attempts to contact her. Two years ago she'd sent him the final, brusque e-mail that had smothered the tiny flame of hope that had kept burning in his heart.

I have nothing to say to you and I don't care to listen to anything you have to say to me. If you ever cared about me at all, leave me alone and stay out of my life. Forever.

He'd finally realized then that he'd lost her for good and stopped trying to contact her. A part of him was still terrified he'd never break through that icy wall again. She was so cold, so distant, it filled him with something close to panic. He indicated the couch with a tilt of his head, fighting back the fear and desperation clawing at him. "At least come sit."

She didn't budge from her spot. "I'd prefer to stand, thanks."

So she could open the door and throw his ass out the moment she'd heard enough to seal the coffin on their dead relationship. He didn't intend to make it that easy for her to dismiss him. "All right, then *I'll* sit." He tugged his pant legs up at the thigh and sank into the couch cushions, stretching one arm across the back of it in a pose that made him appear far more relaxed than he actually was.

Grace didn't move, only raised one fiery brow at him expectantly. "Well?"

Shit, it was killing him to finally be alone with her after all this time and have this unbridgeable distance between them. It was all he could do to stay where he was instead of rushing over there to wrap his arms around her again. If he could just touch her, reach her through that cold mask she'd put on to protect herself, maybe there was still a chance for them. He couldn't give up on that hope, couldn't accept that he'd truly lost her. "I hated lying to you," he began in a low voice.

She stared at him, unmoving, unblinking. But he could see the anger and resentment simmering in her eyes.

He pushed out a hard breath, got right to the heart of it. He didn't blame her for holding a grudge. She had every reason to hate him. "When we met I was working undercover using my nickname. I was named after my father. My middle name is John, but my parents always called me Jack."

No answer. Just that hard, cool stare that had him squirming inside. His muscles tensed as he fought the urge to reach for her. He couldn't stand seeing the hurt and anger in her eyes, knowing he'd put it there. He'd give anything to make it right. "So yeah, I lied to you about my name and what I was doing on that op because I had to, not because I wanted to. But everything else was real."

"Except for the part where I stupidly thought you were falling in love with me, but it turned out you were just using me to get close to people in my social circle you suspected were funding terrorists in Kenya."

The acid in her tone hit him harder than that icy look on her face. Alex's gut tightened. He wished he could punch her ex-husband in the face for telling her that. His hands curled into fists and he drew in a steadying breath. "It wasn't the way he made it sound."

"No?" She widened her eyes in feigned shock for a moment, then narrowed them. "Because it sure seemed that way to me when you abandoned me there in that hospital."

He lowered his arm from the back of the couch and leaned forward, every instinct screaming at him to walk over there, wrap his arms around her and hold her until he broke through this invisible fucking wall between them. A dozen volatile emotions battled for supremacy inside him. Anger, fear, grief.

He shook his head, fighting to stay calm, keep his voice down. "You think I wanted that? I didn't have a *choice*, Grace. By showing up there my cover was blown, and I didn't care. What does that tell you? Your husband—" God, he hated saying that word, because they'd been legally separated and Robert had been anything but a husband to her long before that—"was going to have me arrested. He had the cops waiting there for me when you came out of the O.R.. I had to pull every string I knew of just to get through security and be let in to see you in your room the next day."

"Am I supposed to be grateful for that?" She shook her head in bewilderment, thrust an accusatory finger at him. "The man I *thought* I knew wouldn't have let that stop him. He would have stayed no matter what. If you'd really cared and wanted to be with me, you would have found a way."

"I tried!" He swallowed a snarl of frustration, ran a hand through his hair as he sucked in a harsh breath. He realized she had a low opinion of him now, but how could she believe *that* of him? That he would ever willingly walk away from her when she'd been distraught and recovering from bullet wounds he should have prevented? "God dammit, it *killed* me to leave you like that. Ripped me to pieces, Grace."

She lowered her arm and swallowed, her eyes still full of accusation. "You swore you wouldn't leave me. You *swore*." Her voice broke on the last word. She looked away, put a hand to her mouth.

Alex was on his feet moving toward her before he even realized what he was doing. Grace saw him coming. She shook her head, tried to stave him off with an upraised hand and a sound of protest, but he couldn't stay away from her a second longer when she was hurting. Just couldn't.

Even when she backed away from him and came up against the door with nowhere to go, he still didn't stop. He halted only when he stood inches away from her. The warm vanilla scent of her hair and skin rose up to torture him. He could see the apprehension in her wide eyes, the dread, and it broke something inside him to see how afraid she was of being hurt again—of *him* hurting her again.

"Grace," he whispered unsteadily, staring into those beautiful clear eyes. He had to undo the damage, win her trust back. There had to be a way. If she shoved him out of her life for good after this he didn't know how he'd survive it. He wanted her forgiveness, yes, but what he wanted—needed—was to have her back in his life for good. Without her, he'd only been going through the motions of living. His life had been empty.

She angrily brushed a lock of hair from her cheek. "You left me there. I don't care about why you did it, I just know that I was alone there for days, in pain and afraid. And you. Weren't. *There.*"

Alex couldn't speak, his throat was too tight. He was on the verge of losing it, totally breaking down and sobbing like a fucking pussy. Everything she said was true and he knew he deserved it. Nothing he ever said could change that. It felt like someone had their hands wrapped around his throat, squeezing until he could barely breathe.

He struggled to find his voice. "I know. I know you were and I'm so sorry. More sorry than you'll ever know." It had broken something inside him to imagine what she'd been going through all alone during the aftermath. Hearing it confirmed from her own lips was ten times worse than anything his imagination had conjured up.

"Why?" she whispered, shaking her head as she searched his eyes, looking for answers he couldn't possibly make her understand. "Why did you do it?"

"The NSA pulled me out. By blowing my cover I'd exposed myself and the rest of the team. They had us all out on a chartered flight an hour after I saw you that morning, and it was either that or be arrested." And when he'd tried to reach her by phone and e-mail, she'd never answered. Not that he blamed her. "It shredded me, Grace. Leaving you, especially like that when I knew you needed me was the hardest thing I've ever done. But I need you to believe that I would never have left you by my own choice." He raised a hand to touch her, powerless to stop himself, but froze when she flinched.

"Don't." A whispered plea. She shook her head once, panic and denial flashing across her face. Her hands came up to block him, her palms hitting the wall of his chest and he could feel the tremor in them. He ached to touch her, take her pain away.

Alex's own hand shook slightly as he reached up to cradle her cheek in his palm. She flinched at the contact but didn't shove him back as he'd feared. He stroked his thumb gently across the silken curve of her cheek, dying inside because he needed so much more. "It was *me*," he whispered back. "Whatever I did and didn't tell you back then, it was still me." He wrapped the fingers of his other hand around her palm, pressed it to his chest over his pounding heart. "I'm still the man you knew, no matter what else has happened."

Grace squeezed her eyes shut and shook her head again as she tugged her hand from his grasp. "Back up and give me some space. I can't breathe—I can't think when you touch me."

But he couldn't back away. Not now.

Instead he leaned in closer and put one hand on the door, caging her between it and his body. "I don't want you to think, I want you to feel. *Feel* me, Grace. Feel *this*." He grabbed her hand again, pressed it tight to his chest. "Feel that? The connection? It's still there, you know it is, because it's *real*. Whatever else I lied to you about, I never lied about this. Us."

She drew in a shallow breath, and just when he thought she would shove him away or scream at him, instead she opened her eyes and looked right at him. The sheen of tears he saw in them shredded his heart. "And here you are again, showing up out of the blue right when I'm in the middle of something important. How do I know you're not just using me for my connections this time? How can you expect me to believe anything you say?"

Fuck. The lump in his throat was the size of a fucking baseball now. He understood why she'd doubt him, even knew he deserved it in light of everything that had happened. It drove him insane that there was no clear way to fix this, to get it through her head that he would rather die than hurt her in any way. Now she was here in front of him once more but she was so afraid, so skittish. The unfamiliar burn of tears started at the backs of his eyes.

Fighting for control, Alex closed his eyes and bent his head until their foreheads touched. He could feel her trembling there against the door, and his body screamed at him to soothe, to protect. "You already know why I'm here. And I wouldn't do that to you. Not ever. Not even to get Hassani, I swear it on my life." The hoarse words held a desperate edge, a reflection of exactly how he felt on the inside. "I didn't use you last time, either. Meeting you through my CIA contact was as much a surprise to me as it was to you. What Robert told you was a lie. I already had my contacts in Mombasa—if anything I was using them as an excuse to see you."

She'd never see that him blowing his cover for her told her everything she needed to know about what he'd felt for her, and he didn't expect her to. And the guilt, Christ, the fucking guilt was still eating a hole in his gut. "When I heard about the attack..." He stopped, swallowed again as the memories swamped him. The sheer terror of knowing he couldn't get to her in time. "We were in the final planning stages of an op to take the terrorists down when we got the call. I grabbed a team, broke every traffic law in the country getting there and when I saw you lying on that stretcher covered in blood…"

He exhaled, shook his head. "I've never been that afraid in my life. I didn't want to go, Grace. I wanted to stay—so many days I've thought about what it would have been like if I'd been there. I would've done everything I could to help you through that. I would've held you, been there when the nightmares and flashbacks came, fed you by hand, even washed your hair and given you sponge baths in the hospital because I know you can't stand to feel dirty. I'm so fucking sorry I wasn't there to do any of that, or be there for you afterward."

Something in his words or his tone must have reached her through that wall, because she made a little choked sound and twisted her face away to bury it in his neck. "You don't know how much I want to believe that."

His heart swelled painfully. "Believe it." He needed her to. Needed that more than he needed air to breathe. He couldn't take her hating him anymore, thinking the worst of him.

She didn't respond but she didn't pull away either, so he took a chance and slid one arm around her back. He could feel the tremor in her muscles, heard the hitch in her breath as he gathered her close. Alex almost groaned aloud at the feel of her against him, all soft, generous curves. The fragile truce between them was tenuous, but it was there, he could feel it.

He bent his head to nuzzle her temple, breathed in her warm, sweet scent. "I missed you so much, Grace. Every day, I never stopped. I hated that you wouldn't talk to me, even though I understood why."

The fingers resting on his chest curled into his shirt. Hope rose so swift and fast it nearly choked him. "I was lost without you for so long," she whispered, the past tense twisting that knife embedded in his chest harder. "You broke my *heart*."

He squeezed his eyes shut, tried to tell her everything he felt for her with his embrace. Holding her close, he released her hand to slide his into her hair and cradled the back of her head. "I know." He kissed her temple, the edge of her hairline, then trailed his lips to her cheek. She made a sound of protest and buried her face harder into his throat. But he could tell she was affected by his nearness and what he was doing to her. And he wasn't above using her body's response to him if it helped weaken her defenses. This was too important—he'd use any means necessary to get past her shields.

He nuzzled the side of her neck, lingered at that sensitive place where it curved into her shoulder. The exact spot that had always melted her before. He'd discovered it the first night he'd kissed her, two days after meeting her at that dinner. At her hitching gasp he paused, his lips grazing her soft skin, breath caressing her. A sudden burst of erotic awareness arced between them. He could feel it pulsing in the air, a pool of accelerant waiting for a source of ignition. A single spark that would send them both up in flames. She trembled, tensed in his arms.

Let me back in, baby. Let me back in just a little.

He raised his head to stare down at her, urging her face up to his with the hand in her hair. She searched his eyes and he saw the battle raging inside her. Confusion, wariness, *need*.

The need he could satisfy, right here and now. Lowering his gaze to her mouth, he slid his hand from her hair to sweep the pad of his thumb across her plump lower lip. Slowly. Gently. Watching her eyes all the while. Something in them heated, ignited. Alex removed his thumb and leaned in close, until only a breath separated their lips. Everything in him demanded he take her mouth, stamp his claim on her and remind her of what they could have together. Instinct held him back. She was too skittish, too mistrustful of him now. He had to take this slow, as much as it tortured him.

He closed his eyes, leaned in that last inch and touched his mouth to hers.

She jolted, drove her palms into his chest. "I can't," she whispered, the words breathless and full of pain as she turned her face away. "I can't."

Alex pulled in a deep breath and stayed there, her lips so close to his own. He opened his mouth to argue but froze when his cell phone buzzed in his front pocket.

Grace's fingers tightened on him, something close to regret flashing in her pale eyes as she met his gaze. The phone buzzed again, sounding angry, insistent. "You gonna answer that?" she whispered.

The only reason anyone would call him at this hour was for an emergency. Yet Alex held her stare for another few seconds while the phone buzzed, letting her know how tempted he was to ignore it for her, even though it might possibly be the most important call of his career.

Reluctantly he eased back, noting the way her shoulders sagged in relief as he moved out of her space and pulled the phone from his pocket. "Rycroft," he answered, still staring at Grace.

"I think we've got a lead," Evers said without preamble.

"What is it?"

"Possible sighting in Lahore. The intel's fresh, only five minutes old, and it's from a trusted source we've been paying off for years."

"I'll be there in twenty minutes." He hung up, still focused on Grace. "I have to go."

She nodded, didn't ask why or what he'd found out. He was simultaneously relieved and irritated by that.

His jaw clenched. "Give me your number." When she hesitated, he pressed. "You're only in town for how much longer, until the weekend?"

She swallowed, then admitted quietly, "I fly out Sunday morning."

Three days. Just three days until she left, and he was in the middle of a critical manhunt. "This isn't over, Grace, and you know it. Give me your number. I'll call when I can."

Again a hesitation, and he could see her weighing the decision as he waited. Finally she relented with a sigh and held her hand out for his phone. He gave it to her, waited while she input her number and handed it back. He checked the number, looked back up at her. "Is this your real number?"

At his teasing tone she huffed out a laugh, the action softening her features. She knew perfectly well he could get her number on his own if he needed to. But that crack in her veneer made him ache at the reminder of how easy things used to be between them. "Yes, it's real."

He slipped it back into his pocket. "I'll be in touch as soon as I can. I need to see you again." Before she could argue he reached out to tuck a lock of hair behind her ear, the shiny auburn strands glinting in the lamplight. "Take care of yourself."

She nodded. "You too."

"Oh, and there's something else I want to say."

"Yeah?"

"I haven't been with anyone since you."

She blinked at him as the full meaning of that sank in, her face going blank with shock. Four years since he'd had a lover. Though he'd had plenty of opportunity and interest from the opposite sex, no one could ever compare to Grace. No one else had interested him, no one else would do. She was it for him, and until he knew there was no chance with her, he couldn't move on.

Though it felt like he was being torn in half, Alex forced himself to walk out the door. The second he was in the hallway he heard the sound of the dead bolt sliding into place. As he headed for the elevator, he sent up a silent prayer that she hadn't just locked him out of her life for good.

CHAPTER FOUR

"Do you need something for the pain now?"

"No." Malik stayed where he was on the sofa and stared warily across the room at the man who'd appeared at his hospital bedside and whisked him out of the facility. "What else has happened that I don't know about?"

The thirtyish man stepped to the window of the humble house they'd stopped at, pulled back the blinds to peek out into the darkness. "We don't know who we can trust from the old network."

Malik arched a brow, irritated that he was forced to rely on this stranger and the others while not knowing exactly what was happening. The lack of control made him extremely uncomfortable. And angry. "Expecting someone?"

He turned from the window to look back at him. "Shortly, yes."

"Who?"

"A friend you'll recognize." He crossed back to the other side of the room and sat on one of the armchairs.

Malik settled back into the cushions and took stock. The armed men outside guarding them were from the most elite branch of the Pakistani police force, all of them military trained. They'd made the nearly four hour drive here to the outskirts of Lahore with no one following them on the road, but there could be drones or satellites tracking them at this very moment. They'd given him clothing, food and water, and hustled him into this safe house. He'd ordered the place swept for bugs and all the blinds and curtains remained closed. He was as safe as he was going to get, for the moment at least.

"Once I get the call, we can relax a bit more," the man said as he drummed his fingers on the wooden arms of the chair. "If I don't hear from him in the next half hour though…"

They'd move Malik immediately to a different city. Malik stared at him from across the room. So far he'd done everything in his power to ensure the rescue went off without a problem. Malik still didn't trust him. Until he knew who his true allies were now, every one of these men was a possible suspect to him.

The man's phone shrilled with an incoming call. He answered, smiled when he looked over at Malik. "He's here," he said as he hung up.

Moments later Malik heard the sound of an engine close to the house. Doors slammed shut, and the guards outside led someone into the hallway. Malik tensed slightly as he waited to see this so-called "friend". The door swung open. Bashir's personal lawyer stood in the opening.

"Malik," he said with a smile as he rushed over to shake his hand. "It's so good to see you."

It wasn't often Malik was surprised, but he definitely was. "You? You orchestrated all this?"

He nodded. "It took some doing, but Bashir had this all laid out prior to your capture."

Malik hid a smile. Bashir had always been more cautious than him, always making contingency plans just in case. This one had paid off in a huge way. "And he managed to arrange this from prison?"

The lawyer pushed his glasses up on the bridge of his nose. "He told me where to find the information I'd need. Once I found that, it was only a matter of contacting the names on the list and coordinating everything."

Incredible. Malik shook his head. "Well then you have my thanks. How is he?"

A shrug. "He's doing the best he can. No torture that I'm aware of, and he's being fed and well cared for so far. Though I think they'll be doubling his security now that you're out."

No doubt. And Malik couldn't leave his closest friend—his only friend, really—to languish behind bars when he'd shown such loyalty. "Once things are in place, I'll make sure to free him."

The lawyer nodded, seeming pleased by Malik's response. "You still have many trustworthy sources in the police force and some in the military. One or two politicians as well." He paused. "I also have information about who sided with the Americans."

"General Sharif," Malik said in disgust, the name leaving a bad taste in his mouth.

"Yes. I bet he's feeling nervous with you on the outside again."

Malik nodded. The traitorous bastard should be nervous. He would pay. "I have arrangements of my own to make. I'll need an encrypted phone—" The lawyer reached into his inner coat pocket and pulled a cell phone out for him. Malik took it. Once he was alone he'd examine it more closely to ensure there were no tracking devices. Even if he used it, he'd be careful to keep the conversation short and use code words in case anyone was monitoring the call. "What of my body-guards?"

"Both died in the tunnel the day you were captured."

They'd been two of the handful of men Malik had allowed close to him. No matter. His increased mistrust of his so-called "allies" would only make him harder to target in the future. "Any word on the situation in Islamabad?"

"Everyone is looking for you, of course. If you plan to stage the coup now, you'll have to set it up quickly and act using the police and whatever military forces you can rely on."

Malik nodded, already mapping out the steps he'd need to take. "There are a few things I have to take care of first." Things even more important than seizing the reins of power.

The man's gaze sharpened. "I also have information on Rycroft."

At the mention of that name, Malik's muscles tightened. "What about him?"

"I received a report from the police earlier today that I thought may interest you." He dug in his briefcase and pulled out some papers, handed them to him.

Malik skimmed the report. A minor traffic accident in Islamabad, involving an American, Grace Fallon. She worked for the UN. He flipped the page, froze when he saw the image there.

The picture was taken from behind her. A Caucasian woman with chin length auburn hair stood with her back to the camera. And holding that woman was none other than Alex Rycroft. His arms were locked around her in an embrace that no one who saw it could misinterpret as anything other than possessive and protective.

Malik glanced up at the lawyer and smiled as excitement rushed through his blood. He finally had the weakness he needed to exploit. "Find out everything you can about her, what she means to him and where she's staying." He couldn't go after Rycroft directly without serious risk of being captured or killed. But he could bait a trap with the right lure and make Rycroft come to him.

Malik was getting ahead of himself though. Before he could enjoy the pleasure of crushing his most hated adversary, he had another sentence to deliver.

Alex drained the cold dregs of his fourth cup of coffee and set his mug on the conference table where the team was assembled. "I want security tightened on all of us. Hassani was unpredictable before, but now that he's desperate and on the run, he's a total wild card." And since Alex knew him better than anyone else in the room and still couldn't guess what would happen next, that should speak volumes to the other team members.

There was no evidence yet that the lead about Hassani being in Lahore was true. Two teams were converging on the city now to check it out. "Any questions before I dismiss you all?" They'd all been without sleep for two days. There was nothing more they could do for the time being so they might as well grab some much needed rest. He looked around the table at Evers, Hunter, Gage and several other FBI and NSA personnel.

When everyone shook their heads, he nodded. "Okay, be back here ready to go at eleven hundred. Keep your phones on and with you at all times in case something changes."

He went to the truck with Hunter and Gage. Gage drove them back to the hotel as the eastern sky began to lighten with the coming dawn. Up in his room, he crawled between the sheets and closed his aching eyes. Within minutes he was fast asleep. He woke what felt like only moments later when his phone buzzed against his hip. Sighing, he pulled it out of his pocket and squinted at the display. According to his phone he'd been asleep for nearly an hour, but he desperately needed more. The name on the call display compelled him to answer, however. "Zahra? Everything okay?"

"Sorry, I know it's early. Are you still working?"

He sat up, rubbed at his eyes with his free hand. "No, it's fine. What's up?"

"It's…Sean. He's not doing so well." Her voice hitched on the last word.

Aw, hell. Alex had been bracing for this. He just hadn't expected it so soon. "Want me to come in?"

"Would you? I know you've got a lot on your plate right now but I don't know what else to do and didn't know who to call."

There was no way Zahra had missed the increased security he'd placed outside Dunphy's room. She knew something big was happening, and he hated that she had another thing to worry about on top of everything else. "It's no problem. I'll be there within half an hour." After he hung up he grabbed a fast, hot shower and dressed, keeping his tactical vest beneath his dress shirt so it wouldn't draw too much notice. With Hassani on the loose once more, he couldn't take any chances with his personal safety. He texted Hunter and Gage to tell them where he was going, then arranged for a couple of Feds to tail him and caught a cab to the hospital.

He found Zahra standing in the hallway beside the closed door to Dunphy's room, the two men standing guard there doing their best to give her privacy. Her long dark hair was pulled back into a ponytail and her eyes looked bruised underneath. One look at her and he could tell she'd been crying. She looked exhausted and fragile and impossibly young. When he reached her she went straight into Alex's arms. He felt the way her shoulders shook with silent sobs she was trying to hold back, and cursed as he tightened his hold.

"That bad, huh?" he murmured against the top of her head.

She nodded, her breath hitching. "I hate that I can't help him. I know why he's trying to push me away and I know I swore I wouldn't let him, but he's so goddamn mean right now part of me wants to walk away and let him suffer all by himself."

"I bet." He held her until she calmed and finally stepped away, wiping at her eyes. "You're done in, honey. Why don't you grab something to eat downstairs, then head back to the hotel and get some sleep for awhile? I'll hang with him for a bit. Here." He reached into his pocket and handed her some cash to buy some food. "You'll both feel better if you give each other some space for a while. One of the guards can take you up. Go to the hotel, go unwind for a bit. It'll be worth it, trust me."

She looked like she was going to refuse, but after a long moment she nodded. "Thanks. I really appreciate this—don't know what I'd have done without you these past few years."

"Don't thank me for that, it's insulting," he said, giving her one last hug before releasing her and sending her toward the elevators with a gentle push. "Go on, now. I'll handle the bear."

She tossed a weary smile at him over her shoulder and walked to the elevators as he called one of the guards over and explained the situation. Once she and the man were inside the elevator, Alex turned and strode past the remaining man posted at the door. He didn't bother knocking, just opened it and strode right into the room. The smells hit him first, stale air, some kind of chemical cleaner, and the underlying scent of dried blood.

Dunphy was lying on his back in the narrow bed, still awake, his dark stare fixed on Alex. His eyes were completely ringed with purple and black from the bruising he'd suffered in the concussion of the IED's blast. Beneath the blankets, Alex could make out the shapes of the metal external fixators the surgeons had used to put his legs back together. Legs Dunphy couldn't currently feel, and might never be able to use again.

"What are you doing here?" Dunphy muttered. "She call you?"

"Yeah."

"Well you can leave now. I'm not interested in having company at the moment."

From the hostile look in the former FORECON Marine's eyes, Alex could see he was spoiling for a fight. Even though he understood why, Alex was tired, frustrated and pissed off enough to give him one.

Reining the urge in, he glanced over at the rolling table set beneath the windowsill. "I see the boys delivered their get well gift." A box of Mrs. Fields brownies sat next to a card with a picture of Van Halen on the front of it, the four band members' heads replaced by pictures of Gage, Hunter, Ellis and Dunphy. Alex knew these brownies wouldn't be laced with laxatives like the last ones they'd given Dunphy. Poor bastard.

Dunphy grunted in response, glowering at Alex.

Alex set his hands on his hips as he faced him once more. "Wanna talk about it?"

"No."

Alex wasn't at all surprised by the punch of anger in that one word. He was more than ready to do the tough love routine, however. "It's too early to give up hope. It's still only been a few days."

"I'm very much fucking aware of exactly how many days it's been."

Alex studied him for a long moment, noting the tension in the other man's jaw, the tight set of his shoulders. Hostility and resentment burned in those dark eyes. The guy was stressed to the max, ready to split apart at the seams. "Zahra's gone."

Shock, and maybe a tiny bit of fear flashed across his face before anger snuffed them both out. "So?"

"So I told her she didn't have to put up with your shit anymore, and for her to go."

Dunphy's mouth twisted in a bitter smile. "My *shit*, huh?"

Alex nodded. "Yep. She's been through enough of her own with what her father did to both her and her mother. You know exactly what I'm talking about, and then there was that whole episode in the woods a few weeks back when she took a bullet in her leg. She's suffered too much already, she shouldn't have to put up with abuse from you too, especially when she's done nothing but be there for you, try to help you."

"I don't need her fucking help," Dunphy snapped, eyes blazing, nostrils flaring. "I can lay here doing piss all by myself day in and day out without her *help*. I don't need to see the fucking pity in her eyes to know I'm just gonna wake up tomorrow exactly like this, and the next day, and the next—"

"You wanna have a pity party, that's your choice. But when you turn on someone as kind and loyal as Zahra, that's over the line."

Dunphy let out a disbelieving laugh. "What is this, the overprotective father routine?"

"Guess so." It was common knowledge how he felt about Zahra. He didn't deny it, wasn't ashamed or embarrassed by it.

"Well, don't bother. Just leave me alone and get the hell out. All of you, just leave me the fuck *alone*!" He slammed his hands down on either side of him, making the whole bed jump.

Alex would leave, but not until he'd driven his point home and lanced the festering wound inside Dunphy before it got any worse. He stormed over, paused at the side of the bed and glared down at the other man. "What happened to you fucking sucks, and nobody denies that. You wanna take it out on someone? Take it out on me, asshole. *I'm* the one who put you in that vehicle. *I* picked the route and put you last in the convoy."

Dunphy's eyes were nearly wild, the muscles in his arms shaking with the rage pumping inside him. "I wish it were you lying in this fucking bed with two fucking dead legs instead of me!"

"Well it isn't, it's you, and it's still not reason enough to take it out on the woman who loves you!"

The door opened and a young Pakistani nurse stuck her head in. Her eyes were wide as she took in the scene. "Sir, what—"

Alex ordered her out of the room with an authoritative thrust of his index finger, never taking his eyes off Dunphy. She gasped at his rudeness but left and shut the door behind her.

Alex shook his head at Dunphy, unwilling to let this go. "Zahra's been beside you since the moment you came out of recovery, is willing to stand by you no matter what, and you're treating her like shit because you're pissed off. I get why you're doing it, I really do, but you need to pick a different target, someone that can take it and dish it right back. Because she can't, and won't. As for me? I'm happy to go fifteen rounds with you if you want."

Dunphy glowered up at him, his muscles still quivering, but glanced away when a sheen of moisture gathered in his eyes. Alex straightened and took a step back, looked away when Dunphy covered his eyes with his hands and fought back the tears. Raw, harsh sounds filled the room as he struggled for control. Then he broke.

Alex turned away to give him some privacy, wincing inside. His heart went out to the guy, it truly did, but feeling sorry for himself and pushing Zahra away wasn't the answer. Dunphy was going to need all the support he could get in the coming weeks and months ahead. Alex refused to let him sabotage that network.

Finally, after a few long minutes, Dunphy seemed to have let the worst of it out. When only sniffs remained, Alex turned back to face him, grabbed a tissue from the table positioned on the right side of the bed and held it out to Dunphy. Dunphy swiped it from him with a baleful scowl. "You asshole," he muttered, but the heat was mostly gone, replaced by embarrassment at having Alex see him like this.

"I know." He grinned. "Can I get you anything?"

Dunphy expelled a breath and let his head fall back against the pillow. His gaze moved to the table beneath the windowsill. "Shit, just hand me a brownie."

Alex took three from the box, handed two to Dunphy. Alex eyed his own chocolaty morsel. "You sure these things are safe?"

Dunphy chuckled. "Pretty sure, yeah." He bit into the first one, sighed as he chewed. "You know I love her," he said after he swallowed.

Alex nodded. "I do." It was the reason he'd come in here and gotten in Dunphy's face.

"I just…God, I still can't believe this is real. I knew plenty of guys who got fucked up pretty bad, lost limbs or wound up in a wheelchair because of shit they sustained in the line of duty. Just never thought it would happen to me." He looked around the room toward the door and Alex could practically feel the weight of depression settling on the man's chest.

Polishing off his brownie, Alex dusted his hands off and reached down to squeeze Dunphy's shoulder. "I can't even imagine what you're going through," he admitted honestly, "and I'm sorry as hell this happened. But I'm not gonna stand by and watch it beat you. So many injured guys I knew let it beat them, and they didn't make it, whether due to medical reasons or because they wound up killing themselves." Dunphy knew the stats as well as Alex did. "I'm not saying it'll be easy, but you know the most important thing for you to do is to maintain a positive attitude. Even if you have to fake it, find something good in your life and focus on that. I don't want to see you wind up a statistic, and I'm not just saying that for Zahra's sake." Alex cared about his teammates. All of them.

Dunphy nodded, patted the hand Alex had set on his shoulder. "Yeah. Thanks."

Alex withdrew his hand and stuck both of his into his front pockets. "And when you do get up and moving again, if you still want to go fifteen rounds, gimme a call."

One side of the man's mouth quirked upward, a spark of humor glinting in his eyes. "I couldn't fight an old fart like you. I'd feel bad kicking your ass."

Alex barked out a laugh. He still had enough juice to hold his own in a fight. Maybe not for a full fifteen rounds anymore, but at least a few good ones. "Arrogant little bastard."

Dunphy shrugged. "It's the truth."

The tension broken, Alex was in the process of pulling up a chair to continue the visit when his cell rang. Fishing it out, he saw Evers's number and answered. "What's up?"

"There's been some recent activity you should know about," the Fed answered.

"Okay." Alex steeled himself for whatever was coming next. Had Hassani gotten out of the country?

"Someone dirty in the police force leaked the details about Grace's taxi accident. Word is Hassani's seen a picture of you with her. You were hugging her, apparently?"

The blood drained out of Alex's face. Someone must have taken a picture of them when he'd pulled her from the cab. He'd been so focused on making sure she was okay, totally occupied with having her in front of him again, he hadn't even been thinking of the possible security risks. God dammit.

"Someone's been digging into her personal information in the past couple hours, her credit and job history. Hassani's gotta know about your involvement with her. And he's gonna know why she's here."

Alex's fingers tightened around the phone. "Get more security on her."

"I've already talked to her staff, it's in the works."

Not good enough. He was already on his feet, his brain compiling a list of everything he had to do to keep her safe. "I'll bring her in." He'd always thought his worst fear was losing Grace. Seeing her hurt again because of him was a thousand times worse. But it was too late to send her away now, even if he was willing to do that to protect her.

If Hassani knew about her and her connection to Alex, then she was a walking target. And as of this moment, it also meant she was as much a threat to Alex as Hassani himself.

CHAPTER FIVE

In the hotel conference room, Grace flipped to the correct page of the report and scanned the passage in question. "No, I think the wording here is fine," she said to David. "It needs to be made clear to them that the international community's not going to allow Syria to mess around with the timetable. Syria has to dismantle their chemical weapons program and destroy their stockpiles by the date given, or we'll do it for them." Of course it wasn't as simple or as easy as that, but there would be no wiggle room on the terms of the agreement.

"Okay. What about section six, part A-two?"

Everyone turned to that page, including Dr. Travis, the Canadian chemical weapons expert and head of their team, and the six other members gathered around the long rectangular table. "I'd like to strike the third point there," Travis said as he adjusted his frameless glasses. He glanced up, his pale blue gaze landing on Grace. "I don't like the wording and I don't think it's necessary. In fact, I think it opens up a can of worms we don't want to have to deal with."

"Agreed. I move to strike it from the report. Second?" She glanced around the table and one of the other members put their hand up. They followed Robert's Rules of Order while David, acting as secretary for the meeting, recorded it all in the minutes.

The meeting with the Syrian envoy was in two days and there was no room for a margin of error. Compliance had been slow in coming and it was Grace's team's job to make them capitulate and sign this new binding agreement. The corrupt regime must be held responsible for its criminal actions and destroy its chemical weapons before it unleashed any further attacks on the civilian population. Seeing the horrific results and the human suffering up close and personal in the aftermath, when the UN had sent her team in days after the attack a few months ago was something she'd never forget. Innocent men, women and children had died horrific deaths. The faces of those dead children and babies in the hospital morgues would never leave her.

As they moved on to the next item on the agenda, her phone rang. "Sorry." She grabbed it from the table and turned it to silent mode, her eyes catching on the name listed on call display. Alex.

A rush of blood worked its way up her neck and into her cheeks. She set the phone down and looked back at her papers, annoyed by the way her heart skipped a beat and that he'd managed to call her while she was in the middle of a meeting. And that parting comment he'd made before sauntering out the door last night—this morning, that is. She couldn't stop thinking about it.

I haven't been with anyone since you.

He had to be lying about that, right? There was no way an alpha male with Alex's looks, charisma and sexual appetite could go for four freaking years without sex. It just wasn't possible. Still, the tantalizing idea that he hadn't slept with anyone since her had tortured her as she lay tossing and turning in bed long after he'd left. Which meant she was crazy, because there was no way it could be true.

But what if it was? What if she really had meant as much to him as he had to her all those years ago? What if she hadn't just been imagining that incredibly intense connection between them?

"Any comments or concerns about this section?" Travis asked them all.

She jerked her attention back to the meeting, hating that she'd allowed Alex to distract her yet again. As they discussed the next item on the agenda, her phone buzzed noisily against the polished mahogany table. Everyone glanced up at her. She snatched it up, intending to shove it into her briefcase if it was Alex again, but then she saw the text message and froze.

Emergency! Call me ASAP.

Even as she stared at the screen, another message came in.

I mean it. Call me NOW.

He wouldn't seriously keep trying to contact her, wouldn't use that wording unless it really was an emergency. That bone deep knowledge started a buzz of trepidation in the pit of her stomach. Her remaining misgivings about him aside, she couldn't take a chance and ignore this in case it was real. She glanced up to find all the team members staring at her. "I'm sorry, I have to take this. Will you excuse me for a few minutes?" she asked, already pushing her chair back.

Once out in the hallway, she called him back, trying to ignore the way her heart pounded. Not just because of the anxiety, but at the thought of hearing his voice again too.

God, why couldn't she let the idea of him go now that she'd seen him again?

He answered on the first ring. "Where are you?"

She blinked at the brusque demand, the tension in his voice. Her stomach muscles tightened. "I was in the middle of a meeting, why?"

"Grace, where *are* you?" he repeated, and this time there was no mistaking the impatience, the urgency in his tone.

"Still at the Serena Hotel, outside the conference room. What's going—"

"Is your security there?"

She glanced down the hall, spotted one of the security agents standing near the elevators. "Yes, why, what's happening?"

"I'm coming to get you."

"What? *Why*?" The anxiety transformed into raw fear. She instinctively glanced right and left, half expecting to see someone coming at her with a gun, but the long hallway was empty. Images flashed through her mind of that night in Mombasa. The explosion of gunfire. Bloodcurdling screams. Agonizing pain. She instinctively placed a hand over her stomach where the scars were and ordered herself to stay calm.

"Can't talk over the phone. Yours doesn't have the right encryption."

Jesus, this had to be very serious. "Is it my team? Are they in danger?"

"No. You are. I'm sending one of the guards to escort you to your room. Pack whatever you need for the next week and wait for me in your room. I'll be there in fifteen minutes. Be ready to go."

"Wait, what—" He'd already hung up. As the phone beeped in her ear, Grace drew in a shaky breath and ran a hand through her hair. She was in danger? How? Why, if it had nothing to do with the UN team? Unsettled and not seeing any way around the fact that she had to leave, she went back into the conference room. She must have been as pale as she felt, because everyone stopped what they were doing and stared at her. Travis rose from his seat, his graying eyebrows crashed together in a concerned frown. "Are you all right?"

"I—no. Can I talk to you for a minute, alone?"

He hurried around the table and walked out into the hall with her. As the door closed behind them he set a fatherly hand on her arm. "What is it?"

There was no easy way to tell him. "I have to leave."

His head drew back in surprise. "Now? Why?"

"I don't know the details, but there's some sort of credible threat against me. Someone from the NSA just called to inform me. They're picking me up in a few minutes."

The frown deepened. "And taking you where?"

"I don't know that either." She rubbed her hands over her arms to chase away the sudden chill. "I just know that I don't have a choice here. I have to go with him." She was at risk, so she had to be smart.

Travis's expression showed not only confusion, but genuine alarm. "Are you sure you can trust whoever called you?"

"I'm sure." Even if she didn't trust Alex on a lot of things, she knew he'd never lie about this. "Look, I'll call you when I can, and I'll still try my best to make all the meetings. Maybe I'll have to be on conference call—I'll let you know. Right now I need to find out what's going on and make sure there's no threat to the rest of us."

Travis nodded. "All right. Don't worry about anything else, just take care of yourself and update me when you can so I know you're okay. I'll tell the other members that there was a family emergency. No sense getting everyone in a panic until we know what's going on."

"I agree, thanks." She blew out a deep breath, noticed a security guard she recognized heading down the hall toward her. "Gotta go." She paused only long enough to slip into the room and grab her briefcase, murmur her excuses to the rest of the team and then headed up to her room with the guard shadowing her. She shoved everything from the dresser into her suitcase and was jamming her toiletry bag inside when a brusque knock sounded at the door. She glanced over her shoulder just as the door opened.

Alex appeared in the bedroom doorway a moment later. The sight of him standing there was still a punch to her senses. He glanced over at her open suitcase on the bed, then back at her. Standing close enough to catch that delicious scent he always carried, she was reminded of how it had felt to be caged in against the door last night, the feel of his lips on her skin. "You ready?" he asked.

Not really. "Almost. Alex, what's going on?"

He gestured for her to get her bag before answering, his gaze sweeping over the room. "Hassani knows you're here."

She whipped around to stare at him. "How?" The meetings were supposed to be secret, which is why they were being held here rather than in the U.S. or Syria. Pakistan had agreed to play host because the UN had wanted another Islamic country's help to sway the Syrians during the negotiations if necessary. As far as she knew, even the media had no idea what was going on.

"He's got deep connections in the military and police, and apparently one of the cops responding to the accident yesterday snapped a picture of us together. Someone leaked it to Hassani's network, and we got a tip that someone was looking into your background." He grabbed his phone from his pocket, and as he did the hem of his dress shirt lifted enough for her to see the ballistic vest and the holstered pistol at the back of his waistband. Her pulse went up another few notches. She knew it was necessary for him to be armed, especially now, but ever since Mombasa she hated guns. "This is what he saw," Alex said as he held the phone out.

Grace sucked in a breath when she saw the picture of Alex embracing her. The look on his face as he stared down at her was intense, concerned. And the possessive way he was holding her was pretty damn hard to mistake. She swallowed, glanced up at him even as the memory of his arms around her sent a flutter of desire through her body. "So he knows…"

"At this point we have to assume he knows everything, from your relationship with me, to the attack in Mombasa, and you being here with the UN chemical weapons team to meet the Syrians."

She gasped. "Wait, how did you—" She stopped herself as the obvious answer came to mind. He was with the NSA after all. But it begged the question, who the hell else knew about the so-called *secret* meeting? Suddenly she felt exposed and unsafe. Because of the security team placed with them by the UN, she'd felt secure. Now she realized how naive she'd been.

"He's been attacking my team for weeks now," Alex continued, "and we're all on his hit list. One of our members is still in the hospital from an IED blast some of Hassani's TTP cell contacts hit us with a few days ago. He may never walk again."

Grace swallowed, didn't know what to say. She was here to make the region safer. She'd mistakenly thought she'd be much safer in Pakistan than she had been in Kenya.

Alex's eyes were grave, his jaw set. "Hassani wants me bad, and he now knows you're a way to get to me. So until he's behind bars again, I'm not taking any chances with your safety. You'll be staying with me until the threat's over."

Her eyebrows shot up. Of all the things she'd imagined him saying, that wasn't one of them. "How's *that* going to make any difference to my safety, if he's targeting you already?"

"Because your team's security isn't good enough anymore, not even close, and they don't know what kind of threat Hassani might pose to you. My team does. So until I can get something better arranged for you, my guys and I will act as your personal security detail."

Okay, that did make her feel slightly better, but… "Isn't that against some sort of regulations for you?" The NSA had to have rules about that kind of thing, and she was pretty sure her safety didn't matter when compared to Alex's or capturing Hassani.

He raised a defiant eyebrow. "I don't give a shit. I care about *you*, and making sure you're safe."

In spite of the threat level facing her, her gullible heart melted a little at the conviction behind those words. He meant it. She felt it in her bones.

Alex shook his head slightly, the way his jaw flexed revealing his inner turmoil. "I screwed up the first time with you, acted too late on the intel and you paid the price." Regret burned in his glittering eyes. "I can't change what happened in the past, but I can damn well make sure you're protected this time. If Hassani wants to take a run at you, he's gotta find you. And even if he does, then he's gonna have to get through me first," he said, stabbing a finger against his chest for emphasis.

Grace could only stare at him. Though she was still wary of his intentions because she knew he wanted to try and win her back, she recognized the sincerity of his statement. Alex would protect her no matter what, even at risk to his career, his own life. At his core he was honorable, but more than that, he truly did still care, and it turned her inside out. As Grace digested his words and the force with which he delivered them, she couldn't think of a single thing to say other than, "Okay."

He must have been expecting an argument, because he blinked as though surprised by her answer. His entire body seemed to relax, that constant hum of energy he carried with him dimming a little. "Thank you."

She nodded, part of her suddenly wishing there was a way to bridge the gap between them. Standing before her now was the man she'd fallen in love with. Knowing he'd risk everything to ensure her safety slipped past every defense she had.

Shoving those unsettling thoughts aside, she quickly finished packing and zipped up her suitcase. As soon as she finished, Alex took if from her and opened the door. She followed him down to the lobby with a security guard and through a service access hallway to a hidden exit at the back of the building. He opened the exterior door and stopped to check everything, then stepped outside into the bright, hot sunshine and held the door for her.

He led her to a black SUV parked close to the building, maybe the same one he'd roared up in yesterday, and opened the trunk to load her bag. After opening her door, he took another look around then checked the vehicle—she assumed for an explosive or tracking device—and finally slid behind the wheel. It surprised her that he didn't have bodyguards with him, but then she noticed another dark SUV tailing them. She relaxed when Alex looked at it in the rearview mirror calmly and realized it had to be a security detail.

He shut his door and immediately the big vehicle seemed smaller, his big frame filling the seat. With his shirt sleeves rolled up, she watched the muscles in his tanned forearms flex as he gripped the steering wheel.

"Where are we going now?" she asked as he fired up the engine.

"My hotel. The rest of my team's there, and two more members should be arriving sometime tonight. We're all staying there under aliases and only checked in two nights ago. We'll be moving again in the morning, just in case, but you'll be well-protected there."

Things were too tense for her to start asking about trivial things like sleeping arrangements. Though she had to wonder, could she hold back from him if they spent the whole night in his room together? The physical attraction between them had been explosive right from day one, and judging by her body's reaction to him just being near, it hadn't lessened one bit. In fact, her body craved him even more now that he'd suddenly reappeared in her life. It remembered what he could do to her with his hands and that muscular body, what he'd shown her about her true sexuality during their short time together in Kenya.

"I still have to make that meeting," she said quietly as he drove. There was no way she could miss it. Not only was she a critical part of the team, she'd been at ground zero days after the attack in Syria. Her professional reputation was on the line. If he tried to keep her from going, he'd have a hell of a fight on his hands.

But he merely nodded, as though resigned to the idea. "I know. We'll figure something out."

Within two days, while he worked around the clock on a critical manhunt and worrying about her security? She glanced over at him, her gaze sweeping over his strong profile. He was as powerful as ever, maybe even more than he had been four years ago. Mombasa had changed him. Hardened him.

Somehow that only added to his appeal, and it annoyed the hell out of her. Even now it was impossible to ignore the emotional connection between them.

When they stopped at a traffic light Alex turned his head and leveled his stare at her. His eyes burned with male interest and an unmistakable possessive light. Tension simmered between them, full of repressed need and old hurts that needed healing. God help her, deep down there was still a part of her that wanted to heal them. For closure, she told herself.

"Do you trust me, Grace?" he asked quietly.

She knew he meant more than at that moment, more than him watching over her now, and there was no way she was ready to go there again. There'd been too much damage, and too much time and distance to repair it. But as far as putting her life into his hands? There was only one answer she could give him. "Yes. I trust you."

CHAPTER SIX

Grace sat up in Alex's hotel room waiting for him to bring the other team members in to meet her. When they'd first arrived almost two hours ago he'd brought her bags in, told her to get settled, then taken her phone and left. She'd unpacked a little, but it felt weird to be here among Alex's personal things. Especially when faced with the wide king size bed he'd slept in. The act of placing her toothbrush next to his at the bathroom sink seemed so intimate, and slightly bizarre considering she was in his inner sanctum but wasn't his lover anymore. That single, unforgettable night they'd shared before the attack was the most bittersweet of memories.

She occupied herself by reviewing the files in her briefcase. They'd been more than two-thirds of the way through the agenda when Alex's call had hauled her out of the meeting. By now her team had wrapped everything up and were probably having lunch somewhere. Her stomach rumbled. How long was she going to have to wait in here? With the security scare, room service definitely wasn't an option.

At the sound of the keycard sliding into the lock followed by an electronic beep, she set her papers aside and faced the door. Alex walked in, two large men right behind him, the ones she'd seen at the accident site yesterday.

"Got you some lunch," Alex told her, handing her a Styrofoam container full of something that smelled aromatic and delicious. "Chicken curry over rice, mild on the spices."

It shouldn't have surprised her that he remembered her aversion to spicy food. Her mouth was already watering from the heavenly aroma. "Thanks." She looked at the other men.

"This is Hunter," Alex said, gesturing to the built, dark-haired man, "and this is Gage." He nodded at the big redhead who'd been driving the SUV yesterday. "Hunt was a SEAL and now co-owns Titanium Security. Gage is former SF, like me. They're my personal security detail and will fill in watching over you if I can't."

Grace smiled and murmured a friendly greeting to the newcomers. "Am I the only one eating?"

"We ate earlier," Alex answered for the others, and pulled a phone out of his pocket. "Use this one from now on. It's encrypted, and we already loaded all your contacts into it. I took the battery and SIM card out of your phone to disable it in case anyone was trying to track you with the signal. You'll get it back once Hassani's in custody."

He sounded confident that it would happen, and some of her anxiety faded. "And what about the meeting with…?" She trailed off, glancing at Gage and Hunter, unsure how much she could say.

"Don't worry about watching what you say with these guys, they're already up to speed on everything. We'll make sure you attend the meeting. As soon as you eat I'm going to run over to your hotel and have a chat with your team's security guys. You can come if you want to talk to your colleagues. Hunter and Gage will shadow us on the way there before they have to leave for a recon job."

"And you'll need to wear this," Hunter added, lifting and holding out a bullet-proof vest. "Smallest I could find, but it might be a bit big on you."

Grace stared at it for a second, her pulse picking up at the physical reminder of the threat. A phantom pain arced through her belly where the long-healed scars were. "Thanks," she murmured, and took it from him. Normally she only had to wear this while in a known combat zone or during the actual inspection of chemical weapons facilities.

"Put it on under your shirt, so it's less noticeable," Alex told her.

Not about to argue, Grace grabbed a T-shirt to wear beneath the vest so it wouldn't abrade her skin, then headed into the bathroom to change. In the mirror her face looked pale, her eyes tired. When she emerged, all three men were waiting by the door.

"Can hardly tell you're wearing it," Gage said in a Southern drawl, giving her an easy smile that put her more at ease. She guessed he was the friendly one of the security team. "Now Alex can relax a little and stop ordering you around for a bit."

"Thanks, but I won't hold my breath on that last part," she said, returning the smile.

"Can you eat on the way?" Alex asked. "I wanna get going on this."

"Yeah, sure." She picked up the container.

When she turned back Alex was studying her, searching her eyes as if he could see the fear she kept buried inside. "You can stay here if you'd rather."

"No, I need to talk to Dr. Travis."

Apparently satisfied by her answer, he nodded once. "Let's go."

She ate as Alex drove her back to her hotel. Hunter and Gage followed close behind in another SUV and the other vehicle of security personnel from earlier stayed behind them. All the men wore earpieces to communicate but thankfully the trip was uneventful. Alex led her into the lobby while Hunter and Gage trailed behind them and whoever was in the third vehicle stayed in the parking lot. Though the weight of the tactical vest was comforting, it was Alex's presence that truly made her feel safe. If he'd been with her the night of the attack in Mombasa, part of her still believed she might never have been shot in the first place. He'd have known what to do, how to protect her and get her out of there.

At the elevators Alex nodded at Hunter and Gage, then ushered her inside the car. They rode in silence to the floor where the inspection team was staying, with her vividly conscious of the man standing beside her. An almost electrical tingle of awareness flowed over her skin and when he put a hand on the small of her back just below the bottom of the vest, heat kindled low in her belly. His hand was warm, the touch both protective and proprietary and she felt that simple contact right down to her toes.

The elevator dinged as it reached their floor and the doors opened. Expelling a breath, Grace stepped out after Alex with his guiding hand firm against her lower back. "Where's Travis's room?" he asked.

"Across the hall from mine." She knocked on his door. She'd called him before driving over, so she knew he was expecting them. Dr. Travis pulled open the door. He glanced from her to Alex, his shrewd blue eyes measuring him before stepping back so they could come in.

"So, does this mean everything's cleared up then?" he asked.

"Unfortunately not." She looked over her shoulder at Alex, unsure how much she was allowed to divulge.

"There's an ongoing investigation right now," he said to Travis.

"With Hassani," Travis answered.

Alex frowned, and Grace was impressed by her colleague's insightfulness. Alex didn't surprise easily. "How do you know about that?"

Travis shrugged. "I'm a reasonably intelligent guy."

Said one of the most brilliant and respected scientists on the planet. Grace hid a smile.

Alex's hand pressed harder against her back. "Does the rest of your team know?"

"That Hassani's missing? Yes. But they don't know Grace's having to leave has anything to do with it."

"I'd appreciate it if you'd keep it that way."

Travis measured him for a moment in silence, then nodded. His gaze shifted to Grace. "So, how are you holding up? What's the plan?"

"I'm okay. Alex just wants me to keep a low profile until Hassani's caught, that's all. He said we can figure out a way for me to attend the meeting with the Syrians."

"Good, because I can't do this without you." He opened his mouth to say something else but a knock on the door interrupted him. "That must be David. I asked him to come." He strode to the door and let her assistant in.

David smiled in relief when he saw her, then his face tightened in surprise when he looked at Alex. The two men seemed to size each other up for a moment and Grace immediately stepped into the awkward lapse by introducing them. They shook hands, but Alex's expression was far from friendly. Letting the other man know without a word that he was the one in charge.

"I've got to meet with your security team," Alex said as he set his hand against her back again. The move was territorial and the other two men couldn't have missed the statement, but for some reason the show of possessiveness didn't irritate Grace the way it should have. "I'll text you once I'm done," he said to her. "You guys go ahead and catch up on whatever you missed at the meeting. I'll post someone outside the door."

Grace nodded, her breath catching a little at the longing in his eyes as he gazed down at her. It brought back all the good memories of him in Kenya that she'd tucked away, reminded her of how intense he'd always been with her from that first kiss in the courtyard garden next to the bubbling fountain. Grace remembered that sizzling moment when she'd first felt those powerful arms around her, when she'd experienced his iron self-control and the blazing passion he'd roused within her so effortlessly as he'd covered her mouth with his and made her head spin.

"I'll see you soon," he murmured, his tone intimate. As he pulled away he grazed his fingers over the thin fabric of her shirt below the bottom of the vest in a tantalizing caress that left tingles in its wake.

Blocking the distracting sensation and the flood of memories it evoked, she faced her colleagues as the door shut behind Alex. "All right, bring me up to speed on what I missed."

They sat around a small circular table to discuss everything. David pulled out the minutes to review and they reviewed the notes and other remaining concerns about the meeting with the Syrians.

"If I can't be there in person, I guess video conference is the best we can do," she murmured.

"That won't work," Dr. Travis said flatly. "Too many security leaks and the Syrians will never okay it. We need you at that meeting."

She was well aware of the possible consequences of her absence. She was a self-professed control freak. They'd worked so long and so hard securing this meeting, the thought of not being there killed her. "Alex will do whatever he can to make that happen, but if it doesn't work out, the rest of you will have to go ahead without me." She hated even thinking of that option, but it might be the only one available to them. She wasn't going to lose her life over this or put other people at risk by being there. "Let's just go over everything again to take my mind off it, okay?"

They spent almost an hour reviewing their strategy, arguments and counterarguments. Everyone knew the timing of this dismantling program was vital. The faster the chemical weapons stores were destroyed, the better. They were just wrapping up when her phone buzzed with a text from Alex. She responded that she was ready, and stood.

Dr. Travis surprised her by giving her a quick hug. He paused when he noticed the vest she wore beneath her shirt. "You be careful," he admonished.

"I will be."

David hugged her next, his reaction far less subtle when he felt the vest. He released her, his brows shooting up. "Is that really necessary?"

"Just for now," she said evasively, wanting to ease the worry she read on his face.

Alex showed up a moment later, spoke briefly to Dr. Travis, then stepped close to her and slipped his arm around her waist. He tugged slightly until she brushed against his side. "Your security team's been briefed about everything they need to know. I'll arrange for backup if they want it. If anything else comes up I'll update them personally." He looked down at her, those silver eyes heating. "Ready?"

"Yes."

He kept his hand on her waist on the way to the elevator but once they stepped inside and the doors closed, it seemed too intimate and she pulled away to put some space between them. He didn't say anything but she could feel that assessing gaze on her all the way down to the lobby. As soon as the doors whooshed open she stepped forward, but he stopped her by slinging that strong arm back around her waist and stepping in front of her.

"You can ignore the pull between us if you want, but your safety comes first and that means you stick close to me," he murmured close to her ear, the feel of his warm breath against her skin making her shiver. His hand tightened on the curve of her waist, his lean fingers flexing there, reminding her of what it felt like when he gripped her tight and worked himself in and out of her body.

He was in full defensive mode as he escorted her out to the waiting SUV. Gage and Hunter were already gone, off on whatever recon assignment Alex had sent them on, but the other vehicle with another security detail was still there to watch their backs. The drive back to Alex's hotel was quiet and tense, the unspoken sexual tension between them impossible to ignore.

"So, you get everything tied up?"

Given her train of thought, his choice of wording made her blush because it reminded her of the way he'd dominated her during that single night of blisteringly hot sex. He'd used the belt from her robe to tie her wrists to the bedpost, and she'd been only too happy to let him. She'd never have guessed that surrendering to a man that way would turn her on, but Alex had damn near melted her from the inside out with his addictive mix of control and tenderness. She longed to feel that freedom and release again. "For the most part. Any word yet on Hassani?"

He flicked a glance at her. "No."

"Is he still using the Taliban and other insurgents?"

"If it suits his purposes he will. But he's not motivated by religion."

"Then what?"

"Power."

"What kind of power? You mean—"

"Grace, stop. I can't."

At his closed reaction she wanted to smack herself. He'd already told her he couldn't discuss an ongoing investigation. But driving alone together with this brittle tension between them was taking its toll on her and she needed something to talk about.

"That color reminds me of the dress you wore that night in Mombasa."

She blinked at the jarring change in subject. Looking down at the cobalt blue top, understanding dawned. He'd taken her out for a quiet, romantic dinner at a fancy resort overlooking the ocean the night they'd had sex. She'd worn a chiffon cobalt dress with a pretty ruffled hem that came to just below her knees. It had made her feel feminine and sexy, the first time she'd felt that way in a long time, but it was the look on Alex's face when he'd seen her that had done her in.

His eyes had heated to molten silver as they raked over her from her head to the tips of her polished toenails revealed by her high-heeled sandals. After weeks of phone calls, texts, secret rendezvous and the hottest make-out session of her life, they'd finally slept together. Well, okay, not slept. The moment his hotel room door had shut behind them, they'd been all over each other. They'd only made it as far as the sitting room before he'd stripped the dress off and had her on her back on the leather sofa in just her underwear and heels. He'd made her come twice there before carrying her into the bedroom and finally taking her, fulfilling untapped desires she hadn't even been aware of, throughout the night until the first rays of dawn streaked across the bed.

She looked away, throat aching at the memory.

Another few minutes of silence passed before he spoke again. "When did you finally divorce him?"

She snapped her head around to stare at him. "What? Why?"

He shrugged, a tight motion of his shoulders. "When I first found out you were in Islamabad I saw you'd taken your maiden name back. I just wondered how long it's been."

She turned her head and went back to staring out her window. "Almost two years."

He grunted. "I'm glad you finally did it."

The buried anger in his tone made her look at him again. "Why?" What the hell was it to him after all this time?

Alex's jaw flexed. "Because he didn't deserve you."

She understood why he thought that. When she'd met Alex, she and Robert were already separated. Alex had seen them interacting at their worst point, when Robert viewed her as a convenient diplomatic partner, someone he could send to various social functions when he was unable to attend. With disastrous results for her. "He wasn't a bad husband. He just…quit trying and fell out of love with me somewhere along the way. I agreed to stay after the separation until the end of his posting to help him save face and avoid gossip that might hurt his career. But then I met you and didn't care about any of that." So very unlike her.

Alex snorted. "He treated you like an employee, not a wife, and he not only completely ignored your needs, he fucking used you to get what he wanted."

The impassioned outburst surprised her as much as it pissed her off. "But you didn't?" she shot back.

His hand tightened on the wheel as he cut her a censuring look. "No, never. And I know damn well you remember how it really was between us."

Yes, she did, and that was the hell of it. She folded her arms, glanced away. "You broke my heart way worse than Robert ever did," she said quietly. He'd gutted her, every bit as much as those bullets and the surgery had.

At her admission his head snapped toward her and the tension in the vehicle became almost suffocating. "God, Grace…" He shook his head, nostrils flaring. "I'm *sorry*. I wouldn't hurt you for anything. You believe that much, right?" He glanced at her again and the anguish in his eyes hit her full force.

She swallowed past the sudden restriction in her throat. She couldn't lie to him about that. "Yes."

He focused back on the road and expelled a weary sigh that twisted her up inside. She *did* believe him. Punishing him for things he couldn't change was not only immature of her, it was cruel. But dammit, learning to live without him had damn near killed her. And there was still that one burning question pinging around in her brain.

"Have you really not been with anyone since me?"

He shook his head, not seeming surprised by the question. "No one."

"Why?" She needed to know.

"I guess I kept comparing every woman I went out with to you, and they couldn't measure up. I dunno, I just…couldn't go there. I buried myself in my work instead."

It was a lot to take in, but she actually believed him. And there was no reason for him to lie about it.

"What about you?" he countered.

"I've dated," she answered evasively, feeling the blood rush into her cheeks. Yes, she'd gone out with a handful of men and yes, she'd slept with some of them. Every time she'd regretted it afterward because with all of them she'd secretly fantasized about Alex. After a few experiences like that where she'd felt ill afterward, she'd given up dating and focused exclusively on her career.

If Alex was disappointed by her answer, he didn't show it. "Did you ever think about me?"

He damn well knew she had. "Of course I thought about you," she huffed. She'd had no choice—he'd ruined her for any other man.

"Well, I'm glad you've got at least a few good memories of me."

She had plenty, but they were like a form of torture. No matter how hard she tried to forget him, move on emotionally, she just couldn't. And each minute she spent in his company her resolve to shut him out slipped a little more. She was terrified of letting him in and then having to deal with the aftermath if he left her again.

The rest of the drive passed in silence. Once they were back in his room he muttered something about having things to take care of and that she should call or text him if she needed anything. Additional security had been hired to make extra patrols on the floor.

Left all alone with nothing to do, she pulled out her e-reader and curled up in the chair by the window. She read an entire book and a third of another. The light outside was fading fast and when her head drooped for the third time she put the reader aside and looked at the clock on the bedside table. It was already after ten and she was exhausted.

She changed into yoga pants and a snug top. Normally she slept naked but that so wasn't happening tonight. She washed her face and brushed her teeth then debated sleeping in the armchair. Since the thought of waking up every few minutes with a crick in her neck held no appeal, she opted for the bed. Alex could take the floor. The maid service had been in to tidy the room but they hadn't changed the sheets because the moment she laid her head on the pillow she could smell Alex's scent on the pillowcase.

She closed her eyes as bittersweet memories rose up to haunt her. The way he'd smiled down at her in the moonlight on the terrace the first time he'd kissed her. That soul deep connection she'd found with him. The intensity of their lovemaking and the way he'd lavished her with pleasure for hours on end that one night. Finally, after tossing and turning for a while, sleep overtook her.

She woke sometime later in near darkness when the bed shifted. She sucked in a breath and pushed up on an elbow, but paused when she heard his voice.

"It's okay, it's just me."

At the whispered words she relaxed, though her heart was now pounding for a different reason. She wasn't ready for Alex to sleep beside her.

He made an annoyed sound. "It's a big bed, and I'm too damn old to sleep on the floor." With that he slid in beside her and rolled so his back was to her.

Grace stared at him over her shoulder, barely able to make out his silhouette in the faint light of the bedside digital clock. The strange sinking feeling of disappointment caught her off guard. She mentally rolled her eyes at herself. *Make up your damn mind, Grace.*

"Stop thinking so hard and go to sleep," he muttered, then yawned.

Acutely aware of him lying just inches away from her and his body heat licking against her spine, she put her head back down and forced her eyes shut. Even as sleep finally overtook her again she was aware of being safe because Alex was beside her.

Strong hands gripped her hips. She lifted up in a tight arch beneath her lover's powerful body, moving as much as her limited range of motion would allow. He held her hands above her head, those silver eyes seeming to stare right into her soul as he pumped in and out of her body. She was desperate to come, so primed for him she could easily have reached release with one more caress against the throbbing bud at the top of her sex but he wouldn't let her topple over that edge.

Her muscles strained as he rode her, slow and steady, his iron control reducing hers to ashes. She writhed in his grip, straining for the release that hovered just out of reach. He made her feel things she hadn't even known her body was capable of, and he got off on making her whimper and beg as much as she did giving him that power over her.

"Relax, angel." The hot whisper against her ear only frustrated her more. She wanted her hands free to grip his wide shoulders, run her fingers over his muscled back. He felt huge inside her, thick and hot, stroking over a spot so sensitive the pleasure bordered on pain. "Give yourself to me."

She moaned and shuddered as he held her there, the pleasure spiraling up, up, impossibly high…

Sudden darkness swallowed everything. She fought the restraining grip on her hands as the blackness engulfed her, tore her free of that strong embrace. Bright lights blinded her, reflecting off the polished marble floor. The ballroom.

She knew what was coming, what would happen. Terror flooded her. She scrambled to her feet, tried to run in her spike heeled shoes, but it was too late. The masked men were already there at the doorway, taking aim at the guests with their deadly black guns. Gunshots ripped apart the silence, replaced by screams. The sickening metal-tinged scent of blood filled her nostrils. Panic drove her to her hands and knees. If she could just make it to the marble pillar, maybe she could hide behind it, maybe—

The bullets slammed into her belly, ripping the scream of agony from her throat.

Grace jerked upright in the darkness, her heart slamming in her ears and a film of sweat covering her body.

"Hey. You okay?"

She closed her eyes at the sound of Alex's sleepy voice. No, she was definitely *not* okay. "Mm-hmm."

Pushing from the bed, she stumbled into the bathroom and shut the door behind her before flipping on the lights. She flinched as it hit her eyes but walked straight to the glassed-in shower and turned the water on hot. Once the water steamed she stripped and stepped beneath the spray, allowing the warmth to cascade over her. Breathing slowly, she forced the fear away and let the tension bleed out of her stiff shoulder muscles.

Worried that Alex might try to come in, she quickly soaped up to rinse away the sweat. Not wanting to linger, she shut off the water, toweled off then put on the robe hanging on the back of the door. She turned off the light and headed back toward the bed, catching a glimpse of Alex sitting up in it, his bare, sculpted chest illuminated in the split second before the room was plunged back into darkness. Her footsteps faltered. Was he naked?

"Nightmare?" he asked quietly.

She nodded, then realized he couldn't see her. "Yeah. Kind of a flashback."

He made a sound of understanding and let the silence stretch between them. "You going to come back to bed, or stand there all night?"

She didn't know what she wanted. It'd been a long time since she'd dreamed about the attack. Maybe the threat with Hassani had caused it. Maybe it was because she was sharing a bed with Alex. She swallowed, opened her mouth to say something when he beat her to it.

"Come back to bed, Grace. It'll be okay."

Her throat tightened at the tenderness in his voice. "I don't—"

His sigh was loud in the quiet room. "Come lie down and get warm. I can tell you're cold."

It would be stupid to stand there shivering and it was clear he had no intention of leaving the bed. She walked around to the far side and slid in, careful to keep the robe tied securely around her as she laid on her side with her back to him. The mattress shifted as Alex rolled to face her back. He ran a gentle hand over her hair.

"Want to talk about it?"

"No." The memories were still too fresh, too raw. *Hold me. Make love to me the way you did before.*

A long beat of silence passed. She realized she was holding her breath, half expecting him to grab her shoulder and turn her to face him. She jolted a little when instead he moved in behind her, his thighs against the undersides of hers, his chest pressed against her back. He slipped one strong arm around her waist and tugged her into him so that she was surrounded by his heat and strength.

She lay rigid, afraid to move, terrified of the needs rising inside her. More than anything in that moment she wanted to erase the emotional distance from him and just feel, experience one last time what lovemaking was like with him. Her muscles knotted with the need to turn over and wrap her arms around him, burrow into his heat and let him burn the lingering fear away. She knew he could do that.

Alex kept his arm around her and laid his head beside hers, his breath fanning the nape of her neck, stirring embers of desire that could burst into flame at any moment. She knew he was aroused, could feel the solid length of his erection pressed against her bottom. But he didn't act on it. He simply held her close and let his presence chase the demons of her past away. The heat of the hand splayed protectively over her stomach burned through the thin fabric of the robe. Slowly she relaxed, took a few deep breaths and closed her eyes to better savor the feeling of security that washed over her.

"That's better," he murmured, the praise in his voice soothing her as much as his embrace. He removed his hand from her stomach to trail his fingers through her damp hair. His fingertips grazed her scalp in a slow, drugging rhythm that sent tiny frissons of pleasure down her spine.

She almost moaned. "Feels good," she whispered.

"Mmm, it does. I love touching you."

Her heart squeezed. He'd never been shy about that, seeming to truly enjoy touching her and seeing her reaction. She'd soaked up every touch, every kiss and caress like water offered to a woman dying of thirst. She remembered his voice crooning to her as he made her blind with pleasure, praising and guiding her through the erotic journey he'd taken her on. Arousal curled deep in her belly at the thought.

He felt amazing and she'd dreamed of being in his arms again for so long. Letting her guard down a little further, Grace snuggled back tighter into the shelter of his body. The hand in her hair trailed down her nape and over her shoulder, following her curves as his palm stroked over her ribs, waist and hip, then back up. Not in a sexual way exactly, but her body didn't care. Her nipples beaded against the robe and a slow, hot throb started up in her core.

It would be so very easy to slip the robe off, turn in his arms and let him banish the lingering fear and sadness with what she knew he could do to her. He still wanted her and she knew he'd take care of her every need. But she also knew having sex with him would be a huge mistake right now. There was still so much she didn't know about him.

"Did you really grow up in northern Virginia?" she whispered.

He chuckled against the back of her neck. "Yeah, I really did. That a problem for you, being a Yankee from Minnesota and all?"

A grin tugged at her lips. "No." Lord, she'd missed him. Missed this closeness and the way he'd made her feel so cherished. She didn't want to have to live without that anymore. How was she going to get over him when they parted this time?

"Glad to hear that."

Fighting the building desire and the powerful yearning for him she'd never been able to quench, she focused on the soothing caress of his hand and let herself sink into the protective cocoon he offered. And when he wrapped his arm around her and slid the other beneath her head, her guard slipped a little more. She was safe here, and her psyche recognized that on the deepest level.

Alex's breathing was slow and even, but she could tell he was still awake. He held her in the darkness without a word as the minutes ticked past, taking her farther and farther away from the nightmare. As she began to drift off she felt the tender kiss he pressed against her hair, heard the deeply intimate tone in his voice as he whispered to her.

"Let yourself go, angel. I've got you."

☆ ☆ ☆

CHAPTER SEVEN

David paced the length of his room as he waited for the person he'd dialed to pick up. He'd already left a half dozen texts and voice messages but the bastard hadn't bothered calling back. The digital ring droned in his ear, each one that went unanswered increasing his blood pressure. Just as he was about to hang up, his contact answered.

"What do you want?"

For a moment David was taken aback by the impatient demand. "I—I have an update."

"It better be important."

"I wouldn't have kept trying you all day if it weren't," David snapped.

A pause. "I'm listening."

He ran a hand through his hair. "Dr. Fallon has been taken away."

"What?" he snapped.

"As of this morning she's not staying here and can't be with the team right now. There's some sort of security situation going down, only I don't know what it is. Travis knows, but he won't tell the rest of us. And then when Dr. Fallon did come back to the hotel a few hours ago, she was with this guy—the same guy who followed us yesterday and hauled her out of the cab in a bear hug right in front of everyone. He's around fifty or so, very intense and scary. I think he's some sort of government agent. Has to be former military. She said something yesterday about him being a ghost from her past, and I'm pretty sure they were involved." The possessive vibe coming from the man earlier today had been hard to miss.

"So?"

"So he's taken her to a different location and I don't know when or *if* she'll be back. The meeting—"

"They wouldn't cancel the meeting because of that. Would they change the time and location though?"

"They might, but…" He took a deep breath, tried to calm down as he voiced the fear that had been eating a hole in him all day long. "What if this is about me? What if he knows about the deal we made?" David's contact had called him the day after he'd been assigned as Dr. Fallon's assistant here in Islamabad, less than a week ago.

"Impossible," the man scoffed.

"No, it's not. What if they had a phone tap or something? What if they've been monitoring my calls somehow?" Or tracked its signal via a satellite or something?

"Relax," the man chided. "I'm sure you're just being paranoid."

David didn't think so. The way that Alex guy had looked at him, it was like he knew exactly what David had done and it had been all he could do not to squirm under the man's intent stare. Whoever he was, he was clearly protecting Grace for more than security reasons, and it was evident he wasn't a man to be messed with. If the threat facing Grace was serious enough to warrant moving her to a different location and taking her away from the team, then it stood to reason that anyone connected to her might be under surveillance. Including him.

David's insides shriveled at the thought of being caught. Dammit, he'd only taken the bribe because he needed the money. He wasn't a bad person, he just had a shitload of debt to pay off and this had seemed like such a harmless, easy way to grab some cash.

"Besides, you should be more worried about them changing the time and location of the meeting. If they do and I'm not informed in time, there's no deal. And you won't like the consequences," the man went on. "If you mess up, I withhold the rest of the money *and* I'll expose you. It'll be all over the Internet by morning."

His stomach dropped. "If they change anything I'll let you know as soon as I can, but it probably won't be until the last minute." No way would Grace's new bodyguard allow any of that to leak. And if he somehow knew what David had done…

"You let me know right away. Understood?"

"Yes." Before he could say anything else the man hung up.

David set his phone on the bedside table and sank onto the mattress. He dropped his forehead into his hands and went over his options, both of them shitty. With all his heart he wished he'd never agreed to this deal in the first place.

General Jamal Sharif said goodnight to his housekeeper as she left and locked up behind her. Alone in the kitchen he made himself a light meal to eat before heading upstairs to shower. His wife was down in Karachi visiting relatives and he looked forward to spending the evening by himself.

In the master suite he stripped off his uniform and laid it over the chair for his housekeeper to have dry cleaned, then strode into the connecting luxury bathroom and turned on the shower. Taking his sidearm from its holster, he placed it on the marble-topped counter out of habit.

He let the water run while he gathered his shaving items and placed them beside his weapon. Steam billowed over top of the glass walls of the shower enclosure. Stepping beneath the hot spray, he sighed in enjoyment as the powerful stream pummeled the muscles in his back and shoulders. Since finding out that Hassani had escaped, he'd been working long hours to try and help both the Pakistani and American authorities involved with the hunt. His decision to turn over the man had been an easy one once it looked like Hassani would be caught, and Jamal had seen the reward money as an easy prize.

He washed his hair and body, paused to let the water flow over him for a few minutes longer. All day long he'd felt a strange prickling along his spine, as though someone was watching him. His security team hadn't noticed anything and he'd taken extra precautions on the way home. Now that he was locked safely away behind these walls with his state-of-the-art security system, he could finally relax.

Still, that prickle of awareness didn't disappear completely. He figured it wouldn't until Hassani was once again behind bars. There was no doubt in his mind that under any other circumstances Hassani would order a hit on him. But as arrogant and merciless as he was, the power hungry egomaniac would never risk capture by coming here.

When he was out and dried off, Jamal wrapped his towel around his waist and took the can of shaving cream from the counter. His fingers had just closed around it when a flicker of movement in the mirror caught his attention. He froze, mouth going dry. He reached for the pistol.

"Don't bother."

Hassani.

Fear shot through him. He immediately grabbed for his weapon, caught only a flash of motion in his peripheral before a hard weight slammed into his lower back. He cried out in agony at the blow to his kidneys and automatically twisted to bring his hands up. Hassani had him by the throat and jerked him to his knees before he could do more than throw out a fist to protect himself. He could see the pistol out of the corner of his eye, the grip resting just at the edge of the counter.

"You sold me out," Hassani growled in a voice that slid like ice water through Jamal's veins.

He tried to shake his head, fought for breath as those powerful fingers closed around his throat like a vise. "No—"

"Betrayed me." The words were like a sharp lash in the deathly quiet room. And the rage burning in those dark, deep set eyes chilled him to the core.

Jamal lashed out with a foot to sweep a leg out to knock Hassani off balance, but the other man had been trained by Special Forces and deflected the blow easily. He could feel the blood pooling in his face from the pressure around his windpipe, his eyes beginning to bulge. There was no one to save him now, no one to hear his screams for help if Hassani relaxed his grip.

That merciless pressure increased until black spots swam before his eyes. "Was it worth it? A measly quarter million dollars for a rich man like you? That's nothing—*nothing* compared to what you could have had when I took power."

A garbled sound came out of Jamal's swelling throat. There was no way he could deny the charge, and with that vise-like grip all but cutting off his airway he couldn't even beg for mercy. Not that it would do him any good. He read the death sentence in the other man's eyes. His guts spasmed in terror.

Those dark, pitiless eyes bore into him, cold, cruel. "*This* is what betrayal feels like."

Hassani's unbandaged hand drew back and Jamal saw the matte black KA-BAR knife at the last second. He opened his mouth to scream, but the blade plunged deep beneath his ribcage, right into the blood-rich tissues of his liver. The blinding shock of pain paralyzed him, stole the last of his breath.

He automatically brought his hands up to grasp the hilt of the knife, but it was too late. Staring down into his eyes, Hassani plunged the blade in to the hilt and twisted it. Agony splintered through him in a sickening burst that turned the world white, then Hassani twisted the wicked blade back and wrenched it out again. Jamal's hands flailed weakly to staunch the flow of blood pouring from his torso as he crumpled to the floor. He crashed sideways onto the marble, his blood forming a crimson pool as it pumped from his body.

He lay on the floor bleeding out all alone, his last view of earth that of his killer's back as he turned and walked away.

Alex quietly entered the hotel room and shut the door behind him as he balanced the breakfast tray with his other hand. He was disappointed to find the big, rumpled bed empty and the bathroom door shut. He could hear a blow dryer going.

He set the tray on the circular table in the corner and pulled out his phone to check his messages, trying to focus on something other than Grace, but it was hard not to think about her. Holding her last night had been like a miracle to him. That simple act, and the implicit trust she'd shown him by seeking comfort in his arms had healed the deepest part of the wound caused by leaving her four years ago. He'd dozed on and off for most of the night, unwilling to miss out on the opportunity to savor the feeling of holding her, not even for sleep.

He looked up as the bathroom door opened. Grace emerged dressed in an ankle length black skirt and a fitted pink top that hugged her generous breasts in a most distracting way. Her shiny hair was perfectly styled, her makeup minimal and understated. Elegant and gorgeous. But my God, those *curves*. She looked like a damn walking wet dream.

"Morning," she said, offering him a little smile that was almost shy.

"Morning. You sleep okay?" There were faint shadows beneath her pretty aqua eyes.

"The second half of the night, yeah." A light flush bloomed in her cheeks. "I'm glad you were here. Or rather, I'm glad I was here," she said with a small laugh that told him she was still a little embarrassed about it. "I really needed that, so thanks."

"Me too, and you're welcome." Though God knew he'd wanted to give her a hell of a lot more than comfort last night. At least the wall she'd erected between them seemed much smaller this morning. He considered that a major victory. The thing that drove him crazy now was the time slipping away from them.

She only had a few more days in country, unless he could convince her to stay longer, and he knew that was a selfish thing to do considering the situation and the long hours he would have to put in. Still, maybe he could lay the groundwork for spending time with her stateside. He couldn't let go of the idea that there was a chance for a future with her if he gave her more time to get to know him again. "You hungry? I brought breakfast."

Her gaze shifted to the tray and her face lit up. "Coffee?"

"Of course, and sugar for you, but I still think you're sweet enough without it."

She cracked a grin at his terrible line and strode over to take one of the large cups. "In the morning I'm sweeter with it, trust me." She sat across from him and added her two sugars, giving him the chance to study her up close. A fierce ache started up in his chest as he drank in the sight of her. Her skin seemed to glow in the morning light streaming through the open curtains. The little laugh lines around her eyes and mouth were a bit more pronounced than they had been four years ago, but they only made her more beautiful to him.

She glanced up, paused in the act of stirring when she caught him staring at her. "What?"

He shook his head. "You're more beautiful than ever."

Her cheeks turned bright pink and she looked down into her coffee. "Thank you. You don't have to butter me up though. I already slept with you last night." Her eyes lifted to his, the humor sparkling there hitting him right in the heart. This was the Grace he remembered. The sharp-witted chemistry PhD, the passionate, generous-hearted woman he'd fallen so hard and fast for from the moment he'd met her.

He huffed out a laugh, wishing he could reach across the table to stroke her cheek without the risk of her pulling away. His gut told him it was too soon, and he wouldn't risk undoing the little progress they'd made by rushing things, even though that's exactly what he wanted to do. "And on the first night, too," he chided. "I seem to recall you making me work a lot harder last time."

She raised one auburn brow at him. "And I seem to recall it being worth the wait in the end."

Oh, she had him there. It had been *more* than worth it. He'd never experienced chemistry like that with anyone, and he'd never felt this insanely protective or territorial before or since. "Touché." He picked up his own cup, raised it in salute before he took a sip.

As she nibbled at the pastry he'd brought her, he watched the laughter fade from her eyes and a serious expression steal over her face. He knew she had something on her mind, so he raised his eyebrows to prompt her.

"What happened after you left Kenya?" she asked, staring right into his eyes.

I dropped headfirst into the worst depression I've ever experienced in my life. "My mom had another stroke. I went back to Baltimore, moved her into a home there, worked myself into the ground…and kept tabs on you from time to time."

She nodded thoughtfully, not appearing surprised by the admission. "I figured you would have still tried to find out how I was doing. And sorry to hear about your mom."

"Thanks. She's still alive, but that's all, and I know she wouldn't want to be if she was aware of what was going on. I tell myself it's not really my mom whenever I go visit her. She'd hate anyone seeing her like that, even me." He cleared his throat, changed the subject. "When you wouldn't answer any of my messages initially, it was either find out what was happening with you or lose my mind. So I used the tools at my disposal." He didn't regret it and he wouldn't apologize for it because he knew he'd do the same thing again. "I had your hospital records, your rehab records, your employment records."

"Did you know where I lived?"

"For the first two years, yes."

"Why only the first two years?"

"Because of that e-mail you sent me. I knew you were still only separated, and that Robert had been back in the picture. I thought you guys had made a go of it again, and given what you said in that e-mail I knew I had to respect your wishes and let you go." Giving up the dream of her forever had been just as hard as leaving her in that hospital. But he hadn't wanted to know any more details once she'd gotten back together with her ex.

Grace exhaled, looked down at her plate where she'd torn the pastry into bite-sized pieces. "No, we didn't make a go of it. He was in the picture at first when I was released from the hospital. He helped get me back on my feet, but not because he wanted to save our marriage or be a husband again. Looking back, I'm pretty sure it was out of obligation and guilt, since he was supposed to be the one at the dinner the night of the attack."

Alex's hands curled into fists to keep from reaching for her. "What?" Even to his own ears his voice sounded low, deadly.

She blinked at him. "You didn't know?"

He shook his head, feeling the rage bubble up inside him.

"He'd double booked himself with another function and asked me to go in his place. Since I had friends already going, I said yes. I was going to ask you to be my date, but then I thought that would just create a scandal since all the rich and powerful were there along with the media, and everyone knew Robert and I had just recently separated." She tilted her head slightly. "Would you have gone with me?"

The question damn near killed him. "I would have, except we were getting ready to do the sting. I had no idea you were attending the dinner. When I found out about the attack and that your name was a last minute addition to the guest list…"

He had to stop, take a deep breath to ease the swell of emotion in his chest.

Grace surprised him by reaching across the table to wrap her fingers around his hand. "It wasn't your fault. I know you would have stopped it if you could have." She squeezed for emphasis and her belief in him almost undid him.

Alex stared at her. Did she truly know that? Did she honestly believe that, or was she just saying it to ease his conscience? "I would have. I would have stopped you from going, then I would have taken those sons of bitches down before they could launch the attack."

Another squeeze. "I know. I never blamed you for any of that. Only that you left me when I needed you the most."

He flinched. "I—"

She shook her head, waved his response off with an impatient wave of her hand. "And I'm not blaming you for that anymore either. I've decided I need to let that go. I guess I can kind of understand why you did it. Sort of." She tipped her head to the side, her soft mouth curved in a teasing smile.

The anvil that had been sitting on his chest suddenly lifted. He felt like a condemned man who'd just been given a stay of execution. They might not be back to where they used to be, but she was willing to forgive him for his mistakes and was willing to try to put it behind her. It was probably more than he deserved. Hell, he knew it was.

Alex couldn't *not* touch her. Her fingers were still wrapped around his left hand. With his right one he reached out and cupped the side of her face, held her gaze. "I bled with you that night, and every day since." Maybe not physically, but his heart hadn't known the difference. "I've missed you so goddamn much," he said hoarsely.

He caught the flash of surprise and tenderness in her eyes, then she put her free hand over his, pressing it against her cheek. Holding him there. "I missed you too. But I'm here now."

The tantalizing words seemed to hang in the air between them, the invitation behind them. Was this real? His throat was too tight to answer her. Instead he let his thumb trail across the satiny curve of her cheek, down to feather across her lips. They parted slightly under his touch and her breath caught.

He lifted his eyes to hers and bit back a growl at the heat and awareness he saw burning there. Removing his thumb from her mouth, he slid his hand around to cup her nape and leaned forward. Her lashes fluttered as he bent his head and closed the distance between them. He covered her lips with his, heard the breathless gasp she gave—

His damn phone buzzed in his pocket.

Her eyes popped open, clear and beautiful and full of needs he was dying to satisfy. She pulled back an inch, resisting the pressure of his hand around the back of her neck. "Aren't you going to check that?"

What he wanted was to hurl the fucking thing against the wall for interrupting them. He closed his eyes for a second, fought back the tide of arousal so powerful he almost couldn't see straight. The phone rang again, the sound grating over his nerve endings. But it might be something about Hassani.

Hating to pull away, he made himself release her and sit back to answer the call. When he saw the name on call display he swore under his breath. "Yeah?"

"We're up and at 'em," Blake Ellis replied in a cheery voice. "You ready for us?"

No. He glanced up at Grace. She was watching him curiously, her cheeks flushed, but that glaze of arousal was gone. He might have told Blake no just to have a few more minutes' privacy with Grace, but he had to get into the office and if he kissed her again he knew neither of them would be leaving this room anytime soon. "Yeah. Come on over."

"Who was that?" Grace asked when he hung up.

"Your temporary security detail." He got up and headed for the door, opened it when he saw his two employees appear in the peephole. "Come on in." Damn cock blockers, both of them, even if they were oblivious to it. Ellis and Jordyn stepped past him into the room. Even Ellis's deep gold skin tone couldn't cover all the fading bruises on his arms. No doubt the rest of him looked the same because he was moving a little stiffly, still not fully recovered from his fall down the cliff during the op when Hassani had been captured. Switching his attention to Jordyn, Alex immediately noticed the ring on her finger.

Well, good for them. Alex glanced meaningfully at it and smiled at them both before making the introductions. "Grace, this is Blake Ellis and Jordyn Bridger, the two other members of the team I told you about. They'll be escorting you whenever you leave the hotel when I can't be here. Blake's a sniper and Jordyn might as well be. They're both former Marines so you're in good hands. You know I wouldn't entrust your safety to them unless I trusted them."

"Yes, and that's very high praise, coming from you," Grace answered, and rose to her feet to shake hands.

"You didn't tell us she was so gorgeous," Jordyn teased him as she shook Grace's hand. "We've been dying to meet you, right, Blake?"

"Dying," Ellis deadpanned in his usual quiet way, though his eyes were brimming with amusement as he shook Grace's hand.

"If you need to meet with someone from your team or go out for any reason, these guys will take you where you need to go. But don't tell anyone you're staying here. I don't want anything to further jeopardize any of my guys. Or girls," he added, when Jordyn narrowed her eyes at him. "I'll be back as soon as I can, but I don't know when that will be because—" He trailed off when his phone rang again. "Excuse me." Leaving Grace to talk with Ellis and Jordyn, he crossed the room and answered the call from Evers.

"Just got a call from one of our military contacts," the Fed began. "Guess who was found dead on his bathroom floor by his housekeeper this morning with a five inch laceration to his liver?"

Alex's heart sped up. "Who?"

"Sharif."

Urgency poured through him. "Was it a professional hit?"

"Nope. Looks like Hassani took care of this personally. Sharif wrote his name in blood on the tile floor and they found prints matching Hassani's at the scene. Cocky bastard didn't even bother wearing gloves."

How the hell had Hassani killed a man like Sharif when he only had one functioning hand? "Then he must be close by still. When did it happen?" Everyone in the room was staring at him now.

"They think around ten o'clock last night."

Shit. Almost nine hours ago. Hassani could be anywhere right now. "I'm coming in. Make sure everyone's being vigilant about their personal security."

"Will do. See you in a few."

Alex ended the call and faced the others. With Grace in the room he knew he shouldn't divulge the new intel but he didn't give a shit. She wasn't going to tell anyone. "Hassani killed General Sharif last night at his place in Islamabad." He watched the meaning of that hit home in Grace's eyes, how close Hassani was and that the threat level against the rest of them had just increased tenfold. He looked at Ellis and

Jordyn. "Give us a minute." They left the room and Alex walked over to Grace where she stood in the center of the room with her arms folded around herself.

He put his hands on her upper arms, rubbed up and down gently as he searched her face. "It'll be okay. We're gonna find him and nail him, sweetheart. Just stick close to Blake and Jordyn if you need to go anywhere and I'll see you tonight." He hoped.

Grace stopped him by putting a hand on the side of his face. "You'll be careful?"

He leaned into her touch and slid his fingers into her hair. "I will." Unable to stop himself, Alex lowered his head and kissed her. This time there was no hesitation, no surprise on her part.

She gripped his shoulders and kissed him back, parting her lips to let him inside her in the only way he could right now. He groaned at the feel of that tiny surrender, her familiar taste. His tongue stroked hers, explored the tender places in her mouth as she lifted up onto her toes for more contact. He wrapped an arm around her waist and crushed her to him, her breasts flattened against his chest. Her quiet whimper of need sliced through him.

At that moment he'd have given anything—anything—to be able to finish what he'd started. Tumble her into that wide bed and take her the way he ached to, hear her moans turn into throaty cries of release as he pushed her over the edge. To have her gaze up at him with that agonizing combination of trust and need that satisfied him on the most primal level.

But they couldn't. Not now. He just prayed he had the chance to share that with her one more time before she left. And once this situation with Hassani was over, he was going to put everything he had into convincing Grace they belonged together.

Holding her head steady, he gentled the pressure of his kiss, paused to lick and nibble at her luscious lips before he forced himself to lift his head. They were both breathing faster and her cheeks and eyes held that gorgeous glow of arousal he'd been dreaming about for so long. He rubbed his thumb across her lower lip, stared down into her eyes. "Hold that thought, angel. I'll make it up to you later."

He left her with Ellis and Jordyn and geared up for the race against the clock that Hassani had set into motion.

CHAPTER EIGHT

Sean Dunphy's eyes snapped open in the dim late evening light when someone turned the latch on his hospital room door. He held his breath, aware of his heart thudding hard against his sternum as he stared at the doorway. When it opened and he saw the silhouette of a woman with a long ponytail, a flood of relief crashed through him so fast it made him dizzy.

Zahra quietly closed the door behind her but didn't approach him, instead shoving her hands into her jeans pockets. Maybe because she wasn't sure if he'd try to bite her head off again like he had yesterday. "Hey," he said.

"Oh, you're awake." She stayed where she was, still hesitant, wary. His fault.

He pushed up onto his elbows, tried not to notice the outline of the legs he could no longer feel beneath the blankets. His whole back hurt with the movement, bruised and battered muscle stretching over achy bones. "Did you get some rest and some decent food?"

She nodded, looking distracted as she pushed her dark bangs away from her forehead. "Have you eaten?"

"Couple hours ago." Though he hadn't had much of an appetite. A lengthy silence ensued and she broke eye contact with him. He hated that, hated knowing he was responsible for her need to protect herself. She should never have to protect herself from him. "Zahra."

Her head came up, her eyes finding his.

He held out a hand. "C'mere."

She stared back at him, started to shake her head.

He beckoned with his hand. "Please. I need you." It was the truth.

At those softly spoken words she made a choked sound in her throat and hurried across the room to go into his arms. A shudder ripped through her as he hugged her. Sean cursed under his breath and laid back so he could hold her to him. He cupped one hand over the back of her head and pressed her face into his neck, squeezing his eyes shut at the feel of her. The way she burrowed into him and held on so tight told him just how much he'd hurt her. "I'm sorry," he whispered, meaning it, even though the words weren't easy for him. "I was a prick and you didn't deserve it."

"Yeah, you were a *total* prick," she agreed.

Sean stroked a hand down her spine. "I'm glad you came back."

She lifted her head to look into his eyes. "You knew I wouldn't stay away long."

Actually, he'd figured she'd at least make him wait a couple of days as punishment for the way he'd lashed out at her. "Once I calmed down enough to think straight, I *hoped* you wouldn't wait long." Even just the past day and a half had felt like an eternity without her.

"Sean, seriously? You thought I'd leave you here all alone just because you'd hurt my feelings?"

He shrugged. "Yeah." He'd certainly deserved it.

She sat up a bit more, narrowed her eyes at him. "I'm so insulted right now. Have you forgotten how tough I am?

Sticks and stones, funny boy. It's gonna take a hell of a lot more than that to drive me away." She searched his eyes. "But you're not going to do that, are you?"

At the note of vulnerability in her voice, the lump in his throat magnified until it nearly choked him. He shook his head, put a hand to her face to stroke his thumb along her angular jaw line. "I'll try my best not to." It wouldn't be easy. Part of him had wanted to lash out at her, vent all his rage and grief and frustration and she'd been an easy target. Now he felt like an asshole.

Apparently satisfied by that response, she laid her head on his chest with a sigh and gently rubbed her fingertips over his heart. He swore it swelled under her touch, so filled with gratitude that she'd come back to him. "Did you get any sleep while I was gone?" she asked softly.

"A little."

"Think you could sleep now?"

"If you lay with me, maybe." He needed that contact, craved it, and he didn't care if admitting it made him look weak. Where Zahra was concerned, he *was* weak. Luckily, she didn't seem to mind.

She sat up, chewed her lip as she glanced uncertainly at his legs. "I don't want to hurt anything—"

"You won't." Even if she kicked him in her sleep he wouldn't feel it, and the surgeons had cobbled his legs back together with titanium staples, plates and screws so it wasn't like she'd do any damage. He grabbed her wrist, tugged until she gave in and swung her legs up onto the narrow bed. She gingerly placed them next to his right leg and lay down on her side facing him. "You're gonna fall off the edge like that," he chided, banding one arm around her to haul her upper body forward until she was draped across his torso.

Zahra sighed and snuggled into his shoulder, her fingers tracing gentle patterns over his chest through the thin material of the hospital gown. Sean closed his eyes and blocked the jolt of grief that welled up inside him. Up until the IED attack, if she'd been pressed up against him and touching him like this he'd have been rock hard and ready to rock her world in a matter of seconds. Now there was no sensation whatsoever from the waist down and every day that passed without any encouraging signs that he might regain feeling or movement in his lower body dragged him deeper into the pit of despair he was trying like hell not to fall into.

The hushed sounds of the staff moving about in the hallway outside reached him, blending with the quiet whir of the IV machine as it administered the cocktail of steroids and antibiotics they were pumping into his veins 24/7. Zahra covered a yawn and shifted. Her warm weight was such a comfort. "Need anything?"

"Just this," he whispered back. During those long hours while she'd been gone, he'd faced the very real fear that he'd driven her away for good. Much as he hated what had happened to him, hated the weakness and the terrifying prospect of spending the rest of his life in a wheelchair, he knew he'd never needed anyone as much as he needed Zahra now.

He ran his fingers through her silky ponytail, trying to envision what sort of a life he could give her now. Until a few days ago he'd had it all planned out. Once they got Hassani and headed back stateside, he was going to take her away somewhere romantic and pop the question. Should he even contemplate that still? She was loyal, and he didn't doubt that she loved him, so he was pretty sure she'd say yes if he still asked her.

But wasn't it selfish of him to ask her to marry a cripple? That was more like a life sentence than a happily-ever-after. Maybe that was partly why he'd lashed out at her earlier. Maybe he *was* trying to push her away because he knew she deserved better than to be saddled with him now, or maybe he wanted to drive her away before she could leave him. He was terrified that she might one day, when it finally sunk in that he wasn't going to get better.

He swallowed hard past the lump in his throat. Blocking those depressing thoughts, he kissed the top of her head and breathed in the clean fragrance of her hair. "I love you, Zahra." So much it shook him. How the hell would he go on without her if she walked away one day?

She pressed her lips to his chest. "Love you too."

It was a miracle, and one he intended to cherish. With Zahra's warm weight snuggled against him, helping to keep the fear and helplessness at bay, Sean closed his eyes and allowed himself to drift.

He dreamed he was running. On a tropical white sand beach. The breeze was warm and soft against him. He was laughing, racing toward something…someone. Zahra. She stood near the edge of the surf wearing a lacy white gown, holding a bouquet of orchids. Her hazel green eyes were full of love and happiness as she gazed back at him. A diamond ring glinted on her hand. His wife.

Sean ran up to her, lifted her into his arms and swung her off her feet. She draped her arms around his neck and laughed as he twirled her. Then her gaze caught on something over his shoulder. She tensed in his arms, her face going stiff with fear. Sean stopped, turned his head to assess the threat. A dark and evil-looking cloud was coming up the beach toward them. Instinct drove him to protect her. She was in terrible danger. He couldn't let anything happen to her. He set her down and pushed her away from him, shouting at her to run.

The sound of the surf disappeared and the beach fell away. He was back behind the wheel of the SUV on the Khyber Pass, the muted roar of the sea replaced by the hum of the engine. A dark shadow appeared in the rearview mirror. Danger was stalking him, he knew it but he couldn't stop, couldn't turn back. All he could do was drive faster, try to outrun it even as he knew it was futile. He had to follow the others, guard their six. The hairpin turn was dead ahead. His heart hammered his ribs as he slowed into the first part of the turn. Instinct screamed at him to stop, to go back. But it was too late.

A huge explosion erupted beneath him. He screamed and threw his hands up to shield his face from the searing heat of the flames just as everything went black. When he came to, the others were staring down at him. Hunter. Alex. Gage. Ellis. Their faces were pinched with worry and he could smell blood and burning flesh.

And his legs. God, his legs were mangled like hamburger when he lifted his head to glance in horror down the length of his body. He braced himself for the pain, but the agony never came. Instead he felt a hot pins-and-needles sensation in both limbs. It ran down both his legs, right into his feet, like a million tiny beestings.

Paralysis caused by spinal shock. The terrible words ran through his head.

He shifted to escape them and the prickling, stinging sensation increased.

His eyes snapped open and he struggled to get his bearings as the dream tugged at him. The hospital. He was sweating, heart racing. Zahra was sound asleep against him, using his chest for a pillow. But that prickling sensation was still there, stronger now.

What the…

He jerked up onto his elbows to stare down at his blanket-covered legs. Was he still dreaming? Maybe he was having phantom pain like he'd heard about from amputees he'd known.

Zahra gasped and shot into a sitting position. "What's wrong?" she whispered tensely, casting a frantic look around.

"My legs."

She sucked in a breath and scrambled away to face him, her expression full of dread. "Oh God, did I—"

"I feel pins-and-needles." It wasn't just in his head. He fucking *felt* something.

Eyes widening, she glanced from his face to his legs and back again. "Are you…sure?"

He nodded, swallowed past the dryness in his throat. It hurt enough to make him break out in an all-over sweat, but that probably had more to do with his racing pulse than the pain, and he'd fucking take pain any day over the horrifying numbness he'd experienced since the blast. "Both legs. And the feet, too. All over, like ants biting me."

She met his gaze once more and he saw the powerful yet devastating surge of hope there.

"Go get the doctor on duty," he urged hoarsely, grabbing the call button to bring the nurse. His heart hammered against his ribs. *Please God, please let this be real.*

Zahra jumped off the bed and raced for the door.

Grace tossed the TV remote aside and laid back with a sigh against the pillows she'd stacked up against the headboard. It was already after nine, plenty late enough for her to take a nice hot bath and change into her jammies for the night.

She hadn't heard from Alex since he'd texted her just after lunch to check in with her, and he might not be returning to the hotel tonight at all. The memory of those kisses this morning had her all revved up inside, and it looked like there wasn't going to be any relief for the ache of arousal she'd been suffering all day.

She'd passed the hours reading, going over files then eating with Jordyn and Blake—she wasn't sure why Alex always called him Ellis instead—before taking a very short walk through the hotel garden with them. It hadn't taken long for her to figure out they were a couple, but it certainly didn't appear to affect their job performance. They'd both been focused one hundred percent on her and their surroundings the entire time. Grace was a homebody by nature and loved to cuddle up for some quiet time, but these four walls were seriously starting to close in on her.

She was thinking about starting that bath when her new cell rang. It was Jordyn. "Hey," Grace answered. "You going to come bring me a chocolate for my pillow then tuck me in for the night?"

"No, sorry, that's not in my contract," Jordyn said on a laugh. "We just got a call from Alex. Apparently Zahra—one of our team members—contacted him. He wants us all to come to the hospital."

Grace sat up, heart sinking. "Is everything okay?"

"It's fine. It's Sean Dunphy, our teammate who was wounded the other—"

"I remember. Alex told me about it." What a horrific thing, for a man like that to become paralyzed.

"Well, something big must have just happened for Alex to call us in there, so we're all heading over there now. Hunter and Gage are going with Alex, and Alex doesn't want us leaving you here alone so he said to bring you with us. We'll be by to get you in five."

It wasn't her place to be involved in whatever was going on with their wounded teammate, but she wasn't about to argue and the truth was she would take any excuse to see Alex again. "Okay."

When they stepped off the elevator at the hospital twenty-plus minutes later, Grace could see Hunter and Gage standing next to a door near the end of the hallway. The nurses gave them hard looks as they passed, apparently none too pleased about such a big group breaking the visiting hours rule, but she followed Blake and Jordyn without a qualm. Alex was here and she couldn't wait to see him.

Hunter and Gage both nodded at them as they walked up. "What's the deal?" Blake said quietly.

"Doc's still in there with them," Hunter answered, and even though Grace didn't know him well, she could see the excitement in his eyes. "Might be good news."

Grace didn't even know Dunphy and she felt hopeful for him. "Where's Alex?"

"Inside." Gage nodded at the closed door. "Zahra wanted him in there with them."

"Blake told me what you guys did, by the way. I can't believe you gave him brownies after what you did to him last time," Jordyn said with a shake of her head.

"Come on, it's totally fitting," Gage insisted, folding those thick, tatted arms across his chest. Grace could make out script in amongst the designs. It looked like people's names but she couldn't be sure. "Mirroring, or whatever."

"Like book ends," Hunter added.

"Book ends," Gage agreed enthusiastically, pointing at Hunter as he nodded in approval. He looked back at Jordyn and shrugged. "Besides, he got a kick out of it."

"Bad pun, man," Hunter said wryly. "Really fucking awful."

Gage shrugged but looked a little chagrinned as he realized what he'd said. "Just came out. Sorry."

"Wait, what's this about the brownies?" Grace asked when no one filled her in.

They all looked over at her, but Gage was the one who answered. "Dunphy's the team clown, likes to pull practical jokes on everyone. Since he's younger than the rest of us, Hunt and I decided to teach the little shit a lesson." He grinned.

"With brownies?" she asked, not getting it.

Gage's smile widened. "Yeah. Laced with a box of extra strength laxatives."

"Oh…" Grace didn't know what else to say, other than that seemed pretty damn harsh retaliation for a few practical jokes. "And so did he, uh…"

"Learn his lesson?" Hunter interjected. "Nope. Not a surprise to anyone that knows him. Only person who seems to be safe from his sick sense of humor is Zahra. So far, anyway." He said it fondly, and Grace knew he actually got a kick out of Dunphy's antics. "But you didn't spike the brownies you gave him now, right?" she pressed.

Hunter shook his head. "Nah. Just wanted to remind him how much we care, right, Gage?"

"Right," Gage said with a decisive nod.

Yeah, because nothing says love like a reminder of what had to have been an epic and seemingly endless bout of diarrhea. Grace shook her head at them. Alpha males were so weird.

"You have to know Dunphy to get it," Gage said to her in their defense, then waved a hand dismissively. "It's a guy thing."

Apparently. Grace couldn't help but smile. "Does Alex do that sort of thing?" She couldn't envision it.

Gage looked surprised for a second as he thought about it. "No, not that I've seen." He looked at his teammates. "You guys ever seen him…"

Everyone glanced at each other then shook their heads.

"Huh," Gage mused, and directed his attention back on her. "Maybe not now, since he's the boss, but I guarantee you he did back in his Army days."

"Now that I can believe," Grace acknowledged. She'd seen a playful side to Alex and could easily picture him doing something similar to his soldiers back in the day.

"You gotta admit, that hot sauce thing Dunphy pulled was pretty good," Blake put in.

"Yeah, and Hunt's reaction was the best of all," Gage added with a chuckle. "Probably had heartburn for a week straight after, but he ate every damn bite just to show the little prick he could take it."

Grace was lost again. The team members stood talking amongst themselves for a few minutes until finally the door opened and Alex walked out with a dark-haired young woman with dusky skin. He had his arm around her back, his head bent as he whispered something to her while she had her face buried in his chest. A jolt of alarm spiked through Grace, but then Alex looked up at her and the answering smile on his face made her breathe out a sigh of relief.

"So, what's happening?" Hunter demanded before anyone else could ask.

Alex squeezed the young woman tighter, his embrace protective, almost fatherly. This had to be Zahra. It was clear she meant a great deal to Alex, and while she wasn't jealous of the woman, Grace was definitely curious about their relationship. Though he'd kept secrets from her, she knew it was rare for him to show that kind of attachment openly. Alex glanced up at Grace, his obvious pleasure at seeing her warming her to her toes.

"Dunphy just had a major uptick in his prognosis." Everyone seemed to hold their breath as they waited for him to continue. He murmured something else to Zahra, who was trying to get herself together, and she nodded. "Doc will be out in a minute and then you can go see him."

Not wanting to interfere, Grace stayed behind the others as the doctor came out and shook hands with Alex. Alex squeezed Zahra once more and she went back into the room with everyone else.

Grace erased the distance between them and smiled. "So, good news?"

"Looks like." His lips turned up on one side in that sexy grin of his and he drew her into his arms. "How'd you make out today?"

"Fine. Bored to tears, but that's as bad as it got." She wrapped her arms around his waist and leaned her head against him, let out a soft laugh when her cheek touched the dampness on his shirt. "I found the wet spot." She wiped her cheek and looked up at him. "Was that Zahra?"

"Yes. She's worked for me for a few years now."

"She's special to you."

Another grin, this one full of pride. "Yeah. I guess I kind of took her under my wing after I recruited her. She's been through a lot, and I'm damn proud of how she's handled herself. One of the best cryptologists I've ever seen, too."

Wow, okay then. "I don't think I've ever heard you speak so highly about anyone before."

His smile widened. "That's only because you've never heard me talk about you."

A warm bubble of pleasure rose inside her. The man could be so charming when he wanted, but she knew that wasn't just a line, and she could see the sincerity in his eyes. "Well, I'll consider myself flattered then."

"You should. It's well-deserved." He started nuzzling the tender spot just beneath her ear. Such a simple thing, but it sent a wave of pleasure through her entire body. Delicious little shivers cascaded over her skin, tightening her nipples as she pressed closer to him. Lord, she'd never get her fill of the feel of him, so strong and vital, and her arousal level had been at a simmer all day.

She jerked back guiltily when the door behind them opened and Hunter stuck his head out, his hard features lit with excitement. "Get back in here."

Alex quirked a brow at her but took her hand and led her into the room despite her initial resistance. The entire team was gathered around the man lying in the hospital bed. His eyes were nearly as dark as his black hair and beard, and even though she'd never met him, she could tell the sparkle there was pure joy. "Look what I can do!" he blurted to Alex.

Alex kept hold of her hand as he walked to the foot of the bed where Zahra sat perched on the edge, a huge grin on her face. She drew the blankets back far enough to expose Dunphy's right foot.

"Watch," Dunphy instructed, his face screwed up in intense concentration as he stared at his foot.

All traces of awkwardness for intruding on such a private moment gone, Grace watched closely and caught the tiny flicker of movement in the big toe.

Dunphy grinned at Alex, clearly elated. "See?"

"Hell yeah, I saw," Alex chuckled. "That's awesome, man. But don't overdo it. The doc said you need to keep resting."

Not in the least deterred by Alex's words, Dunphy turned his gaze on her. "And who's this?"

"This," Alex answered, tugging her close to his side, "is Grace."

At that Zahra stared up at her with wide eyes. "*The* Grace?"

"The one and only," he affirmed.

Grace glanced back and forth between them, wondering what he'd told Zahra about her and their relationship. She stuck her hand out. "Nice to meet you."

Zahra shook it. "*Very* nice to meet you." When she looked back up at Alex, her eyes held a happy, almost wistful expression. The understanding and very pleased smile she gave him touched Grace deep inside. Whatever he'd told Zahra about her, it must have made her seem very important to him. She liked that thought.

Alex flicked her a telling glance, the pride and hunger there stealing her breath. Then he looked back at Dunphy. "Get some sleep and keep up the good work in the morning." He reached down and gave Zahra's shoulder an affectionate squeeze. "Call when you've got another update or if you need anything."

"I will."

He faced the others. "Come on, everybody out so these two can have a chance to get some sleep. I'll drive Grace back myself." Grace watched as identical expressions of surprise showed on everyone's faces. Except for Blake, who looked purely amused as he stood with a muscled arm draped over Jordyn's shoulders. Her eyebrows were hiked up under her hairline. Gage let out a soft chuckle.

Hunter's cheek creased in the hint of a grin and he nodded. "We'll follow you back. All right, let's rock." They all followed him out of the room.

As they walked toward the elevators Alex held her back to put space between them and the others, his hand warm and sure around hers. She glanced up at him questioningly. “Shouldn’t we stick close to them?”

“We will, but not that close.” His silver eyes seemed to glow in the dim lighting as he looked down at her. “I want you all to myself for the rest of the night.”

Grace shivered in anticipation and shut her mouth.

CHAPTER NINE

Alex glanced sideways at Grace as he drove them back to his hotel, amused by the slight grin on her face as she studied him. "What?"

She held up a hand in self defense. "Nothing. I guess I just never realized you'd told anyone about me."

"Only Zahra, and only the Cliff's Notes version. The PG version," he added wryly.

"Still. I just…it surprised me."

It shouldn't have, but he could see why she'd feel that way. Maybe now she'd realize she meant something more to him than a fling and a means to access the wealthy and powerful set in Mombasa. "Then I guess I'll have to keep showing you how I feel about you until you actually believe it."

For a moment he thought he'd gone too far, that she'd shut down and retreat from him emotionally, but instead she studied him with an almost wistful expression. "How do you feel about me?"

It was too soon to pull out the L word, even though he knew he still loved her. Too much time had passed, there was too much hurt, and in many ways they were strangers again. He had to give them the chance to re-learn about each other, rediscover all the reasons they'd fallen for each other in the first place, which was why this damn time crunch bothered him so much. With every hour that passed he was acutely aware of the time slipping by him. So he pushed the hesitation aside and laid his heart on the line. "You're the only woman I want, and I'd do anything for you."

The look in her eyes softened, warmed, and he thought he caught a sheen of moisture there before she glanced away. "I don't know what to say."

"Just say you'll give me another chance." If he could get that much, he knew he could capture her trust and heart again.

She glanced over and he caught a flash of hope in her gaze, warring with the indecision. He tightened his hands around the steering wheel to stay the impulse to reach out and touch her. Last thing he wanted was to make her bolt now, when he was so close to earning another shot. *Come on, angel, let me in one more time and I swear you'll never regret it.*

But Grace didn't tell him what he longed to hear; she cleared her throat softly and changed the subject. "So, Dunphy seems in good spirits."

Hiding his disappointment, Alex let it go for now. "Hell of a lot better than he was, that's for sure."

"What's his prognosis now?"

"Still uncertain, but the nerve pain and movement are good signs. I hope to God he keeps gaining more motor control and that they can get the swelling around the spinal cord all the way down. There was a single compression fracture in one of his lumbar vertebrae, but that's not the problem. They think the pressure from the swelling on the cord is causing the paralysis. Spinal shock. But the longer the compression lasts, the higher the chance that the damage will be permanent."

"Well I'd say he's off to a great start. I hope he regains full use of his legs again. At least he's got Zahra there. She seems good with him."

"She loves him. She's as loyal as they come, so she'll stick by him no matter what. I only worry that she'd put up with too much bullshit if he develops full blown depression. Had a little chat with him yesterday to set him straight about that, though. Think it might have worked, too," he added with a faint smile. Though if Dunphy didn't regain use of his legs, depression was a certainty.

Grace smiled back at him. "Like I said, you're just full of surprises. I wouldn't have pegged you as the fatherly type, but you certainly wear it well."

He shrugged. "I've always been that way with my guys. Comes from my ODA commander days, I guess. But Zahra's special. I think we've been good for each other, and acting as her mentor early on got me through a really tough stretch after you and I…" He trailed off, leaving that sentence unfinished because they both knew how it ended.

Grace was silent a long time, but he could hear the wheels turning in her head and wondered what she was thinking about. "Do you ever regret not having kids?" she asked a few minutes later.

The question took him by surprise for a second. "Sometimes. But my marriage wasn't really a marriage for a long time before we finally split, and we both knew it wouldn't have been fair to bring kids into that. I was gone so much, I wouldn't have been there for them enough."

He had her full attention again, even though she wasn't looking at him. "You never really talked much about your ex."

Another shrug. "She was a good person, just couldn't deal with the lifestyle and the long absences. Not that I blame her. It all took its toll over the years until I came home one time after a three week mission and all her stuff was packed. I realized then that we were essentially strangers bound by law and vows neither of us meant anymore. I'm not proud of it. I know I could have tried harder, and I might have if she hadn't already had someone else waiting in the wings. As far as divorces go mine was pretty amicable. I think honestly we were both glad it was over." Those were mistakes he'd never repeat with Grace. If she let him back into her life, that is.

Curious, a little hesitant to ask in light of the emergency hysterectomy the doctors had been forced to perform during the surgery to save her life, he stole a glance at her. "What about you? You ever wish you'd…"

She nodded, still staring out the windshield. "Sometimes. Since I was over forty and my marriage wasn't great I'd given up on the idea with Robert, but after I met you I wondered if maybe…" She blew out a breath and Alex's gut knotted when she put a hand to her abdomen.

Unable to help himself he reached out and gripped her hand, squeezed. "I'm so sorry that choice was taken from you." And that he hadn't been able to prevent that loss.

She pressed her lips together, gave another little nod, and he knew she was battling the ghostly memories swirling between them. Thankfully she didn't pull her hand away. Instead she curled hers fingers around his and stroked her thumb across his knuckles. "Well. No sense regretting all of that, because we can't go back and change the past."

"No," he agreed. Which was why it was vital he fix the damage he'd caused, show her how much he wanted her. How much he wanted—needed—her in his life. He couldn't go back to living without her.

They lapsed into silence for the remainder of the drive to the hotel. In the underground parking lot he parked in a secure area and shut off the engine. When she made no move to undo her belt, he glanced over at her. She was staring at him with an unreadable expression, still holding his hand, and she didn't seem to be in any hurry to exit the vehicle. Alex quickly scanned the lot and contacted Hunter via their earpieces as the Titanium team leader parked the other SUV close by. The threat level here was minimal. He could see two uniformed guards posted at the lot entrance and knew there were others. "We clear?"

"Clear," Hunter responded.

The lot was secure, well-lit and patrolled by guards, and nothing had tripped Alex's internal radar. It was clear Grace wanted to talk, so if she wanted to stay here for a bit, he was fine with it. "You guys go ahead, but post one of you inside until we join you. We'll be in shortly."

"Roger that." Two spots over, the other SUV's doors popped open. Hunter, Gage, Ellis and Jordyn climbed out and headed for the stairwell entrance.

Having given them as much privacy as he could considering they were in a parkade, Alex focused back on Grace. "You okay?" She looked like she wanted to say something but either didn't know how or wasn't sure if she should. "What?"

As she gazed at him, a new tension filled the quiet interior. Arousal buzzed over his skin like a low voltage electrical current, crackling with sudden awareness. She seemed to be measuring him, her pretty eyes glittering in the light from the tall lamp posts that trickled through the tinted windows. Before he could prompt her again she undid her seatbelt, leaned forward, and pulled him down into a hot, hungry kiss.

Momentarily caught off guard, Alex recovered fast and swallowed a groan at her outward display of need and desire. As her fingers speared into his hair he took her face in his hands and seized control of the kiss, parting her lips with his tongue to slide inside and taste her. She made a soft sound at the back of her throat and kissed him harder, her fingers tightening in his hair. Heart pounding, Alex let his right hand trail down her jaw to her neck, paused to feel the rapid pounding of her pulse with his fingertips before he skimmed his hand down to follow the generous curve of one breast.

Her answering gasp was lost in the ravenous kiss. She tasted faintly of mint and smelled like sin. She arched her back to press that soft mound of flesh harder into his palm. Remembering how sensitive and responsive she was, Alex cupped her, squeezed and explored gently before sliding his thumb over the hardened center pushing against her bra and shirt. A strangled whimper escaped her. She scrambled up onto her knees on the leather seat and plastered herself against him, trapping his hand between them.

"I've been thinking about this all day. More," she demanded breathlessly against his mouth.

Fuck yes.

Alex took over. He climbed over the center console, grabbed her seat release lever and dropped the top half back as far as it would go. Grace gasped and grabbed his shoulders for support, her eyes wide and full of arousal at his move as he followed her down and stretched out on top of her, settling his hips between her legs. The contact was torture, not nearly enough with her snug skirt restricting her movements and blocking access to where he wanted to be. Grace licked her shiny lips and stared up at him during a long, charged silence.

When he saw the knowledge that she was trapped and at his mercy register in her eyes and the shot of pure heat that followed, Alex dipped his head and took her mouth again. He pinned her with his weight, reveling in the way her arms came around him and the little noises of enjoyment she made.

His cock was hard and full against her pelvis. With a frustrated groan, Grace raised her hips to rub against him, wanting more. The friction through their clothing wasn't nearly enough for either of them. Easing away, he reached down, grabbed the hem of her skirt and yanked it over her hips to bunch around her waist. There was just enough light for him to make out the skimpy black panties she wore, offset by the paleness of the fine-grained skin of her upper thighs above the lace bands of her sheer black thigh highs. He swallowed a groan at the sight of her and those soft, rounded thighs that would fill his hands perfectly, give him something to squeeze as he rode her to ecstasy and back.

He smoothed a hand over their satiny curves, watching her face as he hit the sensitive spots he knew would make her even hotter. The way she bit her full lower lip when he came close to the edge of the fabric covering her sex sent a thrill of power through him.

Without giving her time to surface from the arousal, Alex buried his face in her neck and breathed her in, giving her little licks and nibbles that made her squirm in his arms. Christ, she was so soft, it drove him nuts. He wanted to feel her naked against him, bury himself as deep into that softness as he could get. He trailed his tongue up the side of her neck, chuckled softly when she gasped and threw her head back to give him more access.

Only when she was twisting against him, fighting for more friction, did he finally lower his hips into position and wedge his erection tight against the scrap of fabric between her thighs. At the contact Grace gave a broken cry and dug her fingers into his back. The scent of her arousal swirled around him, making his head spin.

"Oh, God, touch me," she begged breathlessly. "Please."

Alex suppressed a growl at the raw need in her voice. Making her fly like this was one of the greatest thrills and pleasures of his life. He loved seeing her this way, protective walls down, craving him so much she let her pride go and surrendered to pure sensation. He quickly lowered his hands to the hem of her top and pulled it upward until the shiny material of her bra was revealed to his ravenous gaze. He paused only a moment to enjoy the view of her ample cleavage displayed so erotically in the black satin cups before reaching behind her to undo the strap. She helped him by wiggling out of it and her breasts spilled free.

This time he couldn't hold back his groan. *Oh, hell.* He'd always been a breast man, but Grace's were fucking spectacular. Creamy and plump, topped with tight deep pink nipples. Cupping the luscious mounds reverently, possessively, he buried his face between the heavenly softness and drew in her warm scent as he kissed her smooth flesh. Her breathing turned choppy, her hands clutching at his back through his shirt as he swirled his tongue over the velvety skin and moved in toward the rigid nipples that begged for his mouth.

Alex hummed in enjoyment at the sweet taste of her, reveling in the way she squirmed against him. Normally he'd draw it out, make her wait, but he needed this as much as she did. He dragged the flat of his tongue over one hard tip as he slid an arm beneath her hips to hoist her pelvis upward. He shifted his body to hold her in place with his weight when she bowed up and rubbed against his groin. God, she felt and tasted even better than he'd remembered. Closing his eyes, Alex drew the taut peak into his mouth and sucked, flicking his tongue over the sensitive flesh in the way he knew she loved. Grace let out something close to a sob and arched her neck in a long, lovely line.

He was in heaven. His erection pulsed heavily between his legs as he rocked against her center, his mouth teasing her tender nipples. Her breathing hitched. She reached down to dig a hand into his ass, rubbing her pelvis against him in frantic little circles. He could tell from the sounds she was making and the tight expression on her face that she was getting close already. So was he. It'd been so long; he was so worked up from having her willing beneath him that he could easily come in his pants if he kept rubbing against her like that.

Alex broke the kiss and lifted his head. Grace watched him through heavy lidded eyes, her lips shiny and swollen from his kisses, her gorgeous breasts still cradled in his hands, rising and falling with her rapid breaths. Her nipples were stiff and swollen from his mouth, deep pink morsels he wanted to taste again. And again. He was breathing hard himself, one hand braced on the backrest beside her right shoulder. His cock was so hard it hurt, instinct demanding he finish this, here and now. That wild, hungry glint in her eyes almost undid him, but there was something else he needed first.

"Say my name," he rasped out. She hadn't said it yet. Not once. He needed to hear her call him by his real name, acknowledge who he truly was, not as Jack.

She blinked up at him, those slumberous aqua eyes locked on his. "Alex," she whispered. The hoarse, needy edge to her voice stroked over him like a lazy tongue.

He growled in satisfaction and took her mouth as he rubbed his cock against her center in slow, deliberate circles. Grace moaned into his mouth and brought one leg over his hip to get more contact. Heat built higher, those sexy little mewls of pleasure she made threatening to snap the last shred of control he was clinging to.

At the thought he shook himself. Fucking her in the front seat of the SUV wasn't what he had in mind and it definitely wasn't smart. Once he got inside Grace, there was no way he'd be able to focus on his surroundings, and he'd already let his guard down more than he probably should have under the circumstances. But Jesus, in that moment he'd have given anything to open his pants, pull that damp scrap of lace and silk between her legs aside and plunge into her as deep as he could get.

No. He'd taken so much from her already—whether inadvertently or not, it didn't matter. Now he needed to give.

Fighting for the legendary control he always seemed to lack around her, he forced himself to come up on his knees. She lay there panting beneath him, those gorgeous breasts on display, those fucking sexy thigh highs and heels making him want to dive between her legs, pull those sexy panties aside and lick her until she came screaming. Instead he brushed a lock of her hair back from her forehead, drinking in the sight of her and the way her eyes glittered with pure lust. Once he got her upstairs into the privacy of his room, he was going to show her exactly what she meant to him.

He lifted her into a sitting position, helped her get decent again and grabbed her hand. "Come on."

Grace barely remembered the trip up to Alex's room, too distracted by the blistering sexual need he'd lit inside her to notice anything but him as they passed through the brightly lit lobby. He kept her close to him the whole time, pulling her up against his hard body and skimming his hands all over her in the elevator. By the time they reached his door she felt frantic and edgy, her skin violently sensitive, as if it was stretched too tight. She remembered with vivid detail how it had been between them before. Those silver eyes delving into hers as he pushed her to the brink of release and pushed into her.

Let me love you.

The memory of those words, whispered in that deep voice, made her throat tighten.

"Stay here," he said in a low voice as he opened the door. He went inside, presumably to ensure the room was still safe, and as she stood alone in the hallway, the euphoric haze began to evaporate. She was already deep under his spell, and having sex with him would only bind her tighter to him. She knew herself well enough to know that she could never keep her heart out of the equation. With him it could never be just sex. A moment's indecision made her pause. Was she making another huge mistake?

Alex appeared in the doorway. The sheer heat in his eyes made her mind go blank, and when he tugged her inside and grabbed her close for a hot, deep kiss, she couldn't think at all. His arms were taut around her, one hand buried in her hair to hold her head still, the other gripping her ass as he pulled her flush against him. He pushed his tongue between her lips to stroke hers, caressing the inside of her mouth in a way that left her wet and aching for him.

With effortless ease he guided her backward until the backs of her knees hit the edge of the wide leather ottoman. She sank onto it and lay down, but came up on her elbows with a sound of protest when he didn't follow. Alex stayed her with a shake of his head and stood towering above her. "Take off the skirt and top," he ordered in a low voice that sent a shiver of longing through her.

Her body pulsed all over as she remembered the incredible pleasure he'd bestowed on her before. Except this time she felt a little shy with the lights on and him watching her so intently. She slowly drew the hem of her top up and over her head. Alex let out a deep growl, his eyes fastening on her cleavage. Her nipples tingled in response, dying for the feel of his mouth on them again. Next she lifted her hips to reach back and undo the fastener on the waistband of the skirt. But then she hesitated. She was forty-six years old, had put on weight since she'd last seen him and the surgical scars on her belly were—

"Off," he bit out.

Her hands trembled slightly with a mix of nerves and desire as she drew the snug material past her hips. As though sensing her hesitation, Alex sank to one knee before her and took over. He peeled the skirt down and off her legs, leaving her in only her bra, panties, thigh highs and heels. A low sound of approval that turned her insides molten rumbled up from his chest, but when his gaze snagged on her scars for a moment, she instinctively covered them with her hands.

His eyes flashed up to hers, the muscles in his jaw flexing beneath the silver-flecked stubble. "Don't. Don't ever hide yourself from me." Before she could protest he took her wrists in a firm grip and pulled them away, then surprised her by burying his face against her abdomen. She gasped. His breathing seemed unsteady as he took several deep inhalations. Grace's stomach muscles clenched. She swallowed at the feel of his warm breath on her most hated reminder of the attack. "Baby, I'm sorry," he whispered, his voice ragged as he nuzzled the puckered flesh. "So, so sorry I couldn't stop this from happening."

Her heart squeezed tight and she immediately wanted to reassure him. "Wasn't your fault," she whispered back, needing him to forgive himself for that.

Alex shook his head, his lips brushing over her skin in a whisper soft caress. "Wish I'd been there to help you heal."

Grace blinked back tears and pulled one hand free to stroke his hair gently. "You're here now." Helping her heal the deepest part of the wounds, even if he didn't realize it.

He stilled at her words for a moment, then began kissing and nuzzling her belly. She softened, relaxed against the leather. His lips and tongue following the length of the scars, telling her without words that he wanted to take the memory away and that she was still beautiful to him. Her throat tightened, arousal chasing away the chill inside her. The self-consciousness fell away, replaced by the heat licking across her skin.

His tongue was warm and damp. She wanted it lower, soothing the terrible ache between her legs. A tremor ripped through her. She ran her hand through his thick hair, exhaling as she allowed herself to lay back and savor what he was doing to her.

As though he felt the change in her, Alex kissed the spot just above her belly button and raised his head. The desire and longing she saw reflected in his gaze melted her inside. He lifted a hand to trace one long finger over the curves of her cleavage, his expression focused, absorbed. She curved her spine when he slid his hands behind her to unhook her bra and draw it off. Those big hands cupped her flesh reverently as he rubbed his thumbs over the throbbing peaks, sending an electric current right to the ache between her thighs.

"So sexy, Grace," he whispered, and bent to take a nipple into his mouth. Grace closed her eyes and gripped his head tighter as the pleasure shot through her. He sucked and nibbled one then the other, until she was squirming against the leather and tiny whimpers were coming from her throat. More. She needed more or she'd die.

One strong hand curled around her hip in a dominating grip as the other trailed slowly over her ribs and side. His palm skimmed over her pelvis to the inside of her thigh and traced up and down the sleek, sheer thigh high. The sensation was even more intense because of the thin barrier. She ached so badly for him to slip those skilled fingers beneath her panties and stroke where she was wet and hot. Her legs began to quiver.

Alex made a soft sound of reassurance and trailed his fingers over the silk panel at the front of her panties. She was so wet, almost embarrassingly so, and there was no way he hadn't noticed. Grace bit her lip and prayed for him to end her torment as he continued to tease her. Then, just when she thought she couldn't take anymore without begging, he finally slipped his fingers beneath the satin and lace to trace through her damp folds. She sucked in a breath and raised her hips, squeezing her eyes shut at the erotic torture. So damn *good.*

"Okay, angel," he murmured against her breast, and eased a finger into her. He pushed slowly, letting her feel each sizzling millimeter of the penetration. Before she could enjoy it fully he pulled out and added another, curling them to find and stroke the glowing pulse inside her.

"Oh…" Grace dug her fingers harder into his scalp and tried to remember to breathe as the beginnings of release started to coil deep in her core. She whined when he withdrew his fingers, whimpered when he slid them up to circle her swollen clit. She was trembling, already beginning the climb and it wouldn't take much for him to send her over the edge. It was so effortless with him, and yet unbelievably intense. She'd been craving this for so long…

Alex pulled his hand free and released her nipple from the heat of his mouth. Grace lifted her head to protest as cool air washed over her heated flesh, but stopped when she saw the intent look on his face as he grasped her panties and tugged them over her hips and down her thighs. She knew that look, knew it meant she would come screaming when he finally allowed it and she couldn't wait.

He drew them all the way off and tossed them aside, then put those powerful hands on the insides of her knees and pushed, opening her to his heated gaze. The muscles in her legs automatically tightened as her mind rebelled at being so exposed. He killed all her resistance with a single, blistering look and moved between her thighs to drape her knees over his broad shoulders, her high heels resting against his back. Stretched, held open, she could only quiver in his grasp and watch as he lowered his dark head and put his mouth to her softest flesh.

A sob of need shot out of her at the first melting kiss he gave her. Slow. Seductive. No man had ever taken this kind of pleasure in doing this to her, but Alex clearly got off on it as much as she did. She reached for him once more, grabbed fistfuls of his hair to anchor herself as he reduced her to quivering mindlessness. His mouth was hot, that wicked tongue laving her nice and slow, giving her just the right amount of pressure as he licked his way up and feathered across her straining clit. *Oh. My.* God.

Alex answered the unintelligible plea she made with more of those decadent caresses, using the flat of his tongue to make her shudder and writhe. And he wasn't nearly done. His fingers bit into her hips as he plunged his tongue deep inside her, stroking that hidden hotspot along her inner wall. Grace bucked her hips and mewled, helpless under the growing tide of pleasure. Not about to be rushed, he held her steady and continued tormenting her, alternating between deep licks and tender sucking kisses around the swollen bundle of nerves at the top of her sex.

The muscles deep in her belly drew taut, her thighs trembling on his strong shoulders as the pressure grew. Only when she was desperate, when every muscle was locked in a plea for release and raw moans tore from her throat did he work two fingers inside her and settle that wicked mouth over her most sensitive spot.

Her hands clenched in his hair as her inner muscles clamped around his fingers. She was so close. "Oh, Alex…*God*," she choked out.

He made a low sound of approval and increased the pressure of his lips as he sucked, his tongue flickering oh so softly against that swollen bud…

Grace bowed up and let the cries spill free as the powerful orgasm took her. Shuddering waves tore through her, shooting out to all her nerve endings. She heard the sounds she made, knew they were echoing off the walls and didn't care who heard her. Alex knew just how to touch her, knew exactly how to draw it out to keep the orgasm at its most intense.

He stayed with her, lips and tongue cherishing her, fingers still buried inside her until the waves began to ebb at last. At last she collapsed against the butter soft leather with a ragged groan and fought to get her breath back as the world spun around her. Alex withdrew his fingers and smoothed his hands up her legs, over her hips, her stomach. He pressed a trail of hot, lingering kisses across her abdomen and this time she was barely aware of her scars.

Grace opened her eyes and looked down the length of her torso at him. Her legs were still draped over his shoulders, the thigh highs and heels making her feel wickedly sexy and feminine. But it was what Alex had just done that made her feel cherished. Loved.

Her throat tightened. As the realization hit home she ran reverent hands over his hair. She adored this man, believed he'd hated leaving her. She'd do anything for him.

Alex lifted that silver stare to hers, burning with needs not yet quenched, his sexy mouth curving in a wicked smile. "I love doing that to you."

Another wave of heat flashed through her. She slid her legs off his shoulders and sat up to reach for him, wanting to tear his clothes off and feel him inside her, but he threw her off guard by easing away and standing. Before she could protest, he bent and scooped her up into his arms. Sighing at the effortless show of strength, Grace wound her arms around him and snuggled close to his chest, wishing he was naked so she could feel his skin against hers and wrap her hand around that erection bulging against the front of his dress pants. But when she snaked a hand down between them to grab at his belt, he blocked her with his arm and made a quiet negative sound.

Confused, she studied his face as he strode to the wide bed and placed her in the middle of it. He slid her heels off and tossed them on the floor, then slid her stockings off and dropped them beside the bed. He flipped down the covers, kicked off his shoes and laid down next to her. Grace rolled into his body, sighing in bliss when he wrapped those strong arms around her and cradled her. He kissed her temple, her cheek and jaw, nuzzled at the side of her neck where it sent shivers cascading through her.

She didn't understand why he'd stopped at foreplay. "Don't you want more?" she whispered, unable to hide the uncertainty in her voice.

He snorted a laugh against her skin. The thick length of his erection pressed insistently against her stomach. "Yeah. But it's been four years since I got to do this and I'm not done savoring you yet." He lifted his head, gazed down at her with a possessive tenderness that turned her heart over.

She ran her hands over his shoulders. "Take your shirt off. I want to touch you."

He hesitated a moment, then sat up, unbuttoned his shirt and tossed it aside. When he turned back to her she drank in the sight of those powerful muscles he still worked hard to maintain. She placed her palms against his chest, enjoying the heat and power under her hands. For a few moments he seemed content to let her pet him. Then he took her chin in his hand, tipped her face up and claimed her mouth once more.

And with that he started arousing her all over again, worshipping every inch of her from the top of her head to the tips of her toes that curled when he hit just the right spots with his fingers and tongue. He built the pleasure relentlessly, pushing her higher and higher, then held her there on the knife's edge of release for endless seconds before at last easing her over into ecstasy. Reduced to a limp, trembling puddle of bliss in the aftermath of the second orgasm, she let herself drift.

Grace was vaguely aware that the lights were off as he settled her into the curve of his body once more. Despite her resolve to stay emotionally detached, something inside her had shifted and she realized she no longer needed to protect her heart from him. Her eyelids were too heavy to keep open. Warm, sated and protected, despite her best intentions she lost the fight to stay awake.

CHAPTER TEN

Malik sighed as he settled back into the sofa with a hot mug of tea. He rested his left hand atop his stomach and examined the new, light bandage he'd wrapped it in. The incisions were sore, the entire hand swollen but he could already flex his fingers a little more than yesterday.

The safe house where he was hidden was quiet and well-protected, tucked into an affluent, residential neighborhood where everyone kept to themselves. For the first time in days he felt safe and relatively relaxed. Authorities all over the country were searching for him but he'd managed to slip out of Islamabad after disposing of Sharif. He and the handful of men with him were using throw away phones and kept calls to an absolute minimum to decrease the chance that anyone hunting him could ping the signal and triangulate his location.

As expected, at the pre-arranged time, his phone rang. He already knew who it was without looking. "Good to hear from you again."

"I see you've been keeping busy," his ISI contact replied in a wry tone.

Sharif, he meant. "It was a detail that I needed to take care of personally," Malik answered with a shrug. Afterward his security team had whisked him out of Islamabad and driven him to Karachi, where he could escape by either air or water if necessary. At the safe house he'd slept most of the morning away. Since waking he'd been dealing with testing various contacts, trying to get a feel for who was still loyal to him in the Pakistani regime and the military. Sharif's death would no doubt send shockwaves through the entire institution, but it would also send a critical message: no one crossed Malik Hassani and lived. He was fairly certain the message had been received.

Now he had other, more important, things to attend to.

"And what about Rycroft?" the contact asked.

Malik had already decided against a personal attack. Sharif had been alone, and easier to eliminate than he'd anticipated. Rycroft would be even more on guard now, especially since he knew Malik had been in Islamabad last night. He hoped the NSA agent was worried. Malik would find him and kill him eventually, but not in any way Rycroft anticipated. "It's too much of a risk right now. We'll use the woman to make him come to me. I assume you've got everything in place?"

A slight pause. "There may be a hiccup."

Malik didn't tolerate hiccups, particularly from a man as connected and resourceful as this one. "Explain."

"The security presence has been stepped up. Both for the team and the new venue."

"So?"

The man huffed out a grudging laugh at Malik's lack of concern. "So, it will be harder to take them all off guard now. It's possible that someone has leaked our plans."

Doubtful. Not this quickly, not unless the man speaking to him now was responsible for a leak. Which Malik also doubted, since he had already been promised a posh job as head of intelligence once Malik took power. From experience he knew that was the best way to gain people's loyalty. "Then make sure we have sufficient force there to carry out the operation." He wasn't worried that it might fail. Rycroft and his team wouldn't be there, and he would only have been able to bring in minimal additional security. Even with the handful of trained men Malik's ISI contact had assigned to the task, with the way things had been planned out, they should be able to carry out the op without much difficulty. "Any word on Bashir?"

"Nothing new. He's in good condition, still undergoing interrogation."

Malik disliked the thought of his old friend being subjected to that sort of treatment. If not for Bashir's bold plan, Malik would be undergoing the same kind of intensive questioning. After his escape, the authorities would have looked to Bashir for answers. And now that they must realize he had something to do with Malik's escape, the authorities would be even harsher with his friend. "They're torturing him."

"Food and sleep deprivation, perhaps some water boarding. Nothing too extreme. Not with the Americans involved so heavily." The man sounded unconcerned.

That didn't lessen the burden of guilt Malik carried. He'd seen plenty of CIA and NSA brutality against prisoners in the past. And during his time in the ISI, he'd ordered such harsh measures many times. So had Bashir. If there had been a way to free him now, Malik would have done it. But his friend was just going to have to endure his situation a little longer. "And what about the other part of the operation? Is everything in place?"

"It took some doing, but yes. I've got a small team equipped and standing by."

"Good. And the two other generals? I can still rely on their support for this?"

"My people have been monitoring them. By all accounts, both still remain loyal to you."

Loyalty was a relative word, of course. He knew that better than anyone. "Perfect." He smiled, took a sip of his tea.

All that remained was putting this plan into action to clear the final hurdle between him and the seat of power in the Pakistani government. Alex Rycroft was the only remaining adversary who Malik considered a real threat to his security and success. Stage two of the plan would occupy Rycroft long enough to allow Malik to make his way back to Islamabad on a private jet and stage the coup within hours. The remaining key generals would use their troops to ensure Malik seized power. Though part of him wanted to stay and kill Rycroft himself, it was highly unlikely the NSA agent would survive the impending attack anyway. "Anything else?"

"Nothing for now."

"Good. Contact me once the first stage is complete. I'll expect your call." He hung up and set the phone next to him.

Enjoying the quiet, he savored the heady thrill of anticipation that slid through his veins. All the planning, all the suffering and tumult were worth it because they'd led him to this moment. If all went according to plan, he would be the new head of government by midnight tomorrow.

If not, at least he wouldn't be around to suffer the humiliation of defeat a second time.

David sat bolt upright in bed and lunged for the ringing phone on the nightstand. He grabbed his glasses, squinted at the digital clock. After midnight. He checked the call display before answering, the number there making his pulse thud. "Hello?"

"I got your message," the man said without preamble.

David ran a hand through his hair for the thousandth time that evening. He was already thinning on top. Right now he was so stressed he wouldn't be surprised if his hair started falling out. "I only found out an hour ago."

"You're sure this is the correct location and time? It won't be changed again at the last moment?"

"I can't say, because I don't have any control over any of that." That Rycroft guy did though. David would bet everything he had that the government agent was behind this last-minute switch. David wouldn't put it past him to change things again in a few hours just to throw off anyone tracking the UN team's movements.

"You'd better hope it doesn't. I've had to assemble a new crew to cover it now."

"I told you I'd update you if things changed, and I did," David said, sounding defensive even to his own ears, but he didn't care. This asshole had essentially blackmailed him into cooperating and now it was too late for David to get out of the mess he'd stepped in. And something else was bothering him. "You haven't told anyone else, right? That was part of the deal." It was the only way he'd agreed to this in the first place.

"Don't worry about it—worry about the final time and location instead," the man replied in a hard tone.

A sick feeling took hold in the pit of his stomach. "You *told* someone? Who?"

"I said, don't worry about it. Call me if you hear anything else. I'll be in touch after the meeting." He hung up before David could demand more answers.

David swallowed and set his phone in his lap, then closed his eyes. What the hell was he going to do? If that guy had leaked the new information, there was no telling how many people knew when and where the meeting was going to be held. Then a more unsettling thought occurred to him. He swallowed.

It was possible that information had somehow reached the wrong people. The ones Rycroft was trying to protect Grace from. Shit. He'd never thought this might happen—he would never have knowingly placed her in danger. When the man had called to make the offer, David hadn't yet been aware of the extra security threats against Grace.

He wiped at the sweat that beaded his upper lip and stared at his phone. What if he'd just put them *all* in serious danger? It wasn't too late. He could call Grace or Dr. Travis. They could alert Rycroft and he'd take the necessary steps to negate the threat, probably move the location again.

But then they'd all know what he'd done.

His reputation would be in tatters, his career ruined before it even had the chance to take off. No one of any worth would hire him if this came out. He'd have nothing but a shitload of debt and a name worth nothing.

That's still better than being dead.

His heart was pounding out of control. God, and what if he was just a loose end now? Once his contact arrived at the meeting location there was no guarantee he'd pay David the money anyhow. He'd royally screwed himself and now maybe others as well. Why the hell had he made such a stupid decision?

Because you were desperate.

David chewed his lip in indecision. The chances of him endangering the team were small, he reasoned. They already had increased security for the team, and there was hardly any time for anyone looking to harm Grace to plan something. If he stayed quiet, chances were the meeting would conclude without any problems. His contact would get what he wanted, and David would get the money he'd so selfishly gone after by agreeing to this damn deal. No, he had no choice now but to roll with it and pray everything worked out.

Pushing out a deep breath, he set the phone back on the nightstand and removed his glasses to rub at his tired eyes. The doubt and guilt wouldn't leave him alone. He liked Dr. Fallon. As a person and as a scientist, as someone who was trying to make the world a better and safer place. If anything happened to her because of him…

He lay back against the pillow and stared at the ceiling, knowing he wasn't going to get any more sleep for the rest of the night.

When his phone buzzed on the nightstand, Alex rolled away from Grace and grabbed it. He snagged his shirt from the floor and slid it on as he hurried into the bathroom, shut the door and flipped on the light. The display told him it was nearly five in the morning, and Claire—Gage's fiancée, currently working back at the NSA headquarters in Fort Meade, Maryland—wouldn't call him at this hour unless it was urgent. Alex had sent her home the day after Hassani's capture, wrongly assuming Hassani would remain locked up. He did up the buttons on his shirt as he answered. "Hey. What's up?"

"Sorry to wake you."

"No problem. What've you got?"

"I've been looking into some of the flagged signal intercepts we've been monitoring. Hassani's voice print matched a call a few hours ago from someone in Islamabad. When we pinged the phone Hassani used it showed he was in Karachi."

Alex stilled, all his muscles tensing. Karachi was on the Arabian Sea. Was the bastard going to try to leave the country by boat? It didn't feel right, because Alex's gut said Hassani's power hungry ego would send him to Islamabad for another attempt at a coup rather than escape. Hassani was many things, but he wasn't a coward. "You're sure?"

"As sure as I can be. We'll keep running the diagnostics, and I'll send you the report."

"Great. Good work. And what about the caller? Any info on where the call came from or who it might be?"

"Still looking into that. Nothing so far. They're using burner phones."

They would. "Okay. Keep working on that, it might lead us to whoever Hassani's been using in the ISI. That's the one source we're still trying to pin down and we need to find them ASAP." He could charter a flight, be down in Karachi within a few hours. "Call Gage for me, tell him what's going on. I'm going to alert the Paks, have them increase security at the port down there, then I'll arrange a flight to get us down there." Once he ended the call he texted Hunter. He was sharing a room with Gage so they'd both be up to speed within minutes.

Alex called Evers next to alert him, and gave him the job of alerting the Pakistani military and other authorities in Karachi so they could keep an extra eye out at the port and the marinas, plus all the outlying airfields. After shooting a text to Ellis and Jordyn to wake them up and let them know what was going on, he finally sent a quick text to Zahra. While she couldn't do much to assist them from the hospital, she and Dunphy were still members of the team and deserved a heads up.

When all that was done he set up a flight for him, Gage and Hunter at oh-seven-hundred out of a private airfield on the outskirts of the city, then arranged a second flight for Ellis and Jordyn to take once they escorted Grace to the meeting with the Syrians. Knowing Hassani was likely still in Karachi made Alex breathe a whole lot easier about Grace's safety. Since Sharif's murder here in Islamabad he'd been even more on edge.

He had to go after Hassani, and he needed his team with him when he did. They understood the stakes, knew how Hassani worked, and they were some of the best operatives he'd ever worked with.

Catching sight of his tired-looking reflection in the mirror, Alex rubbed a hand over his face. He'd already done everything he could to ensure Grace's safety at the meeting by changing the time and location twice. With the increased security for the UN team and the new hotel venue's own security to be alerted an hour prior to the meeting, he felt much better about leaving her while he chased down Hassani at the other end of the country. But he was also acutely aware that Grace was due to fly back to the States tomorrow morning and chances were he wouldn't be back by then. Which left them with a little under two hours together before he had to leave for the airfield. His chest felt heavy at the thought.

He shut off the light and opened the bathroom door, surprised to find the glow of the bedside lamp illuminating the bedroom. Grace stood near the foot of the bed dressed in a hotel robe. She tucked a lock of hair behind her ear as she looked at him. "Bad news?"

"No, finally a solid lead. We've traced him to Karachi." He saw her eyes flare with relief as he walked up and put his hands on her upper arms to rub gently. "So, good news."

She nodded, but didn't look happy. "Except you're going down there after him."

Alex's hands paused. He couldn't lie to her. "Yeah. Flight leaves at seven. Ellis and Jordyn will stay behind to take you to the meeting, then head out on a different flight after they drop you off."

Grace searched his eyes, regret flashing across her face. "I leave tomorrow."

He exhaled. "I know." He settled his hands on her shoulders, squeezed lightly. "I'll get back here as soon as I can, but I don't know if—"

She stopped him by placing her hand over his mouth. "After he's caught, will you be going home?"

Alex kissed her fingers and nodded. "Not for at least a few days afterward though." There was no telling how long it would take to corner and capture the bastard again, however. And once they did, he'd have to stay behind and wrap up all the bureaucratic red tape into a neat little bow before he flew back stateside. God only knew how much longer that would take.

Setting her hand on his right shoulder, Grace continued to study him. "And what happens then?"

He lifted a hand to trail his fingers down her cheek. "I come get you and never let you go again." Even as he said it he saw the worry, the uncertainty in her eyes. He wanted to erase that forever before he left this room.

"Then I guess you'd better make this one hell of a goodbye to tide me over." With that she slid her hand into his hair, went up onto her toes and crushed her mouth to his.

Alex caught his breath at the urgency of the kiss and took her face between his hands. He could practically taste her desperation, could feel the frantic need that made her muscles rigid. He kissed her back just as hard, meeting each stroke of her tongue as he held her face. Her hands slid down his neck to his shoulders and she made a frustrated sound as she ran them over the fabric of his shirt. Alex wanted them both naked, needed to feel her skin against his.

Before he could reach for his top button she gripped the two halves of his shirt at the collar and yanked, hard enough to send the buttons flying. He let out a startled laugh, delighted by her impatience, but all humor vanished when she pulled back enough for him to see her eyes. Fear lurked behind the desire. A deep-seated dread that this might be their last time together. Alex's heart twisted painfully.

Vowing to eradicate that fear for good, he covered her mouth with his and picked her up by the hips to carry her over to the bed. He laid her down in the middle of it and yanked his ruined shirt off, then buried his face in her neck a moment to catch his breath and savor the feel of her soft hands sliding over his naked skin. She ran her palms over his shoulders and chest, down his stomach, her expression hungry, almost worshipful as she stared at his body. Damn, she made him feel twelve feet tall when she looked at him like that. He let her stroke him, didn't stop her when she reached for his belt, undid it and then his pants.

Quickly shucking them off, he knelt beside her near her feet. Her gaze swept over the length of his naked body with such hunger that he nearly shuddered at the need pounding through him. Alex grasped her wrist and lifted her hand from his body. He brought it to his mouth to kiss and lick the center of her palm, and their eyes locked. Holding her gaze, he reached down with his free hand and tugged the belt of her robe free, then pulled the edges apart. His cock jerked at the sight of her naked body revealed fully to him, all those gorgeous full curves he couldn't get enough of, those pretty pink nipples standing up and demanding his attention.

He took her mouth again, gliding his tongue against hers as she slid her hand down his body to his cock. She wrapped her slender fingers around his straining length and squeezed, pulling a tortured moan out of him. Her touch felt so damn good, even better than he remembered.

She lightened the pressure slightly to glide up and down the rigid flesh. He let her stroke him a few times as he explored her silky soft skin, pausing to tweak her sensitive nipples and earning tiny mewls of pleasure in return. But when he went to pull her hand away from his throbbing length she moaned in protest and shook her head, then sat up to push insistently against his shoulder. Alex straightened but she followed, her mouth seeking his and he gave her another deep, hungry kiss as she got to her knees and pressed both hands to his chest in a clear request.

Obliging her, he eased back into a reclining position and stretched out as his heart tried to pound its way out of his chest at the blatant need in her eyes. Stroking her hair with one hand, he ran the other up and down her spine as she trailed kisses and caresses over his chest and belly, down to his pulsing cock. He sucked in a breath as her grip firmed. The molten heat in her gaze as she looked up at him had his pulse tripping, and then her tongue stole out to lick the underside of the swollen head.

Inhaling roughly, he held back a growl as pure pleasure shot up his spine. His fingers flexed in her hair, pulling slightly, and her gaze filled with longing. Those thick lashes fluttered down against her cheeks and then he felt the incredible heat as her soft pink lips closed around the head of his cock. At that first sensuous pull of her mouth he let out a deep rumble of enjoyment and rubbed his fingertips against her scalp.

Grace seemed to melt at the caress, her body relaxing as she sucked at him and swirled her tongue around his most sensitive spot. She did it slowly, like she was savoring him and never wanted to stop. So fucking hot. Alex focused on her face as he allowed her to pleasure him for a few minutes, but knew he couldn't take much more without coming in that hot little mouth. He was too primed, he'd wanted this too long and he didn't want to come until he was buried deep inside her and she was shuddering, crying out in release.

But God, her mouth was so sweet, the glide of her tongue so perfect that he had to stop her. He tightened his fingers in her hair until she looked up at him, then reluctantly allowed him to draw her away. As it pulled free of her lips, his cock stood straight up against his belly, shiny and swollen from her mouth. Before she could protest, he pulled the robe off her shoulders and rolled her under him. He loved feeling her beneath him like this.

He settled between the cradle of her thighs and caught her wrists to pin them over her head as she wrapped her legs around him. Grace shivered and licked her lips as she stared up at him, her gaze heavy with anticipation as she relaxed, giving him that first taste of surrender. This was part of it, the trust she yielded to allow herself to be vulnerable with him.

Transferring both wrists into one hand, he used the other to trail down her neck to find her nipples. He played with them gently while he nipped and licked his way down her throat. Cupping one luscious breast, he took the hardened center into his mouth. She moaned and twisted in his grip but he didn't let up, and he caught the flare of desire in her eyes at the feel of being restrained. He got off on giving her this, the freedom to simply feel as she surrendered her body to him.

He switched to the other breast and treated it to the same attention, teasing the nipple with his lips and tongue as he slid his hand down to her smooth thigh, back up the inside. He shifted his hips just enough to graze his fingers across her folds and found her wet and ready for him. Grace moaned and set one foot on the bed, lifted her hips in a silent plea for more. Alex gave her what she wanted, sliding two fingers into her, stroking with firm pressure before withdrawing to spread the wetness up and over her swollen clit.

"Alex," she cried, tightening her leg around his hip, her body arching under him.

God he loved hearing his name on her lips. "Want you so much," he whispered against her breast.

"Don't tease me," she pleaded, moving against him in a desperate undulation.

Sliding his fingers deep inside her, he savored the way her eyes squeezed shut and her body trembled. "Want me to use a condom?"

Her lids lifted to reveal eyes heavy with desire. "Not unless we need one," she managed hoarsely.

"I'm clean."

"Then no. I just want to feel you inside—"

Alex smothered the rest of what she was going to say with a deep, hungry kiss. He pumped his fingers inside her, slid them out to circle the fragile bud at the top of her sex. Grace hissed and twisted upward but he held her firm, using her accelerated breaths and gasps to gauge how close she was to coming. He waited until her breath hitched and a soft, helpless moan spilled from her lips before pulling his hand free. He quickly knelt between her thighs, still holding her wrists prisoner.

She watched him through heavy-lidded eyes as he lifted the leg curled around his hip and pressed her knee back toward her shoulder, exposing the flushed folds of her sex to his famished gaze. She was open, wet and ready for him and more than anything he wanted to plunge into her, balls deep, and stay there until they both exploded.

Fighting for control, Alex released her leg to take himself in hand and settle the head of his cock at her entrance. Grace stayed still beneath him, her body tense with anticipation. Holding her gaze, he kept a solid grip on her wrists as he slowly slid into her, inch by inch, not stopping until he was buried to the hilt. He dipped his head to swallow her cry, absorbed the shudder that ripped through her and moaned into her mouth as the pleasure tightened every muscle in his body. She was so tight around him, so hot and wet he didn't think he could take it. He stayed completely still, locked deep inside her as he fought back the tide of orgasm rushing at him.

Only when he was sure he had control did he lift his head to watch her face and begin to move. He eased his hips back and thrust forward, angling himself to rub against her clit at the end of each stroke. Grace made a soft, helpless sound of pleasure and closed her eyes, turning her face away.

"No. Look at me."

At the tight command she opened her eyes and focused on him. Stretched out and pinned in place like this, there was nowhere for her to go but straight into the pleasure he was giving. He watched the acknowledgement of that vulnerability register in her gaze, growled in response as he continued to pump in and out of her. Grace's eyes revealed everything, a dozen emotions flitting across her face as he watched. Need, longing, grief. He needed to unlock them all, break through that last protective barrier that shielded her heart. He wanted everything. For her to be his forever, to marry her and wake up beside her every day.

He rocked his hips forward again. She pulled in a shaky breath and blinked as a sheen of tears gathered in her eyes. Sensation threatened to obliterate everything but he couldn't let go until he made Grace surrender completely. Instinct told him he was close to breaking through that last barrier but she was still afraid to let go completely. He continued to glide in and out in a firm, steady rhythm, never allowing her to retreat.

She blinked faster, bit her lip as she stared up at him, and he knew this was it.

The final wall between them. He was going to obliterate it, wedge himself good and tight into the deepest corners of her heart and bind them together so tightly she'd never doubt him again.

He thrust again, felt the telltale tingles gathering at the base of his spine as she tightened around his cock. Wide open, at her most vulnerable in that moment just before she gave him everything. Her tiny whimper of distress shredded him. He bent to kiss the corner of her mouth, her cheek, murmured to her. "Let it go, angel."

There was no place for her to hide. She trembled beneath him as he drove her higher, higher until the pleasure was near agony and the tears escaped her tightly clenched eyelids to roll down her temples and into her hair. He kissed them away, murmured soft reassurances as he made love to her. He felt the first tremor rip through her, felt her inner muscles clench around him and reached between their bodies to caress her straining clit.

Grace sobbed out his name and shattered with a high, breathless cry, started to come as the tears spilled free in a cleansing rush.

Yes.

Burying his face between her neck and shoulder, Alex released her wrists and knee and slid his arms beneath her. She wound around him immediately, clinging through the last of her orgasm as the tears came. He focused on the feel of her holding him so tightly, as though she never wanted to let him go. He was more connected to her in this moment than he'd ever been before.

Squeezing his eyes shut, he tried to hold onto the moment, make it last, but the pleasure was too much. He drove in harder, deeper now, and she welcomed him with her sweet, fierce embrace. She dug her hands into his back, her heels into his ass and squeezed him for all she was worth.

Alex let out a ragged groan and thrust faster, giving free rein to the hunger driving him. His cock swelled even more as the pleasure expanded until it exploded in a fiery burst of heat. He moaned against her neck, wondered if maybe he was dying as he emptied himself into her. The waves tore through him as she cradled him close, enveloping him with her softness. When they faded at last he couldn't bring himself to move. Still buried deep inside her clinging warmth, he never wanted to leave. He lay in her arms as his heart rate normalized, basking in the feel of her surrounding him and knew this was as close to heaven as he could get.

Grace's tears had quieted, the shudders in her chest reduced to tiny ripples now. She sighed and finally relaxed her grip on him to smooth her hands up and down his back, over his hair. Alex all but purred at her tenderness. "You'd better come back to me when this is all done," she whispered, and this time he knew it was concern for his safety that drove her to say it, not uncertainty about his feelings for her.

He lifted his head to look at her, slid his arm from beneath her to gently wipe away the tear tracks on her temples. His heart was so full he couldn't keep the words back anymore. "I love you. I'll do any damn thing it takes to come back to you."

Surprise flashed in her eyes, followed by delight, then a tremulous smile curved her mouth. "You mean that." Not a question.

He smiled in victory. “Yeah.”

She stroked a finger down the side of his face, her expression reverent, impossibly tender. “I love you back. So much I think I’d die if anything happened to you. So you’d better come back to me.”

“I will.” He’d already broken his vow to her once; he’d never do it again. “I promise.” He sealed it with a long kiss before forcing himself to get up and leave her warmth.

CHAPTER ELEVEN

Grace folded her hands in her lap to quell the urge to fidget as Blake made the final turn that would take them to the hotel. She wasn't worried about her security, not with Blake and Jordyn accompanying her until they handed her over to the UN security staff. And besides, Alex had changed the meeting time and place to this new location as an added measure. No, the nerves buzzing in the pit of her stomach had everything to do with her upcoming performance at the negotiating table.

If all went well and they got the Syrians to sign the deal, this meeting could potentially cement her reputation in political and academic circles around the world as one of the best in the business. She'd worked so hard for this, believed the world needed to end the manufacture and use of chemical weapons. This was a major step in the right direction.

Blake turned into the parking lot and pulled over rather than driving to the front entrance.

"What the hell's that?" Jordyn said.

Drawn out of her thoughts by the concern in the other woman's tone, Grace shifted over to peer between the front seats. Then she understood. Outside the front entrance of the luxury hotel a large crowd had gathered. A whole host of media crews with cameras rolling, filming footage of protesters holding signs that read Stop Chemical Weapons Now. Grace's eyes widened.

"How the hell did they find out about the meeting?" Jordyn muttered.

"Dunno, but we're not taking her through that circus," Blake said firmly. He turned the vehicle sharply to the left and headed around the back to get a look at what the situation was there. A few news crews had staked out the back exits too, but a contingent of Pakistani police had already formed a protective perimeter there and seemed to be moving their way around the building.

"Let me call David and find out what's going on," Grace offered as she fished out her phone. He was already setting up for the meeting; maybe he knew a secret route for them.

"No, I'll talk to your head of security," Blake told her and got on the hand-held radio to whoever he'd contacted in the hotel. "The media's camping out at all the entrances. What's the story inside?"

"Situation's contained and there's no time to change the venue now. Bring Dr. Fallon around to exit foxtrot and I'll meet you there," a man replied in a crisp British accent.

"Roger that. Stand by." Blake clipped the radio to his belt and turned to Jordyn. "I'm gonna head around front and see what the status is in the lobby, then check out the fourth floor before we let her out." He swung his gaze to Grace. "Just sit tight for a few minutes."

"Sure." Not about to argue, she stayed put while Blake got out, spoke to the officers at the barricade then jogged around the side of the building. Jordyn slid behind the wheel and Grace noted they'd both left the engine running.

Another news van pulled around the corner of the hotel, stopped only when the police blocked it. "Should I call Alex?"

Grace asked, starting to feel uneasy. There was no way anyone should have known about the meeting in the first place, let alone this last minute location. Yet if there'd been time enough for someone to organize a protest, then clearly the information hadn't been as secret as they'd thought.

"No, Blake's already taking care of that as we speak." Jordyn scanned the lot continuously, alert for any threats, but she was so unruffled by the turn of events that Grace relaxed. If Jordyn and Blake weren't worried, then she shouldn't be either.

To lighten the mood a little as they waited, she attempted some humor. "So, Blake actually lets you drive, huh?"

Jordyn smirked and kept looking out the windows. "It's 'cuz he knows I'm much better with all things mechanical than he is, especially if it's got wheels."

Grace huffed out a laugh, knowing from Alex that it wasn't arrogance but truth that colored the woman's words. "Glad you guys have got that even footing thing figured out early."

Jordyn stole a quick glance back at her in surprise, her pretty blue eyes narrowing. "Why, does Alex give you a hard time about your role in your relationship?"

"No, he never makes me feel inferior or anything, if that's what you're asking," she said quickly. "We've just both got a love affair with being in control, so it's…interesting." That being an understatement. Lucky for both of them, she was interested in keeping the peace enough to only dig in her heels if she felt really strongly about something. Otherwise they'd probably wind up strangling each other. Unless they were talking about control in the bedroom. Because they both got off on the power exchange there, and Grace was only too happy to give up control to him. The results were more than worth it, she remembered with a smile.

"Sounds like you're the perfect match for him, then," Jordyn answered with a chuckle. She put a hand to her ear and Grace knew Blake must be contacting her over the earpiece. "I copy. See you in two minutes." She swiveled around to look at Grace. "He says everything's locked down tight inside and the police are already pushing everyone back from the front. Your assistant's already up there. As soon as you get inside and up to the conference room, you'll be safe as a kitten."

Grace breathed a sigh of relief. "That's great." She gathered her briefcase and shawl, covered her hair while she waited.

"Okay," Jordyn said a minute later. "He's coming out now." She put the truck into gear and drove as close to the police barricade as she could. The closest access door at the back of the hotel swung open and Blake emerged, tall and strong and calm. Grace's heart rate settled and she waited until he was almost to the vehicle before reaching for the door handle. "See you," she said to Jordyn. "Tell Alex I said hello when you see him."

"Will do. Good luck."

She hopped out and slammed the door, then followed Blake to the back entrance. Or rather, he followed her, keeping her in front of him until they hit the door. Even with the vest hidden beneath her suit, it felt good to have him at her back, a man she knew Alex trusted with his own life. At the door he stopped her with an upraised hand and went through first, then ushered her inside the bottom of the stairwell.

A much shorter, muscular Caucasian man was hurrying down the concrete steps toward them, his thirty-something features set in an unreadable expression. He wore a coiled wire leading from his earpiece to clip inside his collar. Though she didn't recognize him that didn't mean much because the security guys guarding the UN team had been told to stay invisible.

Blake nodded at the man in greeting, then put a hand on Grace's upper back to urge her forward. "This is Lang, added to your detail by Alex, and he'll be looking after you. Syrian envoy is on its way now, about ten minutes out. I'll come up with you." It wasn't necessary but Grace appreciated his thoughtfulness. She was breathing a bit heavier as they reached the fourth floor, her heels not the most comfortable thing in the world to climb steps in. She followed the other man into the carpeted hallway to the conference room where more security staff in dress jackets flanked the door.

Grace paused to glance over her shoulder at Blake. "Thanks."

He smiled, his teeth a startling white against his deep caramel skin tone, and his golden-hazel eyes were warm. "Anytime. Go get 'em."

She nodded her thanks and passed between the two security guards to enter the room. They shut the door behind her and her gaze immediately landed on David. He smiled and sighed as though in relief when he saw her, then stood to pull out a chair for her at the long rectangular table. "Good to see you," he said. "Sleep okay last night?"

She hadn't had much sleep at all, but couldn't complain, especially because of the lingering twinge of soreness between her thighs that explained her current fatigue. "I got enough." Not enough of Alex, though. She was addicted to him all over again. And right now she couldn't afford to let her worry about him distract her. She set her briefcase down and pulled her chair in. "What's with the zoo outside? Did you get caught in it too?"

At that David stilled and broke eye contact. “I got here early, just as the first crew showed up.”

“The Syrians are bound to be pissed about this.” She hoped that didn’t start things off on a sour note. These kinds of negotiations were always tricky at the best of times.

He winced. “I know.” He rubbed the back of his neck, seemed to weigh his words before speaking. “Listen, I need to tell you something that—”

Whatever he was about to say was cut off when the door opened and Dr. Travis walked in with the other members of the team trailing behind him. Travis smiled when he saw her. “Glad you could make it,” he said with a twinkle in his blue eyes.

“Wouldn’t miss it for the world,” she answered cheerfully. Now they just had to hope the Syrians arrived without incident and security cleared their way through that throng out front so they could get this deal done.

Cruising at twenty-six-thousand feet on his way down to Karachi, Alex sent off a quick text to Grace.

I’d wish you luck, but I know you won’t need it.

The media circus out front bothered him, but Ellis had assured him the security team there had things well in hand and so far none of his contacts knew how the meeting had been leaked to the media in the first place. It had his instincts tingling but there was dick-all he could do about it now. He wasn’t in charge of Grace’s safety anymore and that was all there was to it. Damn hard letting it go though.

His phone buzzed with an incoming text.

Thanks. Gonna get this deal done if it's the last thing I do.

Her choice of wording set off a warning buzz in his stomach. *Just the start of many great things* he corrected, pushing the sensation away. He was paranoid because of the lack of control, that was all.

Syrians arriving now. Gotta go. You be careful. Hope to see you soon. Xo

He smiled at the kiss/hug and sent one back. *Do my best. Go save the world. Xo*

Setting his phone down, he shook his head at himself. He was turning into a fucking sap, putting x's and o's in his texts. Looking up, he found Hunter and Gage staring at him with bemused expressions.

"You poor dumb bastard," Hunter said, laughing at him.

Alex shot a mock glare at them both. "Whatever. Like you two are any better. Now shut up and get back to work." He grabbed the notepad that Hunter had been scribbling on and glanced at the notes. "Locking down that port is going to be next to impossible. When we find him, we have to make sure we block off all escape routes to the water."

"Roger that."

They continued to go over the current intel. The Paks had officers in place right now on the ground in Karachi trying to locate where Hassani might be hiding. They'd dispatched personnel out to all the outlying airfields. This case was so high profile they had half the country out looking for the guy and officials were waving around enough reward money for his whereabouts that someone was bound to turn him in as General Sharif had done.

When Alex's phone rang and he saw Evers's number on call display, he expected it to be an update about the investigation. "Hey. Whatcha got?"

"Looks like the Syrian envoy's been delayed due to the media presence at the other hotel. They're just heading to the meeting now."

Alex frowned, sat up straighter. "What do you mean? Ellis told me they were en route over twenty minutes ago, and Grace just texted to say the Syrians had already arrived."

"Uh, no, they haven't, because I'm looking at them out the front doors of my hotel right now. They're just loading into their vehicles."

Every drop of blood in Alex's body froze. *Grace.*

Panic grabbed him by the throat, choking his airway shut. Hunter and Gage were both staring at him, tense and alert. "Alert the security and get another team over there *now*," he forced out. Shaking, he hung up with the sickening feeling that it was too little, too late, and just like last time there wasn't a damn thing he could do to save her.

Her team was ready. Grace and the others sat around the conference room table as they awaited the Syrian delegation. She kept her hands folded atop her notepad as she waited for them to arrive. Moments later the door opened and a group of middle-aged Middle Eastern looking men in suits entered, special security ID tags pinned to their right breast pockets. Someone closed the door to give them privacy.

She stood with her team and offered a smile as the introductions were made, a part of her wondering why she didn't recognize any of them. Had they changed the delegates since she'd last seen the list? The five Syrians shook hands with Dr.

Travis and she held out her hand to the first man. A tiny flicker of unease threaded up her spine at the intensity of the man's gaze as his hand closed around hers. His grip was dry and firm but something in the way he stared at her turned the disquiet into a warning tingle in her brain.

Her smile faltered.

Before she could pull her hand free the strong fingers tightened and tugged her toward him. Caught off balance, she let out a squeak and threw out a hand to catch herself on his shoulder just as the unmistakable roar of gunfire exploded out in the hallway. She was aware of the sudden swell of panic, the shouts and struggles from the other members of the team as the man raised a hand and plunged something sharp into the side of her neck.

A needle.

He stared down at her with dark, satisfied eyes as she crumpled against him, then everything went black.

CHAPTER TWELVE

Alex couldn't stop pacing the length of the plane's small cabin. For more than ten minutes now he'd been in an agony of suspense. All he knew was that there'd been a massive attack on the fourth floor of the hotel where Grace was and that there were many casualties. He was trapped, helpless to do anything as he waited for word.

No matter how much he wanted to order the plane turned back to Islamabad, he couldn't. They were three-quarters of the way to Karachi already, and much as it killed him, the U.S. government valued Hassani's capture more than the lives of Grace and her teammates. For now, all he could do was pray his gut was wrong. That Grace wasn't dying right now, lying there bleeding out on the floor of the conference room.

Except his gut was rarely wrong.

Hunter and Gage were going over some maps together near the cockpit. They looked over at him every so often but didn't say anything and gave him a wide berth, probably aware that he was on the verge of losing it. Alex ignored them and the two security personnel at the back of the twenty-seater who sat on either side of the prisoner, and kept pacing. He didn't dare stop moving. If he sat down he'd explode.

When his phone finally rang, nearly fifteen agonizing minutes after the first news of the attack, he answered part way through the first ring. "Is she okay?" he blurted to Evers, aware and not giving a shit that his voice was rough. He didn't worry about the prisoner overhearing. Even without the earmuffs and hood blocking out light and sound, Alex was too far away from him to be overheard above the jet's engines. Alex had brought him on a hunch that it might be beneficial to the plan. Now the man might prove to be the only bargaining power Alex had left.

"Fuck, man, I'm sorry. She's gone."

Alex shot out a hand and gripped the back of the seat next to him to keep from falling as he squeezed his eyes shut. A crushing numbness filled his chest. Images of how he'd found her lying, bleeding to death on that stretcher in Mombasa, flashed through his mind. The way her eyes had focused on him when he'd raced over and grabbed her cold, blood-stained hands, the plea and the terror in her voice as she begged him to stay. *Don't leave me.* But he had, and he hadn't been there for her this time either. Jesus.

He sucked in a ragged breath, swallowed a sob clawing its way up his tight throat. He couldn't take this. Didn't want to hear how she'd been killed, yet couldn't bear not knowing the details of what—

"The whole team is gone. They took all of them."

Alex blinked, forced himself to inhale. Wait. *Took.* Not took *out.* He swallowed back the bile rising in his throat as a painful bubble of hope swelled in his chest cavity. "She's alive?" he croaked, his voice sounding far away, as though it was coming from the other end of a long tunnel.

"Yeah, looks that way, for now at least. We found syringes loaded with sedatives on the floor. Hit squad posed as the Syrian envoy, took out the security personnel. Only one guy survived—the Brit, Lang—but he took a bad shot through the pelvis and couldn't give us much intel. They're prepping him for surgery over at the hospital now."

Alex barely heard anything beyond that Grace might still be alive. He held onto that hope with everything he had. "Where are they?" he bit out.

"Somewhere on the south side of Islamabad."

His fingers dug into the leather seat so hard his knuckles were white. "How the fuck did they get through security, and what are the Paks doing about it?"

"No one knows how they got through, but from the initial reports it looks pretty sophisticated because they all had proper ID badges and paperwork with them. They must have had help from someone high up."

A setup. But by whom, the Paks or the Syrians? Or was there another major player here that he was missing? "Where's the investigation at?"

"The attackers split up into four dark SUVs and took off, heading south," Evers continued. "They took what appear to be pre-determined routes out of the city. And when police gave chase, militants popped up at four precise locations to engage the cops just as the SUVs passed the same spot. After taking those casualties the Paks have pulled their law enforcement personnel back and are now tracking the vehicles using satellites and a drone. I just sent you guys the satellite footage link, but from all reports it looks like they're still headed south."

Alex's attention snagged on that detail. "How far out are they?"

"Last I heard, about fifteen miles south of the city."

He looked over at Hunter and Gage, still at the front of the cabin. "You guys get the link Evers e-mailed yet?"

"Pulling it up now," Gage answered as he and Hunter stared at the laptop screen.

Alex strode over on shaky legs and held his breath while the footage loaded. He set his phone down and put it on speaker. "Watching it now," he told Evers. Hunter zoomed in on the video of one SUV as it sped down an access highway, the Pak police vehicles chasing it. "Can you get in closer?" he asked, his attention riveted on the rear passenger window.

Hunter tightened the focus on the speeding vehicle but they couldn't see inside the tinted windows, just the shape of the driver's silhouette. Alex stared hard, wondering if this was the vehicle carrying Grace. Was she conscious? Did she know what was going on? Did she know he was trying to find her?

Hold on, sweetheart. Wherever you are, just hold on for me. I'll get you out of there.

As they watched, the SUV rounded a slight bend in the road. When the police vehicles arrived at that same spot seconds later, sure enough, armed men burst out of another vehicle parked on the shoulder and opened fire with automatic weapons. The cops swerved as the bullets tore into their windshields and hoods. Several smashed into each other, others veered off the road and wound up in the ditch. Watching it all on screen, Alex knew the ambush was too well-executed to be anything but pre-planned by someone who knew what they were doing.

"The other three vehicles made a similar escape?" he asked Evers.

"Yes. The Paks are trying to set up roadblocks ahead of them, but it's not easy because no one knows where their final destination is."

"Karachi," Alex finished.

"You sure?"

One hundred percent sure. "Yeah. This is all Hassani. He's going to use Grace to make me come to him." Because the bastard knew Alex would do anything to protect her, even sacrifice himself. He hadn't woken up this morning ready to die, but he would willingly trade his life for Grace's.

"Well, they can't be planning to drive all the way there."

"No," Alex agreed. "Have the Paks search all the outlying airfields around Islamabad and then Karachi. Especially the small or abandoned ones. They'll be hopping a plane somewhere outside Islamabad soon." There had to be dozens of possible sites but they needed a break in the case and that was as good a place to start with as any. Alex glanced at his watch. "We'll be landing in another forty minutes and I'll get things rolling in Karachi. Keep me up to speed."

"Will do."

Alex ended the call and rubbed a hand over his face, then faced Hunter and Gage. They both watched him with grim, empathetic expressions that told him they understood exactly how he felt.

"Whatever it takes, man, we'll nail him," Hunter vowed.

"And get Grace the hell out of there," Gage finished.

Alex nodded his thanks. "Ellis and Jordyn will be nearly an hour behind us. Alert them to the situation while I make some calls." He needed to have everyone alerted and on standby so they were ready to roll the moment his team arrived in Karachi.

Right now he had to get it together and figure out what the hell he was going to do once he landed. Without a doubt Hassani would have everything for his plan in place already. He had the feeling Hassani wanted this to be personal. Did that mean Grace was the bait to lure him into a trap? Or did he want Alex to see her die first?

His stomach twisted at the thought. He wished he had a reliable piece of intel that would help him locate Grace the moment the plane touched down, but he knew Hassani would contact him eventually. Once he did, Alex would do whatever it took to save her.

As his gaze landed on the prisoner in back, a plan began to take shape. It was a long shot, but unfortunately it was the only one he had for now. All he needed was Hassani's location and the chance to put it into action.

Because he wasn't just going to kill Hassani when he found him; he was going to tear the fucker apart for what he'd done to Grace.

Rough hands lifted her, dragged her across something slippery. Grace struggled to open her eyes then realized she couldn't see because they'd blindfolded her. Her mouth was dry, her lips stretched taut from the gag cutting into the sides of her face. Her hands were bound behind her with something. Both ankles were bound together. A sharp, pounding pain drilled into her skull with every heartbeat and her body felt sluggish.

She could hear the sound of an engine, but it was louder, higher pitched than a vehicle. Then she heard a whirring noise and a blast of hot air hit her face. The person carrying her threw her over his shoulder with a grunt, his steps ringing out as though he was walking on metal stairs as he descended. He dumped her across a seat. A moment later something heavy landed against her side. Doors slammed shut and this time she recognized the start of a motor turning over. More doors shut and the vehicle moved forward. Men began speaking in a language she didn't understand, likely Urdu.

The more alert she became, the more her heart began to pound. Cold sweat bathed her spine. She remembered the confusion and panic in the moments before that needle had struck home, the sound of the gunshots out in the hall. Who had done this? And why? Were her teammates lying dead in that conference room? She started to shake. Something moved beside her. She jumped, then realized it was a human body. One of her teammates? She pressed closer to try to convey support without giving away that she was awake. The person beside her stilled.

They seemed to drive for a long time. Finally the vehicle slowed into a series of turns and came to a stop. Grace fought back the dark tide of fear as someone opened the back door and grabbed her beneath the armpits to haul her out. He draped her over one shoulder and began walking. She knew they'd entered some sort of building because the sound of his steps changed, the hollow echo telling her the space was large and open. He dumped her onto a hard seat and then she heard the rip of tape a moment before he seized her bound hands and taped them behind her to something on the back of the chair.

She tried to swallow but the gag had completely sucked the moisture from her mouth. A dark wave of fear threatened to take her under. She fought it, tried to hold onto hope. If they'd wanted her dead they would have done that back at the hotel, or at any point up 'til now. They obviously wanted her for something else. Unless…

Unless they wanted to make her death public and had waited until this very moment.

She shuddered, sucked in a ragged breath through her nose. More men came into the room. She felt a tug at the back of her head and the blindfold fell away. She winced as the overhead light hit her eyes. As they adjusted she made out the four Middle Eastern men standing around her still in their suits—she recognized them as the ones she'd mistakenly thought were the Syrian delegation. They paid her no attention as she looked around. She was in some kind of warehouse and judging by the dust and broken crates everywhere, it looked like it was abandoned. There were windows high up on the walls, so filthy the light coming through them was muted. Glancing around the cavernous space, she spotted a familiar figure strapped to a chair behind her left shoulder, gagged as she was.

David.

She was so relieved to see him and know he was still alive that she closed her eyes for a moment. When she opened them David was staring back at her with pure terror in his eyes, his forehead creased in a frown. Grace turned her attention back to their captors. The men were gathered around something about twenty feet away with their backs toward her, talking amongst themselves. Something about the way they focused on the object sent a tendril of dread down her spine. They moved away a few minutes later and she finally saw what it was. A video camera, strapped to some sort of pole. And beside it, a crate with red writing she didn't understand, but the skull and crossbones symbol was clear enough. Some sort of poison.

She jerked her gaze back to the men as her stomach dropped. None of them looked at her or David. As a group they walked away toward the wide doors at the far end of the building and left, letting the doors clang shut behind them. The sound echoed off the walls and ceiling with an ominous ring, as though they'd just locked her and David in a tomb.

Grace waited a few moments to make sure the men weren't coming back, then set her bare feet against the dirty concrete and started shoving her way back to David. The legs of her metal chair scraped across the floor with hair-raising screeches, but the noise couldn't be helped. She had to find a way to get her hands free. If she and David worked together maybe they could get the duct tape off.

David began scooting toward her as well, frantically rubbing his shoulder against his cheek to try to pull the gag free. A few seconds later he got it loose enough to drag away from his mouth. "Are you okay?" he demanded.

Did she freaking *look* okay? She ignored the question and kept scraping her way toward him, her progress frustratingly slow to avoid upturning the chair and toppling on her back. Her brain kept screaming at her to hurry, hurry, before someone came back or they carried out whatever part of the plan that involved the poison in that crate. Her gut told her that wasn't just a prop to scare them.

"God, Grace, I'm so sorry," David choked out. He was still trying to get to her, but at this pace the dozen or so yards between them seemed impossibly far.

She only paid partial attention to what he was saying, focused on getting close enough to see if they could work the tape free from their hands somehow. There was no time to lose.

"This is all my fault."

At that she glanced up at him, saw the tears in his eyes. Dread curled in her gut but she didn't stop inching toward him.

"I'm the one who alerted the media. I got a call from a producer offering me money in exchange for the meeting time and location. I took it to put a big dent in my debt, but that was before the security scare with you. By the time Alex came to take you from our hotel it was too late to stop it, and the guy threatened me with blackmail if I didn't inform him of the change in venue. I'm sorry." He sounded stricken but Grace shot him an icy glare all the same and he lowered his eyes.

They were halfway to each other when the clang of the release bar on the door made them both freeze. Grace whipped her head around to stare at the doorway, her heart thudding in her ears.

The door swung open. A shadow fell across the dusty floor. Then footsteps, ringing hollowly through the air. Her muscles tightened as the man came into view and the door clicked shut. A stocky, powerfully built man with short dark hair sprinkled with gray and a well-trimmed goatee. He wore a black suit with no tie, his bearing and posture radiating authority. His left hand was covered in a bandage.

Then he stepped into the light in the center of the room and Grace's heart seemed to stop beating.

Malik Hassani.

He held her stare as he approached, his gait confident and a gleam of anticipation in his dark, deep set eyes. "You know who I am?" he asked her in a quiet, deep voice that resonated through the empty space.

Unable to speak even if the gag hadn't been pressed against her tongue, she gave a stiff nod. Hassani's mouth curved slightly and he flicked a glance at David before coming back to her. And then Grace knew. This was about Alex, and Hassani had brought her here to make him suffer. Either through her torture and death, or by Alex's. Maybe both. Nausea bubbled in the pit of her stomach.

He paused at the camera to start it, the little red light blinking as it recorded. Meeting her gaze, he nodded at the crate beside him. "You should be intimately familiar with what's in here."

And then she knew. Knew what was in there and how she was going to die. And it was worse than anything she'd imagined—even worse than the terror she'd felt while she'd lain on that marble ballroom floor with her lifeblood pooling around her.

Hassani walked up to her and stopped within arm's reach. He reached behind her head and undid the gag and she instinctively shrank away when the cloth fell, but there was nowhere to go. She ran her dry tongue over her lips and tried to swallow down the panic clawing at her insides.

In a casual move, Hassani reached into his pocket and withdrew a phone—the specially encrypted phone Alex had given her, she realized with a start. He slipped something into it and hit a few buttons to reactivate it, then pulled something else from his other pocket. The metal gleamed dully in the dingy light and a sharp snick sounded as the blade sprang free.

Grace made a choked sound and shrank away, her skin crawling at the thought of being sliced to pieces. Ignoring her reaction, Hassani stepped beside her, reached down to grip her numb hands and sliced through the tape. Her arms fell to her sides. She flinched at the pain as the blood rushed into her stiff shoulder joints and fiery pins-and-needles shot through her hands and fingers as the nerves woke. Her muscles were too stiff and weak to obey and she couldn't pull free when he grabbed her hand and placed her phone in her icy fingers.

His dark eyes bored into hers, so cold it felt like a burst of arctic air had brushed against her skin. Goosebumps sprang up, denial pounding in her brain.

"Call him," he ordered softly, and Grace didn't pretend to misunderstand. He wanted her to call Alex, let him hear her die while he was helpless to stop it. Her throat moved convulsively and she opened her mouth to tell him to go to hell. Hassani must have seen the spark of defiance in her eyes, because before she could speak he reached behind him and withdrew a lethal-looking black pistol from his waistband.

Without looking away from her eyes he pulled the slide back with his injured hand. The metallic sound was terrible, chilling in the deathly quiet. He raised the weapon and pointed it at David. "Call him or he dies."

David's sharp intake of breath was overly loud in the brittle silence.

Staring into those cold, hard eyes, Grace knew he would do it. She knew both she and David were never leaving this building alive, whether by Hassani's hand or whatever was in that crate. Once she made this call, Alex would come for her. She had to at least warn him about the chemical weapon and pray it was enough to save him.

Quivering inside, she gripped the phone tighter, entered the password and dialed Alex.

CHAPTER THIRTEEN

"Play that back again," Alex ordered Gage. He and Hunter were gathered around the laptop with Ellis and Jordyn, who had just arrived at the makeshift command center in Karachi a few minutes ago. Various others were running around trying to organize the enormous number of police and military known not to support Hassani. Evers was en route on another flight and should be landing within the hour.

Nothing was happening fast enough for Alex's liking.

Gage moved the cursor and hit the play button on the footage that showed one of the suspect planes landing at a small airfield to the northeast of the city twenty minutes ago. On the screen, four small SUVs approached the aircraft as it taxied off the runway and came to a stop in the middle of a field.

The vehicles began circling it, driving faster and faster over the dry ground until they kicked up a huge cloud of dust thick enough to obscure the view of the drone filming overhead. A few minutes later, one by one the trucks peeled away, each driving off in a different direction. When the dust cleared enough to see the plane, it was empty, and there was no way to tell who the passengers had been or which vehicle

Grace had been unloaded into. Alex swore. At this point they had to assume that every other plane carrying the remaining UN team members had been treated similarly. Every single one of those SUVs had gone to different airfields.

Maybe one of the others had caught something he'd missed. "Well?" he asked his team, the desperation eating at him.

"Not a fucking thing," Gage muttered as the others shook their heads.

Alex huffed out a breath and scrubbed a hand over his face. Two hours. Two fucking hours since he'd been on the ground here and all he'd managed to do so far was send the Paks off on a series of wild goose chases after all the vehicles shown in the drone footage. Five other flights had been flagged as potentially holding hostages from the UN chemical weapons team. There was no telling if Grace had been in any of them, or even if she was still alive. But she had to be. Hassani would never have gone to the trouble of orchestrating this elaborate plan if all he'd wanted to do was kill her. So where the hell was she?

One solid lead. That's all they needed to break this case open.

Tamping down the frustration inside him, he gave each of the Titanium team members a list of people to contact, some military, others police. They immediately started calling to arrange coverage, logistics. In the middle of scanning through the dozens of new e-mails that had arrived in his inbox over the past few minutes, his phone rang. When he saw Grace's name pop up on the screen, his muscles went rigid.

He sucked in a breath, snapped his fingers to get the others' attention as he put the phone on speaker and answered. "Grace?" His heart was in his throat as he awaited a reply. His entire team was staring at him, bodies tense, riveted to every word.

"*Alex.*" The ragged note of fear in her voice sliced through him like a razor blade.

He blocked the emotions raging inside him, focused on what he needed to know to find her. "Are you hurt?" he demanded. He had to get the critical info out of her and keep her on the line long enough for them to get a lock on her signal.

"N-no, but—"

"Where are you?" He had to get her to calm down, help him find her. But Christ it had never been so hard to contain his emotions before.

"David and I are in an abandoned warehouse, and there are chemical weapons—" She broke off and let out a fearful cry that made the hair on the back of Alex's neck stand up.

"*Grace,*" he shouted.

"She's done talking," a familiar male voice answered a moment later, "but I'm not."

Alex's hand tightened around the phone, gripping it so hard his fingers ached. There was no way he could play this cool. He was too wound up, too terrified for Grace. And Hassani knew it. Bastard wanted vengeance for exposing him in the first place, and then for his subsequent capture and interrogation. "What do you want?" he ground out. "Me?" *You can fucking have me, asshole.* He barely choked the words back. He couldn't tip his hand, not yet.

"Eventually. But I'm not going to make it that easy for you. You've got thirty minutes to trace this call and find her. Then you can die together, if she's not already dead by the time you get here. Much as I'd love to stay and watch, I've got more important things to take care of."

The line went dead before Alex could respond. He jerked his gaze from the phone to look at Gage. "Call Claire," he rasped out, aware that he was shaking, coming apart at the seams and didn't know how the fuck to stop it. Every second that passed bled precious time away from his chance of saving Grace. "Get her to trace the signal." Normally he'd do it but he knew he wasn't thinking clearly enough to risk Grace's life on the chance that he wouldn't make a technical mistake right now. And outside of Zahra, he didn't trust anyone else to take care of this but Claire.

"On it," Gage responded, his phone already to his ear. She must have answered a second later because he started rattling off details.

Keeping one eye on Gage for a signal, Alex called the head of Pakistani security and the officer in charge in Karachi to update them as Gage spoke to Claire. "I need a HAZMAT team on standby," he told the man, "and I need them ready to move with one phone call. Get me whatever emergency response teams you can, get them mobilized and make sure they're ready with enough auto injectors to treat chem weapons casualties." Grace had said Hassani had chemical weapons. What sort, how many and where they were located were anyone's guess. The thought of him unleashing that kind of toxin turned Alex's blood to ice.

As he spoke, in his peripheral vision he saw Jordyn get up and come over to him. He tensed. She hesitated as she watched him, then started to raise her hand as though she was going to touch him in a gesture of consolation. He shook his head sharply and twisted away as he listened to what the man on the other end of the line was saying. Thankfully Jordyn dropped her hand and stepped back, her eyes holding a sympathy he couldn't stand. He knew she was only trying to help but he couldn't take anyone touching him right now. He was so on edge he was about to lose it in front of everyone.

Gage stood up suddenly, his eyes locked on Alex, and gave him a decisive nod.

"Gotta go," Alex blurted to the official. "Call me when everyone's up and in place." He spoke to Gage as he ended the call. "She's got it?"

"Yeah. Hunt's pulling up a map with the signal now."

Thank you, Claire. He rushed over to the laptop, stared at the screen with burning eyes as Hunter enlarged the map. The red dot appeared in the lower right of the screen and Alex's pulse doubled. "That's only a few miles from us." Hope surged again, swelling in a painful bubble against his ribs. His chest felt too tight, his lungs couldn't get enough air.

He reached past Hunter and pulled up a close-up of the area. They all studied the terrain, the layout of the building and the position of the airstrip. Alex grabbed his phone and called the Pak official again to give him the location as the others all jumped up and gathered their gear. But he'd already decided he couldn't ask this of them.

"You're not going in there with me," he said firmly to them when he hung up and met them by the door.

They all stopped and looked at him like he was nuts, even Ellis, who was normally the hardest to read. "You're not fucking going in there by yourself," Hunter growled.

"It's a trap," Gage said, stating the obvious in case Alex didn't get it, frowning at him like he'd lost his damn mind.

But he'd never been so clear about anything, except Grace. Whatever happened, he was getting her out of there alive. "Yeah, and that's why all of you are going to hold back on the perimeter. HAZMAT team's on its way, so make sure you suit up and follow MOPP level four protocol the second they get there. And the prisoner comes with us." He indicated the hooded man flanked by the two guards walking toward them from the rear of the room.

"And what about you?" Jordyn blurted.

"There's no time and I can handle myself," he argued. At this point Hassani was too paranoid to trust anyone, except Bashir, and the man couldn't help him now. Hassani would be acting on his own now, biding his time until he could get up to Islamabad. Alex was more convinced than ever that's what the bastard wanted, more than the chance of escape.

He had less than fifteen minutes to come up with a plan and get to Grace; he wasn't going to waste time arguing. "Let's move. Hunter and Gage with me and the prisoner, and you two following with the guards. Gage'll drop me and the prisoner off and pull back to provide cover while you two stake out an observation position and keep eyes on the building. I'll handle Hassani."

Hunter and Gage exchanged a long look, then the team leader turned his attention to Ellis and Jordyn and gave a tight nod. "Stay close and keep your channels clear."

Alex glanced at the clock on his phone before stuffing it into his pocket. Twenty-one minutes until the deadline. Already heading for the door, he checked to make sure he had a round chambered in his SIG and took the M4 Gage handed him before racing outside with the others to the waiting vehicles.

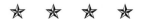

Malik paused at the doors to check the sensors surrounding the old hangar. When his phone showed they were all still intact, he eased out into the long shadows cast by the corrugated metal roofline and cast a cautious look around.

Nothing moved and there was no sound except the distant drone of a small aircraft's engine. He picked up the length of chain he'd left next to the door and wound it through the handles, locking the two doors together with a heavy duty padlock. Then he eased around the back of the hangar to survey the open space he had to cross. He'd hidden his vehicle in an old shed on the far side of the sun-baked field.

Aside from the pilot coming for him shortly and the generals and their men waiting for him back in Islamabad, he was working alone from here on out because he didn't trust anyone. His paranoia about being double crossed was well-earned, having already been turned on once by a trusted ally. He wasn't going to make that mistake again. From here on out, he controlled everything. Including Alex Rycroft's demise.

He'd planned the route to the shed carefully, making sure he would have enough shadows cast by the trees scattered across the terrain to cover his retreat. All he had to do was get into the waiting vehicle and drive the few miles to the LZ where the helo his ISI contact was sending for him would touch down. Then it was only a matter of a few hours before he reached Islamabad and his personal loyal military guard awaiting him there.

Just as he stepped from the safety of the shadows next to the building, the sound of approaching vehicles reached his ears. He froze, flattened himself against the side of the hangar. Peering around the edge of the wall, he saw two dark SUVs roaring up.

No. It couldn't be Rycroft. Not yet. It was too soon.

His pulse hammered in his ears. There was nowhere for him to go now except for the getaway vehicle he'd stashed, and he'd be exposed to whoever was in those vehicles if he moved now. He waited until the SUVs slowed across from the hangar before taking a sliding step toward the shed. The rear passenger door of one popped open. He stopped, watching. He was less than seventy-five yards from the vehicles.

A man emerged. Caucasian. Broad shouldered. Dark hair, gray at the temples.

Rycroft.

Every muscle in his body went rigid.

Rycroft reached into the vehicle, hauled someone else out the door, a man with a hood over his face. Something familiar about the prisoner's stance made Malik hesitate.

Rycroft frog marched the man out past the SUV and toward the hangar, and the vehicle took off with a spin of its tires. Malik's heart thudded in his ears. Had they spotted him?

Rycroft pushed the hooded man ahead of him, one hand holding the prisoner's bound hands behind the man's back, the other gripping a pistol at his side. He walked forward a few more yards and came to a halt. "Malik!"

Malik sucked in a breath and grabbed for his own pistol as he shot a glance at the SUV Rycroft had climbed out of. It was still driving away, abandoning the two men. It had to be a trap. There had to be others positioned around the perimeter that he couldn't see. How the hell had they gotten here so quickly?

He jerked his gaze back to Rycroft, standing out in the open. The ballistic vest Malik wore suddenly seemed inadequate. He felt practically naked as he stood there gauging the distance between him and Rycroft. They stood far enough apart to make an accurate pistol shot unlikely, despite their mutual expertise. He could still make a run for it, still get to the truck.

He took a step to the side, leaned his body weight to the left as he geared up to make a desperate spring for his freedom.

This time he knew Rycroft spotted him. Before Malik could take another step, the man reached over and ripped the hood off the prisoner, exposing his face.

Malik jerked to a halt when he saw Bashir staring back at him.

Rycroft raised the pistol, pressed it to Bashir's temple. His friend was tense, his face bathed in sweat. Malik could read the fear in his eyes even from this distance. Bashir had fought and bled and suffered with him. For him. And then he'd risked everything to secure Malik's freedom. He couldn't abandon him like this.

Despite his instincts screaming at him to run, Malik couldn't make his feet move. Couldn't force himself to run from the only true friend he had left on earth, even though it would likely prove his undoing.

Rycroft would die for this.

Thank you Jesus, the bastard was actually hesitating.

Alex kept his gaze pinned on Hassani, standing in the shadows of the hangar's roofline, and prayed this would work. *That's right, you bastard, I've got a gun to the head of the only person you care about. How does it fucking feel?*

He had Hassani's full attention. Everything now hinged on him holding it for a few more minutes. "Jordyn, go," he murmured to her via the team's earpieces, too low for Hassani to hear.

Alex pushed the rage and fear aside, kept a firm hold on Bashir in case he tried anything, and stared Hassani down. With every heartbeat Alex was aware that Grace was locked up in that hangar just across the runway from him, trapped and terrified with possible chemical weapons ready to be released. During the drive here, Hassani had sent him the live video link that showed Grace and her assistant bound in the hangar. No sign of the chemical weapons she'd mentioned, but he believed her.

He ran his gaze over Hassani, looking for a possible detonator of some sort. He couldn't see anything except the bandage around his left hand, the pistol in his right.

Alex drew in a deep breath and got down to business. "I'm here to do an exchange," he called out, aware of Jordyn hauling ass just beyond Hassani's peripheral vision. She only had about forty yards to cover to reach the shed and work her magic to disable the vehicle. She'd told him she only needed a minute or two once she reached the shed, and Blake and the other guys had her well-covered from their positions. They were under strict orders to kill Hassani only as a last resort. Alex had to capture him, bring him in for more questioning to unravel his network and so the Paks could put him on trial for everything he'd done.

When Hassani didn't respond, Alex jerked his chin at Bashir, thrust him forward a little. The bastard didn't think he'd shoot him? *Don't bet on it.* "Him for Grace and her assistant. You let them go, you and Bashir can walk out of here together. You've still got time before the rest of the backup gets here. Let me have the hostages, and I'll give you Bashir, plus a head start to Islamabad."

A humorless chuckle answered him, and Alex knew if he'd been close enough Hassani would already have taken a shot. "You expect me to take your word for it?"

"Yes." *I know you want me dead almost as badly as you want to take control of this country.* "Your buddy's counting on it." He jammed the barrel of his SIG harder against the man's temple.

"And your girlfriend's counting on me escaping here as planned," the sonofabitch countered with an evil smile. "The bomb's set to go off in eighteen minutes."

Raw fear grabbed Alex by the throat. He shoved it down deep, kept up the pretense of control when it felt like his whole world was crumbling around him. The CIA and NSA wanted Hassani taken alive. But with the shortened timeline Alex had to either disable or capture Hassani within the next few minutes in order to give Hunter and Gage time to disable the bomb and get Grace out of there. Alex still couldn't see a detonator on him. Was Hassani planning to remote detonate it on command, or was it set to an automatic timer? Alex had to somehow convince him that running was futile.

"I've got snipers in position, a gunship on the way and security forces will be crawling all over this place in a matter of minutes. You want out, this is your chance." It was a long shot, but the only one Alex had. It had to work.

Grace's life depended on it.

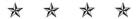

He was lying. Malik knew Alex would never let him walk away after the exchange.

Yet even then something stopped him from turning and running for the shed. Bashir, yes, but also Rycroft himself.

Malik had been hunting him for months. The chances of escaping to Islamabad now were minimal, and even if he did, it was unlikely that he'd live long enough to stage the coup he'd wanted so badly for so long. If there really was a gunship en route, he might not even make it off the ground even if he boarded his incoming helicopter in one piece.

But he could still get Rycroft before one of the snipers got him. Malik knew they wouldn't shoot to kill unless he brought Rycroft down, because they wanted to save the hostages and bring him back in alive. That wasn't happening. None of it.

"Let the hostages go," Rycroft called out.

Malik's right hand curled around the grip of the pistol, his index finger sliding up to find the trigger. Rycroft was wearing body armor; he'd have to get a clean head shot. And though he was wearing a protective vest as well, one shot was all he'd get off before a sniper would put a round through his head. Malik's arm muscles tensed and he started to raise his weapon.

The wail of distant sirens made him jerk his head to the right. Rycroft's backup.

Malik glanced back at Bashir, saw the awareness, the resignation on the man's face. He knew what Malik had to do, knew he had no choice anymore. The sirens were louder now. *I'm sorry, old friend.*

Tearing his gaze away from Bashir, he turned and raced for the shed, using a zigzag route to try to avoid a sniper's bullet. He reached the shed without incident, something that surprised him. Was Rycroft really going to let him go just to save the hostages? Wrenching the rickety wooden door open, he jumped into the vehicle and turned the key. A whining noise answered him. His heart slammed against his ribs. He turned the key again, pumped the gas. Nothing.

Denial and outrage flashed through him as reality settled home. Someone had disabled the engine. There wasn't enough time for him to figure out what they'd done and fix it, not with only one hand. And there was no way he could run out of here on foot.

He was trapped.

Swearing, he yanked out his phone as he exited the vehicle and called his ISI contact. No answer. He tried the pilot next. "Where are you?"

"I'm ten minutes out," the man replied to his frantic demand.

"The rendezvous point is compromised," Malik blurted. "Pick me up at these coordinates instead." He rattled off the location of the old airfield. "I'm in the small shed across from the hangar." And those sirens were even closer now. The snipers had likely moved in closer. Rycroft would be either hunting him or trying to rescue the hostages.

"I copy. New ETA, four minutes."

In four minutes he might be dead. Malik ended the call and grabbed the high-powered rifle from the floorboard of the SUV's backseat. He would not die without a fight, and not without taking Rycroft with him. His girlfriend would die soon enough. Maybe they'd all die after the bomb went off.

"Malik! Come out with your hands up!" Rycroft yelled from somewhere close by.

Never. Malik's lip curled up in a defiant sneer. He gripped the rifle tighter, barely feeling the pain when his wounded left hand cradled the underside of the barrel. If he could stall long enough for the helo to arrive, the gunners could clear off Rycroft and any others on the ground. Three minutes was all he needed—

A shot rang out and the lock on the shed door exploded. The wooden panel swung open slightly. Malik jerked back from the thin slice of light coming inside and raised his rifle's scope to his eye. He waited, slowing his breathing as he got ready to fire between heartbeats.

Another round slammed into the wood paneling just above his head, making him duck. A warning shot. Where was that bastard? Malik wanted to kill him, wanted the satisfaction of putting a round through his brain and watching the life fade from his eyes before a sniper took him out.

"Come out *now*," Rycroft barked.

Was that the faint thump of rotors in the distance? Malik pulled in a deep breath, unsure whether the sound was his helo, or the incoming gunship Rycroft had called in. He wanted his enemy dead, by his hand. The man knew time was running out for his girlfriend; he was running out of patience and wouldn't wait long before swarming the shed. Malik was cornered like an animal again, just like he had been back in those tunnels. Rage built inside him.

When another bullet buried itself into the side of the SUV with a solid *thunk*, Malik's temper snapped. He charged forward and opened fire, spraying the doorway with bullets. Shards of wood flew around him. The door disintegrated, sagged on its ancient hinges to reveal…

Nothing.

Malik's nostrils flared as he sucked in a lungful of air, his body quivering. Those bullets had come at him from his one o'clock. Rycroft should have been—

"Hands up!"

At the shout on his left, Malik spun in time to see Rycroft on one knee, the pistol aimed at Malik's head. The thud of the chopper's blades were clear in the air now, maybe a minute from him.

"The gunship intercepted your ride," Rycroft growled, the satisfaction in his voice scraping over Malik's spine like a dull knife. "You're all on your own. Last chance. Put your weapon down and get your hands in the air."

A wry laugh bubbled up his throat. Really? Rycroft thought he'd actually accept a life behind bars after this? Dying here and now was preferable to wasting away in a prison or suffering through the agonizing death his bomb would cause.

In desperation he swung the barrel of the rifle toward Rycroft and squeezed his finger around the trigger. He didn't get a single shot off before Rycroft's bullet hit him between the eyes.

★ ★ ★

CHAPTER FOURTEEN

Grace tensed when she heard the distinctive popping sounds of gunshots outside the building. Some spaced apart, then a long burst of automatic fire that made her belly shrivel. She stilled and jerked her head up, waiting for an assault or maybe an explosion, but nothing happened.

She threw a frantic look over her shoulder at David. "Hurry!"

"I'm *trying*," he snapped, fidgeting behind him with the tape holding her wrists to the back of the seat. Hassani had re-taped them after the call, but not as tightly as they'd been secured the first time. It was like he wanted her to be able to get free. She frowned at the thought but kept going. She could wriggle her fingers now and the tape seemed to be loosening. Just a little more and maybe she could—

"God dammit, I can't feel what I'm fucking doing," David muttered.

"It's working, just keep going," she urged. "Help is out there but they can't get to us yet. We have to be able to get out on our own." The gunfire was making her heart pound almost as much as whatever Hassani had left in that crate. She wanted as far away from it as possible. *Please let Alex be okay.*

Using his limited range of motion, made extra awkward by the angle his arms were pinned back at, David kept working at the flap of tape he'd managed to pull loose. Each little tearing noise meant she was that much closer to freedom. Grace kept her arms taut and her wrists cocked up to give him the best access possible and had to remind herself to breathe.

David grunted and yanked, nearly fell over, but a long tearing noise shot another punch of adrenaline through her veins. "Almost there," she encouraged, feeling some give in the restriction around her wrists. The muscles in her shoulders and arms were on fire, the joints aching from being held in such an awkward position for so long.

Another tear. "Now?"

She struggled to pull her wrists apart, sweat trickling down her spine and dampening her face and armpits. "Almost…" The slight give was maddening, pure torture. Gritting her teeth, she growled deep in her throat and forced her burning muscles to the limit, pushing, pushing—

Her wrists jerked apart. She sucked in a breath. "Quick! Grab the end of the tape again."

David cursed as he blindly fished around for the end, grabbed it and pulled forward. They struggled and strained together and finally the tape gave with a sharp pop that sent David flying forward onto his face on the concrete. But her hands were free.

Grace twisted them out of the tape, groaned in relief as she brought them forward and bent to frantically rip at the tape holding her ankles to the chair leg. She had no idea how much time passed before she finally got her legs free but it had to have been a few minutes. There had been no more shots from outside. She knew Alex was out there somewhere. Why wasn't anyone coming in after them?

She surged up from her chair and scrambled over to help David. He was lying on his side now, still strapped to the chair, his sweaty face white and his mouth pinched from the pain in his arms. "Hold still," she murmured, heart racing as she attacked the duct tape holding him. She got his hands undone then went at his ankles. With a last urgent rip, the tape came off and she grabbed him by the hands to haul him to his feet. He swayed for a second, then steadied himself and looked around.

"This way," she urged, tugging him toward the window high up overhead. Hassani had locked the doors at the far end—they'd both heard him wrap the chain around them before he left—and the only other way out that she could see was that window. That red light on the damned camera was still flashing, so whoever was watching the feed would know they were both free and trying to escape. She didn't care. She would have kicked it over and smashed it if she hadn't been afraid that the bastard had booby trapped it somehow. If she was going to die, it would be while attempting an escape, not while cowering here like a frightened animal, praying that someone would save her.

Together they stacked old crates on top of each other into a rickety kind of ladder. When it was high enough she climbed to the top, grabbed the wall to support herself and reached a hand down to David. "Get me something heavy."

He ran over to get the folding metal chair she'd been tied to and handed it up to her. Bracing her weight on the wobbly mound of crates, she drew the chair back, legs out, and drove it forward to plow against the glass pane with all her strength. The glass cracked but didn't break. Panting, she drew back and slammed it forward once more. Over and over until her muscles were quivering and she was gasping for breath. But she'd managed to make a softball-sized hole in the window.

"Here," David whispered, thrusting his suit jacket up at her. Grace wrapped it around her hands and shoved at the jagged edges of the glass until they snapped free and fell to the ground outside. She blinked against the glare of the sunlight streaming through the opening, her eyes slowly adjusting to see the line of emergency vehicles and personnel formed a few hundred yards away.

She looked down, surprised and relieved to see the building was dug into the ground so that the drop from the window wasn't as high as she'd initially feared. They were maybe eight feet up. There was no one nearby, no one to shoot at them. "Come on," she ordered David, and reached down for his hand. He clambered up next to her, held the jacket in place over the windowsill to help protect them from any jagged glass as she threw a leg over the edge.

The moment her foot cleared the opening, a long, ominous beep sounded behind them. They both turned their heads in time to see the wooden crate explode with a loud boom she felt in her chest. Whatever had been in that crate was now being released into the air.

Terror flashed through her.

Acting on instinct, Grace grabbed the edge of the windowsill, hauled her upper body through the small opening, and jumped. She hit the ground on her side with a thud, her hip and shoulder taking the brunt of the impact. The jolt of pain stole her breath for a moment, but panic drove her to her feet. She scrambled up, looked back at the window in time to see David shoving through it. His face was white, his eyes streaming, nose running.

He managed to haul himself out and drop to the ground, landing on his back. Grace took a running step toward him, but jerked to a halt when she realized he was drooling. In that paralyzing moment he lurched onto his hands and knees and started gagging.

SLUDGE symptoms.

Grace's heart seized as she suddenly realized exactly what had been in that canister.

Heart in his throat, Alex ran toward the old hangar where Grace and her assistant were being held. Beyond the hangar, a wall of emergency vehicles and personnel stood ready and unmoving. No one was going to approach the building now, including the bomb squad, not with the risk of chemical weapons exposure.

"Give me status," he barked to his team, who were all positioned beyond the perimeter, keeping watch through their scopes. His boots pounded against the sun-baked tarmac as he tore across the open space. The entire place was likely booby-trapped and according to Hunter the latest video footage had showed Grace and David trying to get free. If they tripped the bomb…

He blocked that thought and pushed himself as hard as he could. Seconds later, Hunter's voice came through the earpiece. "Stop. She's coming out the window."

No! He skidded to a halt, changed directions until he could see the back of the hangar. Sure enough, he saw Grace attempting to climb out the broken window. "No!" he roared, the word torn from the deepest part of him, but she didn't hear him, didn't stop. As he watched she hit the ground and struggled to get to her feet. She turned back to help David, who hit the ground. Grace took one single step toward him and froze.

Alex's heart lurched, fear freezing him in place.

Grace lunged forward to grab David's hand, and when she turned back he could see the stark terror in her face, the whites of her eyes showing. "Sarin!" she screamed. "Sarin!"

The bottom dropped out of Alex's stomach.

Swearing, he swerved left and sprinted for the HAZMAT truck. "Give me some auto injectors!" he yelled at the men assembled there. One guy ran over to hand him a few, his expression through the plastic visor of his chem weapons suit telling him just how crazy he thought Alex was. He shoved past one guy who tried to block him, punched another in the stomach when the man grabbed Alex's shoulders.

He tore free and whirled, intent only on getting to Grace. She'd dragged David a few yards but now let him go and ran, tearing her blouse open and yanking it off as she ran. She rubbed at her eyes and nose, and he could see her shoulders jerking as she gagged.

Leg muscles screaming, lungs ready to explode, Alex raced toward her. She wiped frantically at her face again, jerked her head around when she noticed him. The grief and panic in her face tore at his heart. She put her hands up and shook her head, veered away to run from him because she knew the remaining sarin on her skin and clothes could infect another person for up to a half hour.

"Grace, no!" he shouted. Her ragged sobs floated back to him but she didn't stop, didn't slow as she attempted to get away from him. To save him, even as every labored pump of her heart pushed the nerve agent through her bloodstream faster. She stumbled, gagged, and Alex was finally close enough. Using every bit of strength left in his legs, he launched himself at her, caught her in a flying tackle and brought her down. He twisted in mid-air to take the brunt of the impact but it wasn't enough. She bounced against the tarmac and cried out, then turned her head and began vomiting.

Alex rolled to his knees and yanked the safety cap off the atropine auto injector, grabbed her thigh to hold her in place and pressed the needle firmly into her outer thigh, holding it there for ten seconds. He smelled the sharp ammonia scent of urine, looked down to see the puddle forming beneath her.

Fuck, oh, fuck.

Frantic to stop the progression of the symptoms, he tossed it aside and followed the same procedure for the 2-PAM injector. She was vomiting uncontrollably, shaking, her face covered in tears and mucus. As he held the second needle in place he felt his own eyes start to sting, his nose start to run and an ominous tightening in his chest.

He was so focused on keeping that injector in place that he only heard the pounding footsteps a second before someone drove him into the ground with their weight. The loaded syringe fell from his hand as he hit the ground. Strong hands flipped him onto his side.

He cranked his head around, stared up through streaming eyes at Hunter looking down at him through the visor of his MOPP suit. Then the sharp sting of a needle in his lateral thigh. His stomach twisted. He pitched to the side and puked, kept puking even when there was nothing left to come up. His chest was so tight he could hardly breathe, his lungs laboring to draw air as the toxin circulated through his bloodstream.

He felt the sting of a second needle. After a few seconds the tightness in his chest eased enough for him to gasp in a breath between bouts of vomiting.

Hunter began stripping Alex's shirt off him, then his boots, socks, pants and underwear. Someone else stood nearby to stuff the clothes into a plastic bag and seal it shut. Cold water sprayed over him. He lay there shaking at the chill even though the sun still beat down on his naked skin. The nausea slowly faded, then the running eyes and nose dried out enough for him to see. Despite Hunter's growled command to stay still, he turned over on one elbow to look for Grace. Someone else in a MOPP suit knelt next to her, blocking her from view.

"Gage, move the hell aside so he can see her, for Christ's sake," Hunter snapped. "He won't fucking lie still otherwise."

Gage glanced back, shifted enough for Alex to see Grace and his heart squeezed so tight he couldn't breathe for a moment. She was still breathing, her face holding a faint bluish tinge. Those beautiful aqua eyes were still streaming, but they were partially open and looking at him.

"Grace," he wheezed, reaching out a hand toward her. His eyes filled again, but this time not from sarin exposure.

At the sound of his voice her eyelids flickered. She focused on him, her naked breasts shuddering with the force of her distressed inhalations, the muscles in her neck standing out as she struggled for air. Gage placed an oxygen mask over her nose and mouth.

More running footsteps sounded, then a wall of men in HAZMAT suits surrounded them, blocking Grace from view. Alex closed his eyes and lay there as they administered oxygen and started an IV, praying as he'd never prayed before. If Grace didn't make it, he didn't want to either. He'd let her down so much already, abandoned her when she needed him most. Not this time.

As soon as the IV line was in and they were pushing fluids into his bloodstream, he shoved aside the restraining hands on him and crawled the few feet over to where Grace lay.

"Move back," Hunter barked, clearing the way for Alex as the former SEAL banded one heavy arm around Alex's chest and lugged him over. Hunter laid him next to Grace and Alex immediately sought her hand. Her fingers were ice cold and limp in his, but her pupils weren't constricted and she was looking straight at him.

Alex squeezed her hand, his voice breaking. "I won't leave you."

More tears flooded her eyes in response to the ragged vow. It felt like his heart was being crushed in a vise when her fingers squeezed his feebly, so weak. "Hang on to me," he urged, wishing he could somehow infuse his own life force into her, trade his life for hers. "You have to hold on, baby. Please, I can't do this without you." His voice cracked on the last word but he didn't care, and didn't give a shit who heard him. All that mattered was Grace and making her hold on, keep fighting. He held her hand, fighting for every breath along with her, dying inside as he watched her suffer without being able to do anything to ease it.

He didn't know how long they laid there before plastic-lined stretchers were brought out to load them onto. Alex refused to release Grace's hand. Her eyes were closed now, that awful blue tinge around her lips scaring the fucking hell out of him. He was afraid if he let go, she would let go of the tenuous hold she had on life.

Thankfully Hunter and Gage acted as his advocates and convinced the EMTs not to separate them. Hunter's grim face was the last thing he saw as they loaded him and Grace into the back of a specially outfitted ambulance. "We'll see you later at the hospital, brother."

Alex nodded and clung to Grace's hand as two EMTs clambered into the back and someone slammed the rear doors shut. The vehicle took off, lights flashing and sirens blaring. Alex prayed they'd get to the hospital in time.

Grace woke cold, disoriented and alone in an alien world.

She lay in a hospital bed encased by a plastic tent, quarantined from anyone else at the medical facility they'd brought her to. She remembered Alex's voice, the desperate look in his eyes as he'd begged her to hold on. Somehow, she had. But she was so afraid. Was he okay? She didn't know how much of the sarin she'd been exposed to or how much she'd ingested, and being isolated from everyone else was frightening. She'd seen the victims of nerve gas attacks firsthand, but never imagined she'd be one herself someday.

Machines beeped and whirred softly around her. Her breathing seemed better and she was no longer vomiting, though a low grade nausea remained. Her head pounded and her eyes hurt. They'd washed her and changed her into a clean hospital gown. She remembered the feeling of absolute helplessness as her body had whacked out on her, exhibiting the classic SLUDGE symptoms that were the hallmark of a nerve gas attack: salivation, lacrimation, urination, defecation, gastrointestinal distress, emesis.

If Alex hadn't raced after her and tackled her to administer the antidote, she'd have died at that airstrip. Suffocated right in front of him. He'd been exposed too, but probably to a lesser extent. And what about David? He'd gotten a larger dose of the gas than she had. He'd looked bad. Really bad the last time she'd seen him. When she'd realized she couldn't drag him any farther without ingesting a lethal dose herself, she'd left him. Even though she was angry that he'd put her and the others in jeopardy by leaking the meeting details to the media, she still had to live with the knowledge that she'd been unable to save him.

The airlock made a sucking sound as someone opened the exterior door to the room she was in. Her heart beat faster as she stared at the suited figure who entered. As the individual came nearer her heart sank. It wasn't Alex.

The nurse stopped at her bedside, unzipped the plastic barrier and stepped inside, zipping it up behind her. She was middle-aged and had a kind face. She took Grace's hand and put her gloved fingers over her pulse point. "How are you feeling?"

Terrified. "Lucky to be alive."

The nurse smiled. "That you are. Do you remember anything after your arrival?"

She shook her head. The last thing she vaguely remembered was the feel of Alex's hand holding hers in the ambulance. "There was a man brought in with me. Do you know if—"

"The neurological team finished with their initial assessment a couple of hours ago. I saw on the monitor that you'd woken up and wanted to come in and let you know you're not actually as alone as it seems."

Grace gave a weak smile. "Thank you." She opened her mouth to ask about Alex again but the woman continued.

"We've been giving you more doses of atropine to counteract the exposure. You're doing very well."

The airlock opened and more people dressed in protective suits entered. They converged around her talking about her vitals, treatment protocol and then three doctors conducted a series of neurological tests and assessments on her. By the time they finished she was so exhausted she could hardly keep her eyes open. They left her alone to doze.

Her eyes popped open sometime later at the sound of the airlock being opened. This time she lifted her head, a half sob of relief exploding from her when she recognized Alex. He wasn't wearing a protective suit, just a surgical mask and gloves and he stripped the mask off as he unzipped the plastic wall that separated them.

"Alex, no—"

He ignored her and stepped inside, zipping it shut after him then turned to face her. The naked relief in his eyes hit her like a punch to the gut. He didn't crouch down beside the bed as she'd expected. No, he slid his arms beneath her and literally scooped her up into his lap to hold her. He buried his face in the curve of her neck and she realized he was shaking.

She stroked his back weakly. "Alex, you shouldn't be in here—"

"Shh. I swore I wouldn't leave you. I've already been pumped full of atropine and there's no way you're still a risk for exposure." He raised his head to look down at her, his eyes full of torment. "They wouldn't let me near you when we got here. I tried everything I knew to stay with you, but…" He trailed off, looking stricken.

Grace put a finger to his lips. "I believe you. And it doesn't matter because you're here now." He was warm and solid, his arms holding her so tight. "When you came after me I was so scared you would die."

"I can't believe you ran from me." He shook his head, his cheek brushing against her hair. "Or that you thought I'd actually let you go."

"I was trying to protect you."

He huffed out a breath. "God, I thought I would die when you ran from me."

"You chased me down even though you knew you might die."

"Yeah. And I'd do the same thing again if I had to."

Grace turned her face into his shoulder, breathed in the scent of the strong disinfectant soap and the underlying musk that was all Alex. "So you're okay?" She'd never forgive herself if he wasn't.

"I'm fine. And you're going to be fine too."

She lifted her head, met his gaze. "Did the neurologists say that?"

Alex nodded. "Your system's already shed ninety-nine percent of the sarin, and as far as they can tell everything's functioning normally. You'll have headaches, dizziness and some nausea for a few weeks or so, but with any luck I got that antidote into you in time to prevent permanent neurological damage. Another minute or two and it would've been ugly."

She shuddered and his arms tightened around her, his lips brushing against her temple. "Thank you."

"You don't ever have to thank me for that. Not ever. Understand?"

He said it so fiercely that she nodded. "What about David?" Though she was pretty sure she already knew the answer to that. It still didn't stop her from hoping she was wrong.

"He didn't make it," Alex murmured. "But the other members of your team have been freed from the various locations where Hassani had them taken to, and they're all in good condition. No sarin gas exposure or any other injuries beyond what they sustained in the hostage taking. Apparently he'd hoped to use them as leverage for safe passage to Islamabad once he got on that helo."

Grace bit her lip and blinked back tears, her relief about Dr. Travis and the others tempered by David's death. "David said it was his fault. He took a bribe from someone in the media and they were blackmailing him."

"I know. Evers and the team in Islamabad managed to crack the case while we were busy down here. We found out who Hassani was getting help from in the ISI."

"Is Hassani dead?"

"Yeah."

"Did you do it?"

He nodded. "That hangar he had you in was booby trapped. Didn't matter what happened, that canister was going off, either when the time ran out, or when you tripped it by trying to get out one of the windows and doors. If you'd stayed you would have gotten a lethal dose within minutes. It was damn lucky you got out of there when you did. Even though it tripped the sensors when you crawled out the window, you minimized your exposure."

Of course, she realized. Because sarin was heavier than air, it would eventually sink. "Was it an old canister?" It was the only thing she could think of that would explain why she was still alive. Sarin had a short shelf life and degraded quickly when stockpiled.

"We think so. Another thing in our favor, huh?" When she didn't answer he groaned and stretched out, keeping her tucked into his side.

The medical staff was no doubt having conniptions right now from him being in here, let alone without a protective suit. But she was so thankful to have him holding her like this. She burrowed in close, closed her eyes and savored the feel of him, the steady thump of his heartbeat beneath her cheek. "I love you," she murmured. "So much."

He wrapped his arms around her back and squeezed her. "Love you too, angel. Think you can get some sleep now?"

"With you holding me, yeah." With him beside her she felt completely safe. "You won't let me go?"

"No. I'm not going anywhere."

Grace smiled at that. He'd promised not to leave her, and he hadn't, even at risk to his own life. That told her everything she needed to know.

☆ ☆ ☆

CHAPTER FIFTEEN

Stepping through the end of the Jetway at BWI airport, Gage hitched his carry-on bag higher up on his shoulder and entered the waiting area at the gate. The place was dead. Not a big surprise considering it was one in the morning. He cracked his neck from side to side as Hunter stepped up beside him. They headed for the baggage claim where they'd have to wait for their weapons to be delivered to a location separate from the rest of the luggage.

"What day is it again?" Hunter muttered as he rubbed a hand over his face.

"Can't remember," Gage responded. He was done in. The entire team had been going on next to no sleep for the past few days. Alex was still in Karachi with Grace, who was being released from the hospital within the next day or two. Evers, Blake and Jordyn were flying out later today. Zahra was still in Islamabad with Dunphy and a small security team at the hospital, where he continued to make slow but steady progress. Rumor was they'd be sending him back stateside for rehab in a week or two.

After the intense hostage incident with Grace and her assistant, Gage and Hunter had been screened and treated for sarin exposure along with Blake and Jordyn just in case, but thankfully nothing had penetrated the protective suits they'd worn. Even thinking about it made his skin prickle. That chemical weapons shit was scary as fuck, and he was glad people like Grace were out there championing the fight to eradicate them.

"How about you grab the luggage and I'll take care of the other stuff," Hunter suggested. Gage nodded and headed for the carousel where the other passengers were gathering. He covered a yawn, looking forward to getting home to the latest NSA safehouse he shared with Claire and crawling into bed beside her. Though he didn't plan to let her sleep until well after dawn. He'd spent six hellish months apart from her before they'd gotten back together, and this last trip was the first time they'd been separated since. He'd hated it.

"Hunter!"

At the excited shout, Gage turned his head and saw Khalia running toward his team leader, her high-heeled boots clicking on the floor, the hem of her coat and her long dark hair flapping behind her. A wide smile stretched her mouth. Hunt's answering grin was the only outward sign of his surprise as he set down his carry-on and strode toward her, that smile transforming his harsh features as he reached for her. She jumped into his arms with a squeal, grabbed him around the neck as he lifted her from the ground and hugged her tight.

Gage hid a smile and turned back to the empty carousel. Good to see Hunt could still be taken off guard. Finally the carousel buzzed and the bags started feeding down the conveyor. The flight had only been half full so there wasn't much luggage to sort.

He grabbed his big suitcase and Hunt's duffel, lugged them over to the couple who were still wrapped around each other kissing. Gage cleared his throat, raised an eyebrow at

Hunter. The team leader grinned in response and took the bag with a murmur of thanks, one arm wrapped around Khalia's shoulders.

She pulled away from him and crossed to Gage to hug him. He caught the glint of the rock on her finger as she reached up her arms to wind them around his neck. "Good to see you back safe and sound," she murmured.

Gage threw a grin at Hunter. Tight-lipped bastard hadn't said a word to anyone about getting engaged. Looked like there would be a few weddings in their crew over the next while, beginning with his and Claire's. He planned to whisk her away to some place tropical in the next few weeks and elope. He knew she was good with that plan. They'd waited long enough to make things official and he didn't want to wait anymore. "Good to be back. And nice to see you again." It felt like forever since he'd first met her in Islamabad back in September.

"I wanted to surprise him," she said with a grin, looking back at Hunter.

"You did, and that's not easy to do." He settled his gaze on Hunter. The bags holding their weapons were waiting on the floor next to the other carousel. "You ready?"

"Yeah. We'll drop you off," Hunter offered as he walked over to grab them.

"Nah, it's okay, you two go ahead. I'll catch a cab." Nothing worse than being a fifth wheel, and it'd been weeks since Hunter had last seen his girl so Gage figured they could use the privacy.

"No you won't," Khalia replied in a sly tone, and Gage caught the hint of a grin that curved her lips.

Before he could wonder what that comment was supposed to mean, the sliding doors at the end of the secure area opened and he caught a flash of caramel-brown hair as Claire walked in. Her face lit up when she saw him and Gage's heart started to pound. Grinning like an idiot, he dropped his bags as she rushed over and caught her up in his arms, growling low against her neck at the feel of her soft curves plastered to him. Her silky hair snagged against the heavy stubble covering the lower half of his face.

She squeezed him tight then eased back to take his face in her hands, scanned his eyes. "Hi."

"Hi yourself." She and Khalia must have cooked this little welcoming committee idea up. He couldn't stop smiling as he bent to kiss her. Her lips were soft and warm beneath his, parting eagerly for the caress of his tongue. She tasted like cinnamon and he couldn't get enough. When he finally lifted his head, the love and joy he saw shining in her gray eyes melted him inside, chased away the heavy weight of exhaustion that had been pulling at him. She was like a ray of sunshine, lighting up his whole world. "What are you doing here? I told you not to wait up because I'd be home so late."

"Yeah, but as you know I'm not that good at taking orders. Besides, this is a special occasion and I wanted to welcome you home properly."

The special occasion she referred to was the end of Hassani and his terror network, which signaled the end of his days in the field. Gage knew she'd been holding her breath for this day. She'd spent her whole life worrying about the military men in her life. He didn't want her to have to do that anymore.

"It's really over?" she whispered, a hint of uncertainty in her eyes.

He cradled her cheek in his hand, marveled again at how soft her skin was. He couldn't wait to stroke his hands all over her naked body, make her purr and moan for him. "It's all done. I've officially begun the transition to desk jockey-trainer hybrid." Hunter and Tom Webster, the co-owners of Titanium Security, had asked him to come on board in an administrative capacity. He'd agreed to act as a consultant when needed, get new contracts and help train new security members when they were hired. Although he'd miss being out in the field with the guys, he knew it was time to step aside from that life.

He'd done his time; he wasn't getting any younger and he had a life to make with Claire. One where he wouldn't be called out in the middle of the night to fly overseas and put his life on the line in the field anymore. She deserved better than that.

Claire let out a relieved sigh. "I'm glad to hear it. And to celebrate, I brought you a special surprise."

His interest captured, Gage raised a speculative brow at her as a dozen enticing possibilities occurred to him. "Yeah?"

Eyes sparkling, Claire leaned up on tiptoe to whisper against his ear, her warm breath stirring shivers that suddenly made the front of his pants too tight. "Just wait 'til you see what I've got on under this coat. Or rather, what I *don't* have on." She pulled back to waggle her eyebrows at him and his eyes immediately shot to the long black trench coat she had on, the black heeled boots below it.

"Lemme see," he blurted, reaching out to pull the collar of the trench aside and peer down it. He caught just a glimpse of red lace and plenty of pale, smooth skin before she squealed and slapped his hand away.

"Gage, not *here*," she finished in a scandalized whisper, turning three shades of red.

He smothered a chuckle. "In the truck then?" There was no fucking way he'd be able to keep his hands off her until they got home. Zero.

Laughing, she leaned her head against his shoulder and wrapped her arms around his waist. The sweet scent of vanilla drifted up to tease him. "Maybe. If you're good."

"Baby, you know I'll make it way better than good."

She swatted his shoulder, glancing around to see if anyone had overheard. Hunter and Khalia were both laughing at them. Claire narrowed her eyes at him. "You're gonna pay for embarrassing me like this." Her voice dropped to a whisper. "Now I'm going to torment you all the way home."

Visions of her unbuttoning that coat and stroking teasing hands all over her body while he watched flashed through his mind. And one of her leaning over the center console while he drove to unbutton his jeans and wrap her mouth around him. "Totally worth it," he murmured.

Setting his arm around her shoulders, he pulled her close, grabbed his bags and started for the exit with Hunter and Khalia behind them. He couldn't wait to see what Claire would do in the truck. Now if he could just drive them to the house without getting into an accident, but even still, it was a hell of a memorable welcome home.

Seven weeks later

Grace opened her eyes as she turned over in the wide, cozy king size bed and found the other side of the warm flannel sheets empty. She didn't hear the water running or Alex moving around downstairs. Yawning, she stretched her arms over her head then sat up. It was still light out but already late afternoon, the sky outside the cabin's loft bedroom turning a soft red-gold above the snow-capped evergreens.

It was quiet out here on Whiteface Mountain, near Lake Placid in the Adirondacks of Upstate New York. The only sound was the slight whisper of the wind buffeting against the windowpane. Alex had to be downstairs. She smiled to herself. Now was the perfect time to give him his early Christmas gift.

She was still tired, could easily have slept the rest of the day away, but she was getting stronger every day. It was likely she'd suffer fatigue and headaches for months from the sarin exposure but she couldn't complain because those symptoms were on the extreme mild end of the spectrum.

She knew she was lucky to be alive, and though she hadn't been able to attend the meetings, her UN-sanctioned team had gotten the deal signed by the Syrian delegation. The dismantling of the chemical weapons stockpiles and facilities was already underway. After the holidays, she was scheduled to go to Syria with the team to inspect the progress, and Alex would be back at work on his next assignment. In the meantime, she was going to savor every hour of this stolen time her recuperation gave them.

But Alex would be waiting for her downstairs and she had a gift to deliver, so she climbed out of the warm nest of the bed and took a shower in the adjoining master bath. They'd rented the cabin for the week leading up to Christmas, and she loved getting away with him like this, away from everyone and the demands of their jobs. It felt like the honeymoon she'd always dreamed of, and she secretly hoped she'd be having a real one within the year. Right now though, she was going to make this the most memorable Christmas Eve Alex had ever had.

Grace took her time washing her hair and shaving her legs. Once she was out and toweled off, she rubbed her favorite sugar and spice lotion into her skin and blew her hair dry. She brushed her teeth, put on more eye makeup than she normally did to accentuate her eyes, then took the special bag out of her suitcase she'd been saving for this occasion. Pulling on a knee length satin robe, she opened the door and nearly ran face-first into the thin red ribbon strung across the threshold.

She stepped back, finally noticing the handwritten note dangling from the end of it. She smiled as she read the familiar block printing.

Follow the trail to find your present.

For a moment she stood there with a stupid, sappy grin on her face, so touched by his thoughtfulness that she had to swallow the lump in her throat. No one had ever done anything like this for her. When had Alex managed it? After making love to her he'd fallen asleep snuggled up against her back, but obviously he hadn't slept long and she must have been practically unconscious because she hadn't heard a thing while he set this up. That man was just full of surprises.

Feeling like an excited kid on Christmas morning, she took the end of the ribbon and began to wind it around the spool he'd thoughtfully left attached to it. She stepped out onto the upper landing to take a look around. He'd wound the ribbon from room to room, leading her on a quest through the entire upper floor of the cabin before winding it around the banister on the stairs.

"Alex?" she called. "I'm heading down."

No answer. She frowned, paused in the winding. Was he even here? She could smell the homemade lasagna she'd made earlier and popped in the oven to warm before her nap.

Unsure what she was about to find downstairs, she wove the spool in and out of the wooden banister as she descended the stair, her bare feet silent on the carpeted runner. Halfway down she caught the magical glow of the tree they'd decorated the night before and she paused when it came into view. There was more ribbon criss-crossing the living room, but she couldn't help the thrill that went through her at the sight of that tall spruce covered in white lights and the box of decorations they'd bought at a local store. No sign of Alex, but a roaring fire burned cheerfully in the hearth beside the tree so he couldn't have gone far. It was the most romantic, cozy sight she'd ever seen.

Hurrying now, she unwrapped the ribbon from the bottom newel post and followed the trail through the kitchen. He'd been very thorough, she thought with a laugh. When the hell had he had time to do this?

The ribbon wove its way from the kitchen to the study, then to the powder room and finally back into the living room where the tree stood. She followed the trail right into the branches and back out again, finally spotting where he'd laid it along the rug in front of the fireplace and back toward the kitchen. The spool was almost full now. Bending to gather it from the rug, she straightened and stopped short when she saw Alex in the doorway. He was leaning against the wall with his arms folded across his chest—a very muscular chest framed to mouthwatering perfection between the two halves of his open flannel shirt.

He gave her a slow, sexy smile and watched her without a word. Grace belatedly noticed that the ribbon trailed right into his front jeans' pocket. "I can't believe you went to all this trouble for me," she said with a little laugh. She slid her gaze down to where the ribbon ended, right next to a particular package she was very interested in enjoying some more. "So, are you my present?" Because she would love to unwrap him here by the tree with the firelight flickering over his body.

He quirked a dark eyebrow. "Come find out."

Grinning, she sauntered up to him, making sure to put an extra sway in her hips. Alex tracked her with that bright silver gaze, the heated look in them making her sizzle from fifteen feet away. She stopped less than a foot from him, cocked her head. "Hmm, what's in the pocket?" she asked playfully, cupping her hand around the bulge in his pocket, very close to the other, equally prominent bulge behind his fly.

Rather than answer, he reached into the pocket, drew something out, and held it out to her.

Grace forgot to breathe as she focused on the blue velvet box in his hand. The smile froze on her face, the humor evaporated. Elation and a jolt of nerves flooded her veins. This was it. Her heart thudded in her suddenly dry throat.

"Open it," he urged quietly.

She couldn't think of a single thing to say. They'd talked about getting married of course, but she never thought he'd propose so soon. With shaking hands she reached out and slowly lifted the lid. Something shiny and metallic sparkled in the lights from the Christmas tree. White gold, or maybe platinum?

She lifted the lid all the way to expose the item nestled on its bed of velvet and got her first full look at the…

Key.

Grace blinked then looked up at him in confusion, caught off guard by the sharp stab of disappointment. He'd already told her he would propose when she least expected it, but still. She stared at Alex, not understanding what the key meant.

One side of his mouth quirked up in a charming, endearing grin. "Grace, I love you, more than you'll ever know. Will you move in with me?"

He'd warned her about doing the unexpected, and he certainly had. She chuckled softly. Staring into his eyes, Grace felt the relief, the absolute rightness of it click into place. There was no doubt, no hesitation in her mind, and she felt the permanency of what he was asking wrap around her. He wasn't asking her to just share a roof. Their commitment to each other was unshakable; they already belonged to each other body and soul. The ring and ceremony were only formalizations, and she knew they would happen at some point. This step was more than enough for now, and it thrilled her to know that he wanted to live with her day in and day out.

She stepped forward to take the key from the box and wrap her arms around his waist. "Yes. I'd love to."

Alex tossed the box aside and dragged her close for a deep, searching kiss that left her breathless and hot all over. His hands explored her curves through the thin satin robe, leaving her tingling all over. He broke the kiss and leaned back. "I'm a little disappointed. I was expecting some kind of protest or demand," he murmured, eyes twinkling.

"About what?"

He huffed out a laugh. "A key, Grace? Really?"

She frowned. "It's the key to your heart. I got it. Pretty romantic, too. I love the symbolism of it."

He shook his head at her, his eyes alight with amusement. "You're too adorable. Don't you want your real present?"

She cocked her head. "You know I love presents. What is it?"

Still grinning, he reached into his other pocket and pulled something out. He kept his fingers curled into a fist and held his hand out to her. But when she held her palm up, he pulled his hand away and got down on one knee. Her throat tightened and she bit her lip.

"I don't just wanna shack up with you, angel, though I'm looking forward to that too. What I want is for the world to know you're mine forever." He opened his hand, revealing the sparkling round-cut diamond ring on his palm. "Will you marry me?"

She glanced down into his eyes, saw the love and respect there. Dropping to her knees facing him, she slid one hand around the back of his neck. "Yes. In a heartbeat."

Alex growled in approval and kissed her, slow and sweet until she tingled all over. Then he eased away to take her left hand and slide the ring onto her finger. The diamond burned with an inner fire in the reflection of the flames dancing in the hearth. "You're mine."

The possessive way he said it sent a delicious shiver through her. "That goes both ways."

"Damn right it does." He grabbed her close and took her mouth in a searing kiss.

Before she lost her senses completely, she pulled her mouth away from his and dragged in a breath. "I got you a present too. And in my family, the tradition was everyone got to open one present on Christmas Eve."

"Yeah?"

"Mmhmm. I hope you like it." She took his hands and brought them down to her waist where the robe's satin belt was tied into a bow.

His eyes ignited with frank male interest. "Can I open it now?"

"I think you should."

He stared at the belt as he pulled on the ends of the bow and the robe fell apart. Alex let out a soft growl, his eyes flaring when he saw the snug red lace teddy with its row of tiny black velvet bows holding the two halves together at the front. His molten gaze locked on the one between her breasts where the fabric gapped to give him an eyeful of her cleavage.

"You like?" she murmured, amused and delighted by his response.

He met her eyes, the raw hunger there stirring a delicious flutter low in her belly. "Oh, hell yeah."

"I was going to wait until after dinner to give it to you, but—"

He let out a harsh laugh. "I'm not hungry for food anymore." He yanked the robe off her and grabbed her by the hips to tumble her to the rug in front of the fireplace, coming down on top of her to smother her laugh with a sensual kiss that promised many more erotic gifts to come before they eventually got around to eating dinner later.

Much, much later, she hoped as he stared down into her eyes and undid the first velvet bow between her breasts with his teeth.

EPILOGUE

Five months later

"All right, everyone grab your seats. It's about to start."

At Ellis's announcement, Alex walked over and slid his arm around Grace's waist to interrupt the conversation she was having with Jordyn. "Time to roll, angel," he murmured, bending his head to kiss the side of her neck. Her neck and shoulders were bare in the pale aqua dress that hugged her generous breasts and fell to her knees where it ended in a flouncy hem, showing off her shapely calves. He noticed the goosebumps that broke out across her skin and smiled against her neck.

When she twisted around to look up at him, the top of her head coming to his chin even in her sexy high heels, he noted the spark of hunger in her eyes. One touch, one little kiss or caress and she still lit up for him. It never failed to amaze him how hot they burned together. He knew he'd never get enough of her, not in ten lifetimes.

She turned in his arms and gave him a quick peck on the lips, her saucy red-glossed smile promising much more later on. "Okay. See you in a few."

He watched her walk away from him, his stare fixed on that gorgeous round ass and the sway of her full hips. The woman was a walking pinup girl and he was the lucky bastard who got to see her laid out in his bed every night.

"Alex. Quit stripping Grace with your eyes and get in here."

He grinned and turned around to find Claire—Mrs. Gage Wallace now—in her bridesmaid's gown impatiently motioning him into the back room of the private house they'd rented for the occasion. She let him in and quickly shut the door behind him, and the sight that met his eyes made him feel like someone had punched him in the heart.

Zahra stood there in her silky white gown, a bouquet of white orchids clutched in her hands. Her long dark hair was pinned up on top of her head with just a few pieces left down to frame her face. The white veil trailed down to her slender waist. She flashed him a nervous smile. "You ready?"

Not trusting himself to speak, he nodded and looked down at the tips of her pink-painted toes that peeped out from beneath the hem of her dress. Hell, his damn eyes were stinging. He hadn't expected to get this choked up.

Claire cleared her throat. "I'll just give you two a minute."

Alex appreciated her consideration. As the door closed behind Claire, he pulled in a breath and met Zahra's gaze. Her pretty hazel green eyes were bright with tears. Her lips trembled a little. "Damn, Alex, don't make me cry," she warned, flashing a hand up to wipe the moisture away.

He shook his head. "You look so beautiful," he told her hoarsely. Maybe they weren't related by blood but he definitely felt like a proud father. It was his honor to walk her down the aisle.

The quiver in her lips vanished and a happy smile curved her mouth. "Can I get a hug?"

Aw, hell, was she trying to break him? He closed the distance between them and slid his arms around her back, squeezed his eyes shut when her arms wound around his shoulders and hugged him hard.

"Thanks for everything," she whispered.

"No, thank you," he answered in a rough voice. They'd been through so much—all of them had. When she let go he eased back and she grinned when she saw the dampness in his eyes.

"I won't tell anyone," she promised.

"Better not," he said on a laugh. Inhaling deeply, he stepped up beside her and offered his arm. "Shall we?"

She nodded. "Let's do this."

He walked her to the open patio doors that led out onto the manicured lawn and sloped down to the beach where the waves curled against the shore in lazy strokes. The moment they appeared at the top of the stairs the guests all hushed and the violin quartet started up. Zahra inhaled and squared her shoulders, gave him a little nod.

Alex led her over the threshold and out onto the grass. At the foot of the stone patio steps he turned her to face the small group of guests seated in the rows of white chairs. He spotted Grace in the front row beside Hunter and his fiancée, Khalia. Next to them were Gage, Evers, Jordyn and Ellis. Tom Webster, the other co-owner of Titanium, sat behind them. Up front beneath an arbor dripping with yellow roses Claire stood in her pale pink gown beside the minister.

And front and center, flanked by his older brother and the minister, stood Dunphy in his tux.

Alex smiled at the sight of him standing on his own, his legs still in braces and one hand resting on a cane to help steady him. His clean shaven face was leaner from the weight he'd lost, but when he saw Zahra he broke into a proud, almost awed smile that transformed his entire face. He'd been through hell these past few months, but Zahra had also gone through her own hell and walked out the other side. They were both survivors, both stronger for their ordeals because of the other. Now they would walk forward together for the rest of their lives.

Zahra squeezed his hand and he squeezed back, stealing a glance at her. Her eyes shone with joy and a love even Dunphy's ass-clown tendencies couldn't shake. Alex knew they'd be happy together and he couldn't be prouder of them both.

When they reached Dunphy, Alex paused to draw Zahra's veil back then shook the groom's hand. Dunphy's eyes sparkled as he clasped Alex's hand in a firm grip, and he knew it was more than a thank you. It was a vow that he'd always take care of her. Alex nodded and returned to his seat beside Grace.

She was smiling at him fondly as he eased into the chair, obviously aware how emotional it had been for him to give Zahra away. She leaned into his body when he draped an arm around her shoulders. Laying her head on his shoulder with a little sigh, she squeezed his free hand. "You did good, dad," she whispered just before the minister began the ceremony.

With Grace's soft weight snuggled against his side and her fingers twined with his they watched as Zahra and Dunphy exchanged vows. That would be him and Grace soon, Alex thought. Maybe nothing as elaborate as this setup, but he was going to publicly pledge his devotion for life to her *very* soon.

They were flying out tomorrow night. But not back to Baltimore. Grace had no idea, but he was flying them back to Minnesota to see her family for a very special occasion. He, her mother and sister had the wedding arrangements all taken care of and he couldn't wait to surprise her with it. Though they lived together they hadn't seen much of each other over the past few months with her traveling to Syria and Iraq, and him back and forth to Pakistan and Afghanistan to stamp out the rest of Hassani's network. That was going to change after tomorrow night. He was going to marry her in the church she'd been baptized in and attended growing up, and they were going to enjoy every moment of the two week honeymoon in Fiji he'd booked for them.

He couldn't wait to make her his completely, have the satisfaction of seeing her take his name. She'd already told him she was going to keep hers and double-barrel them, but that was fine by him. Grace Fallon-Rycroft sounded damn good to him.

The couple exchanged vows and rings, then before the minister could finish, Dunphy took Zahra's face between his hands and bent to kiss her. And Jesus, it wasn't a PG kiss either. Alex let out a strangled laugh as everyone around him cheered. Hunter stuck two fingers in his mouth and gave an approving whistle while Gage shouted at them to get a room. By the time Dunphy let the girl breathe, Zahra was deep red, her playful glare promising her new husband retribution later.

Holding hands, she and Dunphy turned to face the guests. They looked so happy Alex felt his throat tighten. Everyone here was witnessing hope and love and redemption. A miracle.

Grace laughed softly and squeezed his hand. "Want to borrow one of my tissues?" she teased.

Chuckling, Alex pulled her to her feet and stood with his arms around her middle as the newlyweds passed by up the aisle amid a standing ovation. They moved slowly, Dunphy's strides stiff and jerky, but hell, he was fucking *walking*.

Grace tipped her head back to look up at him, was clearly fighting a laugh. "I love you, you big softie."

He smiled, knowing he was the luckiest bastard on the face of the earth to have this woman's love and get to spend the rest of his life with her. "I know. But are you gonna finally make an honest man out of me someday, or what?"

She arched a playful brow at him and gave him a considering look, though the answer was clear in her eyes. "I think I could be talked into it, yes. And I think it should happen sooner rather than later. We're not getting any younger, you know," she added.

"Hmm, well I'll take that under advisement." He thought of the surprise that awaited her in Minnesota and smiled to himself as he guided her up the aisle after the others.

—The End—

Complete Booklist

Titanium Security Series
(romantic suspense)

Ignited

Singed

Burned

Extinguished

Rekindled

Bagram Special Ops Series
(romantic suspense)

Deadly Descent

Tactical Strike

Lethal Pursuit

Suspense Series
(romantic suspense)

Out of Her League

Cover of Darkness

No Turning Back

Relentless

Absolution

Empowered Series
(paranormal romance)

Darkest Caress

Historical Romance

The Vacant Chair

Acknowledgements

Big thank yous to my amazing BFF and crit partner, Katie Reus, and my fabulous detail-oriented hubby, Todd. Also sending out hugs to Julieanne Reeves and JRT Editing, for helping me make this story shine.

About the Author

NY Times and USA Today Bestselling author Kaylea Cross writes edge-of-your-seat military romantic suspense. Her work has won many awards and has been nominated for both the Daphne du Maurier and the National Readers' Choice Awards. A Registered Massage Therapist by trade, Kaylea is also an avid gardener, artist, Civil War buff, Special Ops aficionado, belly dance enthusiast and former nationally-carded softball pitcher. She lives in Vancouver, BC with her husband and family. You can visit Kaylea at www.kayleacross.com.